Thank you to everyone who requested a second book!
I hope it lives up to expectations.

JANUARY

Wednesday 1 January

The first month of my positive, new life. Watch me rip it open, lick the lid like no one's watching, and savour every morsel. I'm taking it by the horns and wringing every last drop of pleasure out of it; that's my resolution – you heard it here first. I hope you notice that this year I'm not putting off writing the diary, unlike last January when my head was in a different place altogether. However, before you assume I've had a personality transplant, I'll treat myself to a modest portion of ranting, courtesy of that menopause thing – just a quickie, no shouty capitals. But I'm not dwelling on that today. In case you were wondering, my need to rant has nothing to do with my hangover. Oh no, absolutely zilch. I'll try to keep it brief.

Why does a hangover take longer and longer to recover from? You'd think our bodies would be used to it by now but, like everything else, it gets progressively worse. Wine improves with age, drinking wine definitely doesn't. Perhaps it's nature's way of telling us to stop damaging ourselves, or nature being bloody spiteful.

I'm not finished yet. You've seen all that positivity malarkey about January? Now let me tell you that it's usually a tedious month – the one that's sent to try us. Either dreary and bleak with post-Christmas blues nipping at your heels, or bright but sub-zero with Jack Frost doling out chilblains and freeze-drying your skin. The days are short and stark, the nights extreme, allowing emotions to surface. The festive period was either deliciously indulgent and so exciting that you can't bear the thought of normality staring at you with its boring, blank calendar *or* it was a total anti-climax and you're left with nothing but a tight waistline and a hefty credit card bill. It's a time to face reality, to beat yourself up for breaking resolutions, and to rid the body of festive excesses – those toxins and fat that lurk around the organs waiting to pounce, rendering them useless, so we're told! End of rant. This year is different. This year I promise to embrace January and try my level best to resurrect the sparkle, starting with a luxurious wallow in tasty toxins and leftover fat. It's going to be a damp January – I am *not* doing that miserable dry thing.

I hope you're all still with me, my stalwarts, my faithful band of diary-reading residents from Shady Pines Care Home. Did you find this year's diary safely boxed up with the others? Were the diaries from my younger days still with them? You'll take great pleasure in reading those. They are bursting with vitality and optimism and kept me going through some of the darker months of last year. You might actually *be* me, in the care home of my future – hi Lizzie! Whoever you are, I hope you enjoyed reading about the events that led me to stay in Newcastle rather than start a new life in London with Lucas. Future me knew the ending all along. After all, that is the very nature of reading an old diary. I envy your knowledge of what life has up its sleeve for me. Now, don't any of you think about haranguing me from your armchairs about being bloody proactive – it could take a while for me to get going.

Thursday 2 January

You need to cut me some slack because I almost forgot to mention my crushing blow just before new year – how could I! Rob from the Refugee Centre called with the devastating news that there's no funding for the English classes, which means no part-time teaching for me. At first, I thought he was calling to tell me someone had snitched about the illicit relationship with Lucas when I volunteered there. Instead, the job I was looking forward to isn't happening. Karma, fate, or a punishment from some non-existent entity, simply for falling in love? I hear you asking me how a non-existent entity can be responsible if they don't exist? Answer: don't ask *me*, they just can. I'll survive – after all I'm retired and intend to enjoy life, but it's a great pity for everyone at the Centre. I must remind myself of that when I fall into a typical January 'woe is me' mode – I'm very privileged compared to many. Must stop the negative vibe now – it's anti-resolution and, like my relationship with Lucas, it's *so* last year.

From this day forward, life's going to be so good I've decided not to write anything more about Lucas. Why? Because committing it to paper will perpetuate the feelings I'm doing my best to suppress, and I'll miss him even more. Okay I agree it's utter nonsense but might turn out to be a good idea, if only to read it in months to come and laugh at the ridiculousness of it all. No, I'm sticking with plan A – the menopause-induced crazy one, and not write about him. Anyway, I haven't heard from him since he left. We agreed it would be less painful for us both, but we'd make an exception in case of emergency. Now define emergency:

- I need to wake up next to him
- I need to hear him say 'Leezie' again in his Colombian accent
- I need to look at the sea with him
- I need a hug from him

I reckon every one of the above qualifies, don't you? Good, then I am triaging each one as an emergency. Sorted.

Saturday 4 January

I'm trying hard but woke up feeling out of sorts. Part physical. Part emotional. Must face up to the fact that recently, the 'peri' has evolved into the fully blown 'm' word. For those of you who've not yet had to think about it, and for others who experienced it years ago, I'm referring to the menopause – yes, *again*! Been having flashes – more like a blush than a flush, and they're coming thick and fast. Remember your teenage years when the person you were madly in love with that week walked past or (worse) stopped to ask you something? Your neck would glow in scarlet blotches, followed by your face, turning you into a dead ringer for, sadly not love, but a lobster? Well, that. Horrendous! As my old diaries confirm, 'going red' was an everyday occurrence back then. It could also have been non-fancying related e.g. in the French lesson you said, 'Il est très joli,' thinking you described Xavier, the laughing old man in the textbook as 'jolly' when in fact you said, 'He is very pretty.' Then the teacher, with a wry smirk, would explain the error, causing the class to explode and make donkey noises until order was once again restored and the focus of collective derision shifted to the next victim. Such were the joys of hormonal-driven adolescence. Now they've come full circle – no, not to you boys, just to the poor girls – who've done nothing but endure:

- periods lasting an eternity
- pregnancy and the delights of morning sickness
- childbirth and its postpartum complications

Finally, when you're dusting yourself down at the end of it all – ta-da! The body announces the arrival of (guess what?) the menopause and its entourage of side effects. 'Of what side effects does she speak?' I hear the menfolk ask. Well sit back and you will learn, then thank your lucky stars you will never be subjected to such unpleasant, crazy bodily experiences over which you have no control.

I was in the supermarket today, loitering around the frozen veg, when a man said 'Excuse me, Elizabeth, isn't it? Gosforth High?' Straight away I could see it was Paul Murray. I'd been through primary, middle, and high school with him. He was always so funny. A boy with the right amount of naughtiness to make the class laugh, but one who also knew when to stop. Popular.

'Oh, hi Paul…' then I stopped mid-sentence while it gripped me by the throat and ripped right through me, turning my face a perfect shade of fourth year scarlet. Aaaaargh! Now he'll think I FANCY the fiftysomething version of Paul, and I don't. How excruciatingly embarrassing. I couldn't say, 'Sorry Paul, it's only a hot flush,' in case:

a) he hadn't noticed (impossible)
or
b) was embarrassed by the explanation (possible)

So what if he was embarrassed? It's no big deal. But that's the sensible, rational me talking. There's nothing sensible or rational about the menopause and its victims. Menopause is the new menstruation. In the eighties, we taught our male friends that it is perfectly fine to say 'period', talk about periods, and send them to the shop to say, 'Tampons, please,' all in the name of education. By doing this, some learned that the milk would not curdle, nor would the crops fail if there was a menstruating woman in the house. A liberating experience for all; no longer should girls feel embarrassed or dirty as their mothers and grandmothers did, and as too many women around the world still do. However, strictly referred to as 'women's troubles', uttered in hushed tones and accompanied by a nod of the head, the word 'menopause' was never *ever* EVER mentioned in mixed company in the ancient eighties.

On top of our hectic schedule fighting the gender pay gap, sexual harassment and mansplaining, we now have a new crusade on our fair hands: teaching NVQ level 1 Menopause. How we'll cram it all in I really don't know. We are Generation M: having cracked menstruation, it is now incumbent upon us to tackle the menopause with the same zeal. Or rather, with a very slightly diminished level of zeal than we used to – adjusted to account for women in middle age. Mind you, we're still talking a shedload of zeal.

Back to Paul – sorry to digress, droning on, and leaving you stranded in the aisle there. Clearly, he had no idea of the can of hormonal worms he'd opened merely by saying hello. I turned towards a freezer and leaned over it, seeking relief among the chips and felt the waves of air cooling my face to an acceptable shade – from lobster to prawn. I reached down and grabbed a pack of frozen peas, clutched it to my neck as you would a long-lost child, then sneaked it up to my burning cheeks, pressing it on hard. Ahhh – momentary bliss. The frozen bag stuck to my skin, which meant I had to rip it off quickly, before throwing it in the basket, like a live crab and turning round nonchalantly to face Paul.

'Are you okay?'

Lovely, considerate Paul, thinking I was seriously ill or mid-faint, barely keeping upright with the help of the freezer, looked worried.

'Oh, er yes, er I'm just a bit hot, and getting peas,'

Hot and getting peas! Why did I say that, for God's sake?

'It's okay, my wife's the same. It's our age,' he laughed, and very sweetly said, 'Take care Elizabeth,' waving as he rushed off.

Wow! No educating required. Not a patronising, 'It's her age,' or a rude, 'It's your age,' but a perfectly chosen, non-sexist, 'Our.' Camaraderie and sympathy for me, empathy by proxy of his wife. Never mind, it was a positive exchange, and I shall return with your certificate once I've signed it. NVQ from School of Lizzie, or Elizabeth. Just one thing, Paul, I'll probably forget all about it as soon as I leave the shop. The woman at the checkout stared at me. At the time, I put it down to my beetroot face and assumed she was worried I would explode all over the till – but there was more.

By the time I arrived home from the topsy-turvy uppy-downy supermarket trip, I felt like sinking a large wine. Resisting, I made a cup of tea and glanced in the mirror – WHAAAT? The word 'PEAS', followed by greenish, blackish, greyish mess, was smeared across my face! It must say 'SAEP' if you're looking at it, which of course Paul, and the rest of the supermarket would have done. Not that 'PEAS' accompanied by inky mush would be any better. How bloody embarrassing. Lovely Paul must have had a real dilemma on his hands:

'Should I tell her? No, it'll embarrass her. She's already in a right flap about the hot flush. But everyone will see, then she'll feel even more embarrassed when she gets home and looks in the mirror. Not your problem, mate. Let's get the hell outta here.'

Bed. Feel a wee bit calmer than earlier, probably due to medicinal wine. I forced myself to put today's escapade into perspective and do some of that mindfulness stuff – or is it mindlessness – who knows? Anyway, I thought about kittens. But I still feel stupid. Realising I have form with this kind of disaster,

I went in search of my old diaries. It's my escapism, guaranteed to cheer me up. Found what I was looking for. Obviously, I'll have to translate it from teenage-speak to middle-aged parlance, or you won't understand a word of it.

I suffered from earache as a child, not only the type dished out with monotonous regularity by parents, but also the physically painful variety. We lived up a quiet road near a paper recycling business (yes, they had them in the old days too). Eddie, a gorgeous eighteen-year-old (i.e. an older man), worked there and would leave around the same time as I came home from school. If I timed it perfectly and was lucky, I would be able to see him, go red, and swoon all the way home, requiring the aid of smelling salts by the time I got in. My partner in crime Debs 'fancied the pants off him' too, as we graphically described it. I would invite her to spy on him from my bedroom window in the school holidays. This entailed hours of hysterical screaming, ducking down, and peeping round the orange swirly-patterned curtains in the hope of a glimpse of the adorable Eddie, who knew exactly what was going on and stepped up to his role by flirting shamelessly, leading us both on.

Earplugs hadn't reached Newcastle in the seventies. Instead, I would protect my sensitive ears with pieces of scrunched up loo roll – the perfect barrier against the North Sea wind, a vicious creature that reduces the official temperature to a complete myth, creating a chill factor of minus fifty or so. One such wintery day, I plugged my ears for the last leg of the walk home from school and spotted Eddie in the distance, leaving work. My stomach churned with excitement at the thought of ringing Debs later, something that baffled my parents who wondered what we could possibly have to talk about, having spent the entire day at school together. School existed merely to:

- further our social life and experience with boys
- provide craic to be dissected later on the phone
- debate current affairs i.e. which teachers we fancied that week
- *never* be taken seriously

Way too embarrassed to stare at Eddie as he approached, I feigned great interest in my bus ticket, and other assorted pocket rubbish.

'Y'alreet?' came the cheery but typically brief Geordie greeting.

'Yeah thanks,' I replied in as casual a voice as I could muster i.e. not in the least bit casual.

With a pounding heart and purple wind-lashed face, I dashed into the house and headed straight to the mirror.

OH MY GOD! The sight unleashed a torrent of tears, each one brimming with hormones: streaming from my ears in shredded white ribbons, were the toilet roll earplugs – fully unfurled. It looked hilarious, but I was in no mood to see the funny side. I was distraught. How could I ever face Eddie again? He would think I put them there deliberately with zero sense of style or dignity. I had well and truly scuppered my chances of being snogged by Eddie. *Ever.*

During the painful weeks that followed, I timed my journey home with the precision of a brain surgeon to avoid bumping into him. Debs was forced into letting me stay at her house until his knocking-off time had passed – rather like mine, with him.

It's a pity Debs no longer lives up here, but she's vowed to check into Shady Pines with me when the time comes. Anyway, I've cheered myself up after reading the diary and live in hope that one day I'll also be able to laugh about the peas incident. Meanwhile, I'm changing supermarkets.

Tuesday 7 January

Already lapsing on the diary writing front. C'est la vie. How can an innocent breakfast end in a potentially disastrous commitment to something I might bitterly regret? Met Simon this morning at the new café in Heaton on the outskirts of town. Positively urban cool though it may be, I prefer a greasy spoon on Shields Road when it comes to breakfast but the bright, colourful room filled with interesting nick-knacks and arty pieces lifts the spirits on a dull day. Also, I'm grateful for his attempt to drag me into the world of healthier eating, as long as it doesn't cost me an arm and a leg. We ordered something dubbed 'smashed avocado' but it was actually mashed. Nowadays, even plain old mashed potato must be reinvented before it's allowed to appear on a menu. For mash get Smash – as every child of the seventies knows.

I moaned a lot about the lack of direction retired life was taking, now that the English classes are off the agenda. For purely selfish reasons (too many memories of Lucas – DAMN, I mentioned him!) I've decided not to volunteer at the Centre either. However, knowing my aversion to garden centres, Simon came up with a bizarre solution:

'You should get an allotment.'

Once an idea pops into his head, it sticks fast until it either comes to fruition or he concedes defeat after a very long and arduous battle. Take the speed dating last year, he won that one too and I'm now dealing with the ensuing PTSD – or *PSD*TSD.

'Why? I've got a perfectly good garden, thank you.'

'You've got a *neglected* garden, you mean. And that's not a double entendre,' he winked.

At that point, I knew resistance was futile and he ground me down slowly but surely, batting back every pathetic argument I threw out. Persuaded me that allotmenteering is not only healthy, but a communal experience, a hobby. I'll meet more people. Older blokes competitively growing leeks, I argued, are *not* my bag. Yes Simon – prejudiced I may be, and yes it sounds ageist, but the fact is they're more likely to be traditionalists (aka sexist) than their younger counterparts who grew up in a more progressive era. You should know by now that sweeping generalisations are my forte.

Simon was prepared for a prolonged fight, his mouth open and ready to fire the next round of persuasive ammo when I bowled him the googly:

'Okay then. I'll give it a go.'

He nearly fell off his chair with shock.

Now I'm back home I'm already starting to wonder what I've agreed to. Well, I'm not letting him push me around; I won't be forced into anything. Simon's incredibly wily in these matters and knows all the tricks. I suppose I need a new project to fill the gap left by Lucas, something that isn't work. And I don't mean a relationship. Don't twist my words, people. Do *not* twist my words. Must remember not to wear reading glasses when looking in the mirror – it's depressing. I prefer the soft focus with a naked, long-sighted eye.

Wednesday 8 January

I hate new year's resolutions with a passion! I felt lonely today so, in an effort to crank up some wretched positivity, I've cracked under the weight of peer pressure for the second time in a week and got myself a Facebook profile. Of course, I had help from Sam to set it up, but I'm very pleased with myself, nonetheless.

Everyone my age has one – apparently. Oh, so those 'everyone' people can see what I've been doing, where I've been, then stomp off in a big virtual huff when they find out they weren't invited. And vice versa. Not that my social life is ever as exciting, busy, or complex as that, but I can always dream. Something else to look forward to is feeling depressed about the number of 'likes' my photos or posts attract, or don't attract. It has become the scourge of the adolescents. A platform on which to be bullied when you have left the school gates, ensconced in the presumed safety of your own home. An opportunity to be trolled by anonymous cowards. Do I want to be a part of this world? I'm not so sure. On the other hand, I feel excluded when my group of friends are chatting about their latest posts or events they've seen advertised. Then I look at a photo of someone's dinner and change my mind.

Looking to the future though, it will come in handy for keeping in touch with the outside world when I'm in Shady Pines. Will we be constantly checking social media to see what our friends and family are doing when we're unable to get out and meet up with them? We can message, text, and have all manner of video calls with them, to such an extent that every care home will need its own IT person. I'm taking a deep breath, holding my nose, and plunging in. Wish me luck.

6.30 p.m. – 33 friend requests sent.
8.30 p.m. – EXCITNG NEWS! I have 11 friends. They are mine, all mine!

Friday 10 January

Met Sara at the Grainger Market in town, where we stock up on fresh fruit and veg from the indoor market stalls to support small businesses, rather than boosting the supermarket coffers. Maybe next year I'll join them with my allotment produce! It's the first time I've seen my lovely young friend since Christmas. She's always too busy either chasing after or trying to avoid some unsuspecting man or woman. Still, I love her because she's fiercely loyal and unpredictable in an ADHD kind of way.

Sara was bursting to tell me the latest story about her grandad Ernie, a proud, independent man of eighty-seven. She and her mum Jenny had arranged to help him move a wall cabinet and had issued strict instructions NOT to attempt it until they arrived. Yes, you guessed correctly, Ernie started without them. When they walked into his garage, they were shocked to find a pool of blood, the cabinet hanging loosely off the wall, and no sign of the errant grandad. They frantically began ringing the hospitals. Then in came a call:

'Hello Jenny, I'm Marion from the sexual health clinic. We've got Ernie here. He's had a minor accident but he's absolutely fine. He's got a slight gash on his head but nothing to worry about.'

'What the hell's he doing at a sexual health clinic?'

'We used to be the minor injuries walk-in centre, so he got confused, bless him.'

'Bless him. I'll bloody well bless him when I see him!'

Laughing all the way to the sexual health clinic (not a phrase you hear often), they walked through the waiting room to the reception desk, past the young people hiding their heads in their hoods, phones or hastily grabbed birth control leaflets. Sitting on a chair, surrounded by clucking nurses expertly patching up his head with fancy tape, was Ernie.

'Ah man, you lot didn't need to waste ya time coming aall the way doon here! I was just gannin' for the bus,' he said, with a worried face.

Sara says he's so sweet that no one can ever be cross for long – and they'd have had to contend with his team of bodyguards who'd formed a protective circle around him, weapons at the ready. Satisfied there was no need for further action, Ernie was released, with a reprimand, and promised his new fans that he wouldn't 'do anything silly' – until the next time of course.

Sara had heard on the grapevine there may be an allotment in the pipeline and joined in with the press gang tactics.

'There's usually a long waiting list so hurry up and snap it up while you can,' was the instruction.

I'm determined not to let them think I'm at their bidding. Oh no, I refuse to be railroaded into anything just because my friends think it's a good idea.

Saturday 11 January

With my new-found determination to master technology without the help of millennials, I booked an appointment online to view an allotment at a site in Jesmond, a ten-minute walk from my house. It's for next Saturday with a Tommy McTaggart, who sent me a lovely email and a map. It's hardly gardening weather, but I'm secretly thrilled at the prospect of having a new hobby and growing my own food – double bubble. Simon described it as 'very Jesmond' which is a throwback to the area's bohemian, health-food shoppy reputation of the seventies. Am I protesting too much when I say it's unfair and allotments are found all over the city? Anyway, we should all be thinking of our carbon footprint and organic living. Okay I give in. It's very Jesmond.

I feel I may have been lured into a trap for sport where everyone, having encouraged me, will now mock mercilessly, make 'The Good Life' jokes, and say I'm pretentious. Oh well, I guess that's the raison d'etre of true friends. I'm in a state of nervous excitement – which I'm taking as a positive. Seven more sleeps – not sure I can wait that long!

Tuesday 14 January

Despite a few days of good spirits, I've fallen at the first hurdle. A mere two weeks into the new year and I've broken my resolution that I'm now saying was never officially a resolution so it doesn't count – I've been thinking again about Lucas. Okay, drag me to the pillory and hurl your rotten cabbages but make it snappy because I need to get home and self-flagellate.

To ring or not to ring, the age-old question. I want to know if he's okay. We're not teenagers or twentysomethings playing that waiting game, more strategic than eighties favourite *Risk* – a game I usually lost then, too.

Sara – will egg me on, goading like the devil on my shoulder, 'What've you got to lose man, Lizzie?'

Simon – a 'life's-too-short, live-for-today' type. Naturally, he'll say, 'Of course you must ring him! Like, *now*!'

Sam – my fiercely-protective-of-her-mother's-feelings daughter. Fearing a re-run of last year, with a few months spent fretting about my anxiety and depression, will give it a resounding 'NO!' and remind me I have an exciting new interest to occupy my time.

Hilary – naturally super-sensible, pragmatic. Apart from casually dating Malcolm, an online purchase, she's leading an essentially single life in a Quayside flat. My middle-of-the-road-verging-on-boring friend who was unhappily married to Miserable Jeff for twenty-five years, has reinvented herself as a trainee party animal and won't want me disappearing off to That London every other weekend. A definite no-no from her. She'll tell me in no uncertain terms I'm only allowed to see men who live within a thirty-mile radius of Newcastle, which begs the question, 'What about a wildlife ranger living on the Farne Islands? Would he be out of bounds, Hilary?' She wouldn't laugh if I asked her that.

On balance, I've decided not to ring him and throw myself headlong into the allotment project instead – if I like the place, of course.

Thursday 16 January

Went on a reccy to the allotments this morning. I peered through the fence, trying not to look suspicious or weird, which I find hard at the best of times, and found my post-Christmas sparkle: the entire allotment tapestry was covered in frost, twinkling in the rare mid-winter sunshine. It was breathtaking and utterly magical.

Friday 17 January

Doubt I'll get any sleep tonight – I'm overexcited!

Saturday 18 January

I can't stop thinking about the allotment, *my* allotment! Tommy turned out to be a softly spoken man in his seventies with a kind, ruddy face – one of life's gentle souls. He showed me around the beautiful south-facing site, a veritable paradise in an otherwise urban world. Despite the inclement weather and current state of the neglected plot on offer, I was sold. Who wants a ready-made manicured space anyway? It would be boring. I can put my own stamp on this one and am relishing the challenge.

When he turned to me and said, with a wide-eyed, pleading look, 'Well?' I wanted to throw my arms round his neck and shout, 'Ooh Tommy, you had me at 'Good morning'!' More appropriately, I said, 'Where do I sign?'

Haven't the faintest idea where to start so I'll need lots of help from others – or the internet, given my soaring skill level. Simon is as smug as a secret lottery winner. I don't blame him, in fact I ought to have thanked him – maybe that's a step too far. Can't wait to get stuck in. There's a stack of unused gardening tools in the garage so I can crack on as soon as it's official, which could be as soon as Tuesday. I squealed with excitement all the way home – hope no one was behind me!

Tuesday 21 January

A day to remember! Collected the allotment key from Tommy and squeezed it tightly in my hand until it almost drew blood. It's a symbol of opportunity, opening the gate to a new life, where I'll learn new skills, enjoy new experiences. When I last collected a key, I was devastated. Newly divorced and still raw from the trauma of it all, I remember staring blankly at the cheery estate agent when she congratulated me on the purchase of my new home. Poor girl. She wasn't to know. Now, it seems absurd to think I was so cut up about divorcing Twat. It was a release, not from abject misery but from a stale and predictably adulterous marriage. STOP! I'm dragging the mood down here and spoiling my heart-warming story!

It's great that the site is so close to home. Unless it's raining or I'm carrying allotmenty stuff, whatever that may be, I swear to do my very best not to drive after today. Don't judge, it's freezing out there. I've already had the environmentalists in my head tut-tut-tutting for the whole journey, spoiling the moment. They were so loud I thought there was something wrong with the car. Hearing voices? Not a good sign. It's my blethering conscience – never shuts up. I rushed down the main path to survey my kingdom, wondering if there'd be any winter veg hidden among the weeds – broccoli or sprouts maybe? Sadly, no chance of that. In the cold light of day, the plot looked much worse than it did when I was thinking of it last night; my euphoria distorted the reality. It was like a second viewing on a house, when you see the faults of a place on closer inspection and it's not as perfect as you remember it. It was an alien landscape: mounds of earth covered in black plastic, interspersed with bright yellow and brown rotting marrow-type things – at least I think that's what they once were.

Most of the greenhouse windows are either missing or replaced with plastic sheets, once secured with tape, now swinging in the breeze. It's like a cartoon haunted house – neglected, overgrown. Even the rickety sliding door creaked on opening, to reveal more dilapidation inside: broken pots, menacing shards of glass, dead plants, boxes, cartons and empty bottles of plant food, dirty plastic bags covered in snails and slugs – don't ask me why. Tired of tapping on the makeshift windowpanes, the outside world had broken in long ago. Burrowing underneath instead, it invaded the warm, sunny space and reproduced; weeds and grasses galore now smother the rubbish as they grow. I casually pulled at a few strands who resolutely stood their ground, refusing to budge.

'Do you know how much effort it took us to get in here in the first place?' they snapped, then broke into a rousing chorus of 'We Shall not be Moved.'

It was going to be a long, long job, a labour of love. Tommy advised me to dig it over in the winter, ready for the spring. What did that mean, exactly? It's alright for you Tommy lad, but you haven't seen what lies beneath. Yuk. That's what, mate! I discovered an old spade under the carpet of grass in the greenhouse and didn't have to dig deeply before discovering something. 'Ooh how exciting – was it treasure?' I hear you shout. No – something way better – millions of roots – couch grass or 'cooch' some call it. My heart sank. Essentially weeds, every one of them waiting to be removed. Do I really need such a project which, in the world of TV makeovers, is a euphemism for 'one hell of a lot of bloody work you absolute idiot,'? Oh no, I thought you'd all say that.

As I approached the gate to leave, I heard a voice with a soft Northumbrian lilt.

'Just shout if you need a hand digging. You've got a bit of a job to do there.'

I hadn't noticed anyone when I was wading my way through the greenhouse or pathetically prodding at the soil like a seventeenth century princess, but the stocky frame and rugged, older good looks belonging to the voice, had evidently noticed me.

'I'm Hal,' he said, offering a gardening gloved hand. I like shaking a man's hand. It screams equality. I squeezed hard, doing the firm handshake malarkey, and looked him straight in the eye. Then I had a hot flush and scurried off. Shit!

Feeling a warm glow of contentment with life as I sip my glass of wine – I've earned it after my gardening stint.

Friday 24 January

Sam came to see the allotment. Her words were diplomatic, 'Er I can see its potential…'

I was defensive. 'Well, I've only had it four days and just scratched the surface – what do you expect with this weather and the time of year? It's not the Caribbean you know!'

'Keep your hair on, mother – I love your Good Life thingy, without the goats and chickens of course, what with this being *Jesmond* and all that,' she mocked.

Yes, it's already started – sigh. In all the excitement, I'd also forgotten about the prospect of frequenting the dreaded garden centres! I'll have to find one that doesn't look like an ad hoc department store for people who've lost their sense of taste in an accident. My only slightly more depressing retail experience than a garden centre visit was the day BHS closed down – it was even diabolical in its heyday. That will stay at number one in the worst shopping trip charts – until the day I get kidnapped and forced at gunpoint into that dreadful outlet park down the A19 specialising in old ladies' tartan golf trousers with matching caps.

I took a name and details from the notice board and sent an email to The Greenhouse Man, asking him to salvage it. He was recommended by Hal. Apparently, he's a great handyman to know. Hoping he's called Gary so he can be Greenhouse Gaz, but I doubt we'll be quite so lucky.

Walked home via the Town Moor. I expect the 'NO LIVESTOCK' rule at the allotments is more to do with the Freemen of the City who partly own the land, than concern for the neighbours. Although, speaking of greenhouse gas, the Freemen are also responsible for the moor and let their cows roam around on there. The cows were staring at me suspiciously as I skirted around them, trying to avoid eye contact. There are two camps in the cow debate:

Cow-towers (pro):

- cows are harmless – they are gentle, curious animals
- cows are terrified of you – just shoo them away
- respect the cow – worship the cow if your faith dictates

- cows love to lick your dog's nose

Cow-ards (anti):

- cows are terrifying beasts who hang around in gangs waiting for you to make a false move
- given half a chance, cows will trample you into the ground and run away laughing, to make cheese
- fear the cow (search 'cow deaths' online)
- never get close to a cow; if you're wearing red, they will charge and toss you up in the air like a pancake to avenge the deaths of their Spanish boyfriends

I love the way the moor creates the illusion of being in the middle of the countryside when it's five minutes' walk from the city centre. This huge expanse of common land, just as you drive out of the city centre, is actually larger than Hyde Park and Hampstead Heath combined.

My new best friends, Wikipedia, Google, and Newcastle Chronicle online told me some fascinating facts about the Town Moor. It's protected by an Act of Parliament and dates back to the thirteenth century. No one is allowed to build on our precious land. It is there for the humans, dogs, and crazy cows of Newcastle to enjoy walking, running, cycling, and eating grass. There are two hills at one end, made from earth dug out to create the motorway in the seventies, ideal for sledging, snowboarding, and skiing after the slightest covering of snow. With kids and students jostling for space, they're luckily in hobbling distance from the nearest A&E.

We are fiercely protective over the moor and are prepared to forgive its dubious past and misdemeanours of youth, preferring to remember the less harmful occasions it has hosted. After all, we're not always responsible for what goes on around us. However, in 1650, fourteen women and one man were tried and hanged as witches there.

Gender bias in the practice of witch-finding is well documented. Throughout the ages it continued to evolve, seeping into our traditional tales we recount to our children, through to modern day literature and popular culture. *Witch* is still a negative label and applies to women only. Conversely, *wizard* has cuddly, positive connotations. Not convinced? Here are but a few examples:

Witch – child-catcher of Hansel and Gretel, Snow White's stepmother – wicked, terrifying, evil, dangerous, murderous.

Wizard – Merlin, Harry Potter, Wizard of Oz, Roy Wood – appealing, enchanting, exciting, glam rocker.

I rest my case.

The moor has hosted countless horse races since 1721, with a stone grandstand built in 1800 to accommodate the spectators. The area's most famous race meeting, The Northumberland Plate Festival or Race Week, was originally declared a three-day holiday for local miners before it was moved to Gosforth Park Racecourse in 1881. Saturday's Plate Day is the Geordie answer to Royal Ascot Ladies Day (gender bias!) and an excuse to dress up and enjoy ourselves in style, or maybe without style, as the case may be. My mind is now wandering away from history to pursuits of a more frivolous nature: Plate Day! Hope Hilary will be up for a day of summer madness in the last week of June.

It's no coincidence that Race Week is held at the same time as the Town Moor Hoppings – the largest travelling fair in Europe. Having visited it again last year, I can safely say that of all the events hosted by our cherished moor, the Hoppings is my favourite. Originally created as a Temperance Festival, it was a typically Victorian response aimed at lecturing people on the evils of drinking and gambling taking place up at the racecourse during Race Week. Until recently, the Hoppings was alcohol-free – a dry event, apart from the weather, which is guaranteed to be wet.

Tuesday 28 January

More digging today. That's my life at the moment. I love, love, LOVE it! It's therapeutic – forking and turning the black compacted earth, chopping, cleansing, and airing, ripping out the weeds and giving it a new lease of life. Am I the same woman who has a phobia of tending her own garden down the road but treats this one like a newborn baby? A voice broke my concentration.

'You're doing a grand job there, mind,'

Hal – the misdescribed 'stocky' man from yesterday, who today appears well-built and in perfectly good proportion wearing a more flattering coat. Like Paul Heaton, also a reasonably attractive man whose coat of choice (usually an upmarket waterproof jacket with the collar worn up – you know the sort) catapults him into the 'cool and incredibly gorgeous' bracket. Yes, hopelessly fickle it may sound, but it's Gallagheresque nineties cool, which has never lost its appeal for me. The smile matched the voice.

'Thanks,' I replied, 'I'm a novice at it.'

He's younger than I remember, all those twenty-four hours ago, early sixties perhaps, with plenty of wavy grey hair – another plus. I must confess it's not only the coat I'm interested in! Then I made a complete and utter pillock of myself.

'It's going okay but I swear that coat grass multiplies the minute you turn your back.'

'*Coat* grass?' he repeated.

'Oh sorry, I meant *couch* grass,' I clarified.

'Aye, it's a swine, that one. That's good. Thought for a minute you'd found a new weed I never knew about!' he laughed.

What an idiot! It's typical of me these days, saying the wrong word without even realising it. Shit. Now he'll think I'm obsessed with his coat and therefore obsessed with *him* and I'm not. Bloody menopause. I sound like I'm on a blind date! Even if he's single, I'm really not interested and far from ready for another relationship. And I honestly don't fancy him – though he is very nice. I think I'm going mad.

He asked if I'd met any other plot holders and told me about an older woman called Miriam. He described her as a 'dishevelled', sad character who can also be rather rude, and not to take it personally. She comes to the allotment to drink secretly. Thinks her husband doesn't know, but he's apparently a quiet, unassuming man and must appreciate a few hours of down time, if she's often drunk. He explained in some detail how Miriam walks a 'fine line' as far as cultivating the allotment according to the rules and regulations is concerned, but everyone knows it would be cruelty to both Miriam and her husband if she was evicted. Hal strikes me as a stickler for rules, a very proper, upright citizen. Then he said something really strange,

'Most other people are pleasant enough but there's one guy who I'd steer well clear of. Tucked away in the corner over there he is, near mine and right next to Miriam's plot. Thinks he's out of sight. Anyway, he can be very rude as well – never speaks or answers anyone else.'

Then his voice turned all weird and full of intrigue, straight out of a TV drama,

'I reckon he's up to no good. Anyway, I must get on.'

Well! I couldn't possibly leave it at that could I? But however much I pleaded, begged, and cajoled, Hal would not be drawn on it and turned super-serious. I don't think he's got the world's best sense of humour. Something tells me I may be found hanging around other people's plots very soon under the pretence of 'looking for ideas', starting with that one in the top corner.

Friday 31 January

Four months ago, if you'd told me I'd be sitting on a wooden board in head-to-toe mud-splattered waterproofs, picking through the sodden soil (not swearing, just describing so don't tut at me like that) in a little patch of land near the Town Moor, I'd say, 'Don't be ridiculous, I'll be in London with Lucas, rattling around in a one-bed flat wondering how long my pension would last if our combined teaching hours were cut. I'll be going out for meals so rarely that I'll be shouting 'HOW MUCH?' after every bill arrives.'

Instead, I'm discovering a new world on my doorstep. Never been a 'back to nature' or even an outdoorsy type, let alone a gardener. Yet, here in my wild, muddy plot I've been tasked with knocking into shape and taming, I am damn well going to get the better of the beast. Besides, it'll stop me thinking about Lucas and what might have been. That's the plan, anyway. I keep breaking the sodding vow slash resolution thing. See? I always said they were made to be broken in the January curse.

FEBRUARY

Saturday 1 February

I've been researching today! With over five thousand others in the city, our allotments were created as part of the First World War effort in 1917 and were known as Victory Gardens. There's a page on Wikipedia about it. Look at me, discussing websites! When the Great Depression arrived, unemployed men were given plots in order to survive, in the absence of a welfare state (or food banks). Of course, during the next war, along with Dig for Victory posters, women were encouraged to take over the donkey work. Allotments have fluctuated in the popularity stakes over the years and are now very sought-after, as the cost of living rises and interest in organic food grows, alongside the veg.

I'm lucky to be looking after this special piece of land with its important place in local history. My plot would have helped a large family immensely in times of great deprivation. It's a humbling thought, and I'll do my very best to care for it and continue the legacy.

Monday 3 February

A woman with long, bushy, greying hair stomped past purposefully when I was digging this afternoon. I knew immediately who it was and exactly what was clanking in her tote bag. Okay I exaggerate – I couldn't say if it was white, red or fizzy, but it was one hundred (or about twelve) percent wine. I'm putting all my chips on red. Casting a cursory glance towards me, accompanied by a grunt of acknowledgement, Miriam was in no mood for chatting. Perhaps she's shy, I thought at the time. The bag had 'Jesmond' written on it, with a heart in place of the 'o'. Like it was London or New York. I'm not sure I'd advertise that as it would be a sure-fire target for mockery from the likes of Simon, and anyone on the number one bus. I pitied her. She looked malnourished, a grey themed woman: hair, skin, eyes, lips, and clothing – in varying degrees, ranging from Delicate Dove to Gun Metal. A woman whose sense of self-awareness packed its bag and left many moons ago, sadly.

Perhaps she's not well, was my first thought, which is why she drinks. Or perhaps it's vice-versa – we may never know. People who are ill find it difficult to be cheery. Many battle daily with their mental and physical health and struggle to function. We don't know what others are dealing with inside their minds, bodies, or homes. Don't judge, I reminded myself, but was relieved when she headed towards the corner of the site. I could barely concentrate on digging after I watched her disappear into her shed and slam the door. She didn't emerge for two hours. Despite the clanking, maybe she was engaged in another shed-related activity? After all it's a standard joke about men and their sheds. Nothing smutty, just doing man-cave stuff, like whittling and spending hours sorting boxes of assorted screws into boxes, trays or drawers of non-assorted screws. Heaven for those with OCD.

I could see from a distance her plot was neglected, unkempt. Dried branches and black, wilted plants bearing shrivelled fruit, left to rot in the saturated earth. A cruel metaphor for herself. These are the thoughts you have while digging. As you plunge your spade deep into the earth, the thinking flows, provided you don't probe too far amid the stony ground. Just as I was pondering Miriam's life, I looked up and there she was, staring right at me.

'Huh! You don't want to bother with all that, for God's sake,' she slurred in a radio four presenter's voice, which took me aback. Admittedly, there was evidence of a forty-a-day habit there in the low, silky cut baritone, but it wasn't unattractive. Then she spoilt it by cackling maliciously, coughing violently and spitting out the words, 'They'll all be back in the spring. Frigging weeds!' I felt compelled to defend my efforts but thought better of it, realising she was somewhere between six and seven sheets to the wind. Ignoring the helpful advice, I introduced myself. She half slurred, half snapped back, 'Miriam.' Despite the brevity of the reply, the smell of alcohol polluted the fresh winter air. She reeked of it! With the tote bag now empty, I wondered what the inside of the shed looked like. Was there any space for tools or was it wall-to-wall bottles?

'Oh yes, yes, yes it's a constant battle with those barstards!' she laughed again – loudly and inappropriately as only a drunk person can. Taken aback, I adopted my teacher's 'now let's all calm down' voice and said, 'Well, you've got to start somewhere, haven't you?'

It had no impact whatsoever. Miriam shrieked, tilted her head towards the gate and winked.

'He's got no idea, you know!'

'Sorry?

'Don't apologise!' she bellowed and laughed again, 'You've done nothing wrong!'

Now she sounded like a woman possessed.

'Him indoors. He that must be obeyed. It's my little secret,'

She pointed at the empty bag then tapped her nose. I was confused about whether she meant going out in public with the embarrassing bag or drinking but it was clarified with a swigging gesture. Miriam's face was now alive, animated, her eyes no longer dull but sparkling, verging on the unhinged. Red wine-stained lips parted to reveal a row of crooked brown teeth. Hooray – I guessed right!

'Yes, thick as a sodding brick he is.'

And with a final tap of her nose, she wandered unsteadily up the path, muttering and shaking her head. Nice to meet you too,

Miriam. Nonplussed, I watched her stabbing at the gate keyhole several times until she finally escaped.

Wednesday 5 February

I'm not a fan of shopping. Trailing around town is a chore, never a pleasure – until you've been propositioned in Poundland by a younger woman. No, this isn't a figment of my imagination, invented for comedic, alliterative effect to make my life sound more interesting, it really happened, this morning.

These days, under the 'get it where you can' umbrella, I'm more than happy to receive compliments from anyone and anywhere I can. Age rises while standards plummet, in equal proportions. But today was very exciting. I was queuing for the self-service till, triumphant in my quest for cheap foil and reading glasses (yes, they're perfectly fine in case you're wondering) when a woman with pink hair and a basketful of arty-crafty items, asked if I wanted to go in front of her. She was barely at the end of her sentence when she said, 'Oh my God, you look just like Kate Bush – when she was younger of course. I was just looking at photos of her yesterday. She's gorgeous, and so are you. Has no one ever told you that?'

I wanted to say, 'Well actually no they haven't and in truth I think you may be thinking of another Kate Bush,' so instead, taken aback by such flattery, I had a massive hot flush and simpered, 'Er, not really and never in Poundland, but thank you,' at which she giggled like a schoolgirl. Her natural, rounded face complete with rosy cheeks lit up when she laughed, and I felt unexpectedly attracted to her. Before I could decline her kind offer of a queue-jump, she blurted out, 'Let's go for a drink. Or a coffee. Anything. I mean oh my God you've made my day.'

I played for time. 'I'm not actually her, you know, Kate Bush. Sorry to disappoint you.' Then I thought, what the hell? There's no harm in it. She could be clinically delusional but that's going to make it infinitely more exciting. Provided we don't go to a dodgy pub at the back of the Grainger Market where she might blend in with the other customers, used to the odd psychopathic murder taking place in the corner booth, I should be safe enough. Before I could engage the sensible side of my brain, I blurted out, 'There's a café across the road.'

I had to wipe my brow with a tissue when she wasn't looking. I'm now wondering why I did that: did I fancy her and was trying to hide my age and sweaty head, or would I have done it regardless of who was there, out of vanity? We'll never know. I will leave that to you to decide because at that moment, I didn't know what would happen next.

It was exhilarating stepping out of Poundland into the unknown (or the back of the Grainger Market if you want to spoil the magic). From the sheer spontaneity of it all, my heart raced as we crossed the street and entered the café. I opted for a suitably public table.

'Strella!' she announced.

I looked over at the fridge, 'Yes they've got beer.'

'Have they? Ooh I'll have a San Miguel,'

'Er, okay. I'm having a flat white. It's too early for me.'

'Strella's my name, actually. It's a shortened version of 'Estrella' – Spanish for 'star'. They pronounce it es-tray-ah in Spain, but people always think it's Stella – another beer, and not nearly as nice for a name. In fact, it's pure old lady. Don't you think?'

Nodding in agreement, I wondered if she secretly thought of me as an 'old lady'. As she swigged back the mid-morning beer, she was clearly topping up her alcohol intake from the night before, hence the rosy cheeks. Then the life story: Strella's from London, went to university here, settled with a man who was on drugs, then a woman who is a serious alcoholic, but they still love each other. I was interested in those relationships; how they ended and what she feels about them now, but she didn't pause for breath once. Just talked at me non-stop, jibber jabber, jibber jabber, mainly about what a wonderful artist she is. Unrecognised, yet incredibly talented. Yes, she's been told many times before. Who by, I didn't enquire. All she needs is a break, someone to offer her an exhibition space. Self-indulgent, paying lip service to being interested by asking me a question but using it as a platform from which to launch into yet another monologue. She's always in Poundland because she works in a few after-school clubs, hence the craft materials. Not working today though, in case I was wondering (I was), because she doesn't drink before work. It was comforting to realise she must have been DBS checked to work with kids, meaning she hadn't murdered anyone – yet. Zoning out and struggling to follow her ramblings, I felt the attraction drain away as fast the beer in the bottle and wondered how short a time I could stay without upsetting her. When she stood up to go to the 'carsey', I grabbed the opportunity to leave, saying I was sorry, didn't realise the time and yes how lovely it all had been. I pressed more than enough money into her hand and made a dash for the door, ignoring the embarrassingly loud voice shouting, 'Wait! I don't have your number, Kate!'

Thinking I was free, I paused outside the café to gather my thoughts. Before I knew it, Strella's mouth covered mine in a beery, yet highly enjoyable, soft-lipped kiss – my first with a woman. It was a confusing mass of sensations – like trying to escape a fire then being airlifted to safety, through fluffy clouds, by gentle, tweeting bluebirds, some playing sweet violin music, and sipping lager. Brought back down to earth with a, 'Mwah', from Strella, I broke free and rushed up Northumberland Street without looking back.

Wow – I didn't expect that when I left the house this morning: just popping into town for a same-sex snog, oh yes, and some glasses (possibly related). It was certainly in keeping with this year's resolution of seizing the day, living life, and shouting a resounding 'YES' to experience something new, even with an element of risk, or disappointment.

Walking past the park close to home, a wave of sadness welled up in my chest as the stark realisation dawned: I would never again dare to shop in Poundland.

Friday 7 February

3.00 a.m. Woke up boiling – threw duvet off.
3.30 a.m. Woke up freezing – replaced duvet.
4.00 a.m. Woke up boiling – got up to write this fascinating entry:

Margaret Thatcher did *not* choose to have three hours sleep due to some remarkable work ethic – she was menopausal.

Late up due to the crap night's sleep. Last year it was anxiety and depression. I need one of those tee-shirts with 'same shit different day' customised to 'year' for a small fee, provided it costs less than a fiver to change. Though it may be more expensive as it's slightly different shit – it's the perimenopause or full menopause – I don't know, I'm not a medic, I'm a menopausal woman at an undetermined stage. Aaaaagh – now I'm driving myself mad and rambling!

Took a break from digging, but weirdly missed it. Best not to overdo it – said anyone who's never overdone anything.

Hilary asked if I fancied a week of winter sun. Told her that's fine if it's before the growing season begins. Some people have children or pets to consider, I have my allotment.

Monday 10 February

I'm enjoying this new, ready-made community. Today at the allotment, one of those bubbly, cuddly, homely women, straight out of a daytime cooking programme, gave me some shiny red chillies. How kind! I think she said her name is Barbara, or is it Amanda, or neither? These days, I'm forever meeting people, asking their names and promptly forgetting them. I have almost one hundred percent success rate with this. It's menopause brain exacerbated by lack of sleep and mixed in with a generous dollop of age. The perfect recipe for a fuzzy head and enough to send you crazy with frustration. Yep. It's definitely a thing; I've read about it. Hilary assured me it's not exclusive to the menopause because Miserable Jeff was the same and never ever remembered a name. The difference is, it doesn't tend to trouble men – 'so what, I forgot her name, it's not a crime'. Women are different. It's in our social, not genetic, DNA to be people-pleasers. 'What will she think of me for forgetting her name? How could I be so rude?' That is how we are raised and how society sees us. There is a wide spectrum of us, but I am at the extreme end and it gets right on my nerves. I feel acutely embarrassed about it. I'm trying to ask myself why it matters so much but I feel it's impolite to ask their name for the fourth or fifth time. Didn't see Hal today. Strangely I haven't forgotten his name!

Good news: email from Greenhouse Man to say he's coming next Tuesday morning!

Bad news: his initials are NH so sadly not a Gary.

Wednesday 12 February

Hilary called with an interesting proposition. She ditched gentle John after he gave her one half of 'His and Hers' slippers for her Christmas present. 'They were fluffy mules! Anyway, he was getting far too cosy in those bloody awful slippers!' she moaned. I thought it was a cute gesture, but she was having none of it, dumped him and found Malcolm online 'in the sales' as she put it. There was a post-Christmas discount on the dating app.

'Do you fancy stalking Malcolm? He's going off the boil. He's texting less and wasn't *available* when I asked him out for a meal last Friday night at that shipping container place opposite me.'

'Maybe he doesn't like shipping containers. Anyway, people aren't always available, some have lives.'

'Malcolm is, and he doesn't. He claims to be shopping again on Saturday when I know he already went yesterday.'

'Let's do it.'

Poor Hilary. She's led such a sheltered life: a couple of teenage romances then saddled with Miserable Jeff. She doesn't realise every relationship simmers down after the initial twenty-four seven rush to the boil, unless it's cultivated from a friendship, in which case, it's a slow cooker job. Poor Malcolm. He still lives with his mum and does the food shopping every Tuesday morning. According to Hilary, that's the extent of his hobbies, bless him. I very much hope he's worthy of our praise and not doing the dirty on her. Anyway, it could be a laugh, and Malcolm-stalking certainly counts as a new activity.

Saturday 15 February

Hang on to your slippers, people, you're going to love this bumpy ride.

Malcolm lives in a purpose built flat behind Gosforth High Street. Hilary was impressed when he first told her where he lived, before realising his mum was his flatmate. Serves you right, Hils! Gold-digging isn't your style. We took my car and dressed in partial disguise wearing hoodies – a complete waste of time because the hoods were too hot to put up and hide our faces. Luckily it was pitch black. When we parked outside, a wave of nostalgia hit me as I thought back to our days at The County pub nearby. I must dig out my diaries of old because this isn't the first time I've sat outside a boy's house with a friend – I guess that was technically stalking, of an innocent variety. More of that later – there's too much to tell you about last night!

After forty minutes of waiting for him to leave the house, I was beginning to lose the will to live when out came a furtive-looking Malcolm. Hilary scrutinised his clothes.

'He's got changed after work. Why would you do that for a food shop? Does Asda have a dress code? He's got no bags.'

'They'll be in the boot,' I said, hopefully.

Malcolm headed off in the direction of Asda. I was about to say, 'See?' when he turned off.

'FOLLOW THAT CHEATING BASTARD!' came the cry from the passenger seat.

It was half exciting and half terrifying, wondering what was going to happen next. Sadly, I didn't get the chance to do a proper tyre-screechy car chase through the streets of Gosforth, because he sailed away up the North Road then turned off into Gosforth Park.

'He's going to meet someone in that pub at the racecourse. KEEP BACK!' Hilary kept yelling, like he was wearing infra-red glasses and would see us. But Malcolm didn't stop at the pub. He headed for the car park. At that point I felt slightly sick because that car park is renowned for only one thing – *dogging*! As I suspected, Hilary was blissfully ignorant and shouted, 'WHERE THE HELL'S HE GOING?'

My worst fears were realised: there were four cars in the darkest corner of the car park, next to the woods. While Malcolm parked alongside the others, I did a quick u-turn and left the car outside the pub, then we crept along by the wall for a closer look. Malcolm got out of his car and into the passenger seat of another. There appeared to be a woman in the back seat too.

'She must be married,' growled Hilary.

I said nothing. Suddenly, headlights were flashed, and a man got into the back of the same car as Malcolm.

'She's a *he*! Malcolm's a bisexual cheat, or maybe he's gay and I'm a smokescreen. Or non- binary…no he won't know what that means. Why didn't he just tell me?'

'Hilary, I think they might be dogging.'

'Don't be naïve, he hasn't got a dog. He's up to no good.'

My heart sank. I would have to explain dogging from scratch.

'There are no dogs involved. He's watching people have sex.'

'In a car?'

'Yes, it's a thing.'

'A *thing*? You're telling me that Malcolm, who lines up his cereal boxes in order of size, and irons every single one of his sodding grey socks, is in that car watching people *shagging*?'

It sounded like it was the first time in Hilary's life she'd used that word.

'Yes. They're probably strangers.'

'Oh well, that makes it alright then, watching *strangers* shagging is absolutely fine and dandy, isn't it?'

'Shsh – someone'll hear you. We'll get caught …' and with that, Hilary stomped away in the direction of Malcolm, or rather, the doggers, as he evidently is one of them.

BANG! BANG! BANG! She thumped on the roof of the now rhythmically rocking car. The poor occupants must have thought it was a police raid. Not sure if dogging people are the subject of police raids – I'll google that one later. The movement stopped – other car doors opened, and torchlight lit up Hilary's distraught face.

'MALCOLM! I know you're in there. What are you doing?'

'Are you looking for someone, love?' said the anonymous torchbearer, in a squeaky, disguised voice.

A moment of silence, then a *very* sheepish Malcolm emerged from the passenger side – a lamb to the slaughter. I felt for him. Mind you, it instantly promoted Boring Malcolm to Dogging Malcolm the Dirty Dark Horse, which is more interesting, at least.

'I only watch, Hilary,' he stammered, pleading his case, 'I've not cheated on you.'

'Why didn't you tell me you were bisexual?'

'I'm not. That's Da… er… there's a man *and* a woman in there. And we're not harming anyone.'

Malcolm had a point, but it wasn't the time nor the place to argue it. I wondered how the people in the back seat might react to the ambush but thankfully they stayed put. Poor Hilary was lost for words for a moment, her mouth still slightly open. Then she found her voice.

'It's perverted AND illegal!'

'No, Hilary, it's neither – it's just voyeurism.'

'Oh yes, I expect that's what they all call it in Gosforth!'

And with that, she strode back into the darkness with as much dignity as she could muster, under the circumstances. I trotted behind her and sat silently while she ranted and raved all the way back home – and right through a bottle of wine. I don't blame her – it was a lot to take in.

I googled 'dogging and the law'; like Malcolm's sock collection, it's a very grey area.

Sunday 16 February

After a long and unforgettable night, I went to the allotment in the afternoon for a spot of R&R. Not more *rock and roll* – the *rest and relaxation* one. These days may be short, but any time spent outside with three sixty surround-sound birdsong instead of four walls, is food for the soul. I feel my mind expanding, reaching out to the sides of the panorama, filling the space then relaxing. It's tangible. The perfect antidote to the morning aftermath dealing with an angst-ridden post-traumatic dogging stressed (PTDS) Hilary.

She's been on the phone demanding to know why I couldn't see he was a 'total pervert', which is harsh, given that the outlandish hobby is obviously more widespread than you would expect. That said, I wouldn't put it in the 'you're never more than ten feet away from a dogger' category of widespread. My attempt to placate her with, 'Look Hilary he's not a monster and he's not cheated on you,' went down like Dracula in a blood transfusion clinic. Then she blurted out a classic that will stay with me for ever more:

'Lizzie, this is not the time for your default position of defending *the underdog*!'

I kid you not; those were her words. I pinched my leg and held my breath, but it was futile – I snorted the stifled laughter right into the phone. She responded with a sound tongue-lashing about being serious which I batted back with a retaliatory slap-down to remind my naïve friend that creeping through the mud in Gosforth Park like an advert for the OAP's Territorial Army, then being terrorised by the cast of *Deliverance,* is NOT I repeat NOT my idea of a good night out! Think she got the message.

'I need a holiday,' she wailed.

'*Now* you're talking, Hils. I can't wait!'

Tuesday 18 February

You'll never guess who came to fix the greenhouse: HAL! Neil Halford, who signed the email NH, is Hal. He doesn't look like a Neil. Thought it would be amusing to surprise me by turning up and not let on that I sent him the email. It was nice to see him, though it was slightly odd not revealing his identity. He was quite proper, almost formal (must be his work voice?) while explaining the process in rather too much detail. When he asked if I wanted it 'erected in the same position', I had to dig my nails into the palms of my hand in case I burst out laughing. I'm always having to do that. After all, it's not easy being a fifteen-year-old trapped in a fiftysomething body.

Anxious not to be in his way, I dug and weeded at a discreet distance wearing my usual unglamorous old waterproofs, glancing over from time to time as Hal skilfully and silently dismantled the entire structure. It was fascinating. Carefully, he handled the remaining panes of glass as though each one had come from the Sistine Chapel. He then meticulously cleaned them until they looked brand new. If it was impatient, slapdash me, I'd have torn down the greenhouse as fast as I could, broken every one of the precious few panes then, crying and in a fit of pique, dumped all the other bits in a heap for someone else to sort out.

Our lunch break was excruciating because Hal was in 'greenhouse jobs I have known' mode (yes, I found *some* of it interesting) and I hoped and prayed he wouldn't use the 'e' word again. It would have sent me into a tizz, causing me to spit out my coffee. During the course of the afternoon, Hal cleverly *rebuilt* the greenhouse. Painstakingly renewing the glass, every rubber seal, and a myriad of metal clips, he created a shiny, brand new one. I couldn't have been happier with the result, and it gave me such a thrill when I saw the finished product. Oh my God I must be really *really* old – a bloody greenhouse is turning me on!

When I told Sara later, she asked if I was sure it was only the greenhouse and not the Greenhouse Gaz guy that was 'floating my boat'. I assured her it was most certainly not the latter and that Hal is not my type – too quiet, too blokey and definitely not funny. She then asked me why I'd 'gone on and on' about his expert workmanship and how he's so good with his hands. I had a mega-hot flush – or was it? Perhaps it was an old fashioned common or garden blush.

Note: Hal is NOT MY TYPE!

Thursday 20 February

I had a sex dream about Lucas. I'm blaming the greenhouse. It's really thrown me because annoyingly, like all dreams, it felt real at the time. Now I'm miserable and wish he was here with me this morning. I woke up and reached over with my foot as I used to, just to check he was there. At the point of contact, a sensation of reassuring calm would shoot around my body. Today my foot reached the edge of the mattress. No body. No Lucas. Nothing. It's sent me down a dark, well-trodden path towards anxiety city, a route I am all too familiar with.

A sex dream is one of the weirdest phenomena our miraculous brain churns out and if yours works anything like mine, you'll now be singing the Muppets version of 'Mahna Mahna', adding 'doo-doo doo-doo-doo'. Back in the room, please! Where was I? Yes, a sex dream is so real that afterwards you feel one of the following:

a) repulsed
or
b) madly in love with the most unlikely of suspects

Regardless of the above choice, you will feel either:

c) as though you've been unfaithful
or
d) set back miles on the circuitous route towards reaching your goal of being 'over' your ex

There are no half measures in a sex dream. They are designed to shock. In recent years I experienced one from a), one from b) – resulting in c), with last night's qualifying as a definite d).

a) The Walrus

During my later years in teaching, I was haunted for months by the memory of my sex dream about an older, exceptionally unattractive colleague. I usually manage to see the good in most people, but bigoted, beer-bellied, moustachioed, child-hating Walrus was someone who tested my generous nature to the limit. He would leer at the younger members of staff when he thought no one was watching but I was so attuned to his vile behaviour I'd torture myself by watching out for it. He'd enjoy queueing at the photocopier, standing behind the young women, salivating as he looked them up and down. He'd then engage in banal conversation, cracking stupid jokes that were not quite inappropriate enough to report. I knew Walrus wasn't 'just being friendly' as many a court has heard in defence of sexual harassment, because he always ignored me. I was probably dubbed 'an old boiler' in his grubby little mind.

Then one awful morning, out of the blue, I woke up to discover I'd had a vivid sex dream about The Walrus. I was traumatised! I was still married to Twat, although very miserable by then and highly stressed at work. The memory was a nightmare, but the dream was anything but. Perversely, in the dream, I *enjoyed* having a wild, passionate session with that sexist monster! I was a) repulsed as you'd expect and jumped in the shower, frantically rubbing at my skin with equally repulsive sea salt and bladderwrack scrub. Then I had to face him at work. Instead of passing him in the corridor with my usual look of disdain, I blushed. Aaaaghh no, no, please God no! Anything but that. It would have been bad enough, but he must have clocked my scarlet face and reciprocated with a wink. Yes, a *wink*. Like the dirty old pig that he was. I can't bear men who wink at women! It's so seventies and is always followed, in my head, by a Sid James laugh.

It didn't take long to get over the Walrus sex dream. Fortunately, the memory can act as a defence mechanism when it gets its finger out, eradicating traumatic events. However, what possessed my brain to play such a cruel trick by putting them there in the first place I will never know. Luckily, I was neither b) nor d) as I didn't give a damn about Twat by then – every cloud.

In case you're wondering about my b) dream – it was about Alan Shearer, and I've loved him ever since, due to his ninety-minute premier league performance.

I should have gone to the allotment. Physical work absorbs the adrenalin and occupies the mind. My outdoor project is great, but today I'm indoors and I miss Lucas. I want to text him with: *Haven't you had enough of That London yet?* I'm like a child. Wanting something – getting it – rejecting it – wanting the first thing back. Oh yes, I hear your scolding voices now, ringing out from the Shady Pines lounge:

Reader (scolding voice): Just listen to her! She's never content. There's no pleasing that one. You rejected him and now you want him back. Really?

Me (defensive voice): I didn't reject him. I rejected the lifestyle in London and the one-bed flat scenario. I chose to stay in Newcastle with my friends and family. So there. I did *not* reject him.

Reader (scolding voice): Yes, you did.

Me (defensive voice): No, I didn't. Leave me alone and pick up my dummy on your way out.

10.00 p.m. Text from Sam. She's calling round tomorrow, thus affirming my life choice to stay here with my lovely friends and daughter. Ignore the outburst from earlier – I blame it on the sex dream. Quiet has returned to the North Eastern front.

Saturday 22 February

Hal stopped by when I was digging the allotment (I'm sorely tempted to write *dogging*). He brought me two leeks and a parsnip. Purely for slapstick comedy value, I'm disappointed it wasn't two turnips and a parsnip. Then again, it would have brought on a hot flush followed by a massive flap, sending him scurrying up the path under a cloud of awkwardness. Suddenly I'm impressed by a gift of vegetables. I laugh at the thought of my younger self (usually in the form of Sam) who will remind me mercilessly of my advancing years, sometimes with the velocity and brute force of the North Korean army. When does it all start, this 'no need for chocolates, jewellery or flowers, shower me with seedlings and root veg instead'? I remind her that such gifts are not given to impress or flirt, but simply as a friend from the allotment community, a ritual of welcome and acceptance – not romance. Sam is enjoying the teasing, so I'll leave her to her sport for now and put a stop to it in due course. I thanked Hal for all his handiwork (stop sniggering at the back or I'll keep the whole class in at playtime) and he was very modest about it, almost awkward. He's very sweet.

I planted my first ever vegetable in the ground – garlic! Okay, it doesn't take much to impress me these days, but I'm intrigued that you just plant a single clove of garlic, then, hey presto – it evolves into an entire bulb! Yes, someone like God, Paul Daniels, or Derren Brown must have made the very first clove, then nature took over. Apparently, it looks like a leek when it's growing and there's always a fierce debate in July about when to dig it up. I can't wait for that!

Thursday 27 February

This week I've been a digging-eating-sleeping machine, but it's worth every aching muscle to see the progress. It was a race with the sun as to who would finish their work for the day first. I tidied up just before the sky merged with the soil to become one murky blur. I just love being here.

Cleared half the area of weeds and couch grass and it's perfectly level, ready for manure and planting later in spring. And I can confirm that the expression 'mud sticks' is one hundred percent accurate as you'll find out if you ever try and remove it with a casual rinse. My two apple trees are beginning to suggest winter is on the way out with their tiny leaf buds making an appearance, only just visible to the naked eye.

Big news on the holiday with Hilary front – partly good, partly bad:

Good – we're off to some place in Gran Canaria where it's allegedly hot.

Bad – we're going with a complete stranger.

Good – for six nights not seven.

Apparently, Hilary's new friend Chrystal (with an 'h' – cue eyeroll) from her yoga class is joining us. Yes Chrystahl, from yogah. Can you believe the brass neck of Hilary? She didn't check it out with me on the grounds that she knew I'd agree to it. Sometimes I think that woman is on another planet – she ought to be. Of course, she's guilt-tripping by telling me Chrystal is recovering from a very unhappy relationship with a control freak and she'll tell me all about it another time. Now I'm heating up. Damn! A self-induced flush, or flash or whatever the bloody thing's called. I was okay earlier and now I'm whipping up the anxiety till it stands up in white peaks, like meringue. Ooh, I could murder a meringue right now.

Feeling dubious about this for three good reasons:

1. I've never met the friend.
2. The friend sounds ultra-posh.
3. Hilary is a useless judge of character.

What if I can't stand her? There'll be no escape. We're sharing a two-bedroom apartment. I'm not good with brand new people – too worried about what they'll think of me. Sara says it's down to years of Twat whittling away my confidence, gnawing at it like the rat that he is, leaving it pared to the bone.

On the plus side, if Hilary drives me mad, I can do my own thing without feeling guilty, as she won't be alone. Perhaps Chrystahl (must stop calling her that or I'll say it out loud when I meet her) and I will get along famously and be a good influence on Hilary, who can be seriously intense at times. Okay I've talked myself round – or at least three hundred degrees of the way. It's bugging me to hell that I wasn't consulted at all. And another thing – we're going next week which doesn't give me much time to finish preparing the allotment! I've told Hilary we *must* all meet for a coffee before we go; it's only fair.

Luckily, I bought that sausage skin swimming costume last year for the torturous spa day experience (cue anxious knot in stomach thinking about it). I'll see if they've got another colour in the same style and buy it online – yes, I can do that now! I hope you're suitably impressed at how I'm galloping away with my technology skills. All part of the new me. Anyway, buying online will avoid the delights of a blue-white post-Christmas lardy body staring back at me in the unforgiving fluorescent glare of the changing room lights. Strip lighting? I don't think so – said the old me.

MARCH

Sunday 2 March

A very Sunday-ish day, starting with pre-holiday nerves and ending with calm. Friends rallied round, making encouraging noises about the trip. They're a great bunch. Was given a good talking-to from Sam about my negativity towards Chrystal (note dropping of the second 'h') and I'm ready to go. Annoyingly, for the first time ever in her reasonably long life, Hilary has been 'too busy' to arrange an introduction to my future flatmate for six nights. Should I be suspicious? No. I'm naïvely putting it down to Hilary's inability to see life from another person's perspective. At least she won't be my 'roomie'. Hilary has nobly offered to sleep on the sofa bed while Chrystal and I have a bedroom each – I should think so too!

Packing was a strange process. It involved several frantic trips to town in search of items I knew were lurking at the back of the bathroom cupboard but didn't realise they were at least ten years out of date: sunscreen, mozzie repellent, sting relief. Thanks to the ups and downs of the past year, the immodium was very much in date. Then there was the ironing of the scrunched-up summer clothing that only gets an airing four weeks a year if we're lucky, but manages to look old and faded, nonetheless. As I rummaged around the drawer for my passport, panicking in case, like my patience, it had expired, I thought back to the Alan Shearer story and smiled. No, not the sex dream story – this one harks back to a time when our relationship was purely platonic!

Many years ago, when Twat and I still liked each other, we went to Thailand on holiday. It's a fabulous country, populated by the friendliest and kindest people. They exude peace and positive wellbeing, with the added bonus of being non-judgemental, true to their Buddhist beliefs – God will judge you, it's no business of ours. It was there that I first used Alan Shearer as a type of ID card. No, I didn't carry him round everywhere: tickets, money, Shearer – he'd be too heavy for my baggage allowance. All will be revealed in a typical conversation with taxi drivers:

Driver: Where you from?

Me: England.

Driver: London?

Me (sighing): No not London, Newcastle upon Tyne, in the north.

Driver: (silence)

Me: Alan Shearer?

Driver (lightbulb moment): Ah Alan Shearer, Newcastle United!

Worked every time, because back then the Magpies were a force to be reckoned with. Captain Alan Shearer had successfully battled his traumatic upbringing, kicking his ball around the Gosforth hood and was ultra-famous. I can see the puzzled looks on your faces. Those of you who are familiar with Gosforth and its environs, will be raising an eyebrow at that statement. It stems from an episode of Match of the Day:

Shearer, who went to my school, was reminiscing about his childhood after a young, homegrown player had scored the winning goal. 'Yes, I remember kicking a ball around the streets of Gosforth....' while all the viewers in Surrey (where the Manchester United supporters live) are imagining a scene from

The Likely Lads with proper Geordie streets, not the leafy suburbs of Gosforth! Viewers are now wondering if poor Alan was forced to kick his ball around a multi storey car park like the scary one in *Get Carter*. Nowadays he thinks Gosforth's slumming it 'cos he lives in Ponteland – now that *is* posh!

Thursday 6 March

Menopausal madness. Took a record three attempts to leave the house to go holiday shopping – not a difficult task for most of the population:

1. Left without shopping list.
2. Returned to house – retrieved said list.
3. Left house without purse that was put down while searching for list.
4. Returned to house – retrieved said purse.
5. Left house with partial success (see #6) on third attempt.
6. Later, discovered I hadn't fully locked door thus rendering house insurance useless in event of a burglary.

Annoyingly, I'm sounding more and more like an old man with every day that passes.

Saturday 8 March

Whizzed up to the allotment for one last dig before deserting it for a week. Hal was there and I felt the need to tell him about the holiday in case he thought I'd already got fed up with the place and CBA to come. There I go, worrying about what people think again, I'm pathetic. He probably wouldn't have even noticed my absence anyway. Now I'm overthinking that he might think I'm stupid for telling him. Aaagh! I really hate being me.

I read that the menopause can heighten anxiety and reduce your confidence – tell me about it!

Sunday 9 March

Didn't sleep a wink so not in the best of jolly holiday moods to say the least. I'm always on edge if there's a stupid-o'clock taxi journey. Five in the morning is the dog-end of a long night shift; every driver is already dreaming of a hard-earned kip in a comfy bed, and it gives me the willies. This very rational fear stems from a journey to the airport once with Twat. From the back seat, I could see the driver's eyes closing in the rear-view mirror and realised if any of us were getting out of this alive it was my job to keep him awake by talking to him non-stop. Needless to say, Twat was of no use whatsoever as he climbed in the back and continued to sleep like an elephant seal while I singlehandedly saved three lives. Thanks to my heroic actions, we all emerged unscathed. True to form, Twat accused me of imagining it and overreacting.

This morning it was all fine and I needn't have worried. My chatty driver was wide awake to the point of irritatingly chirpy, but at least I knew I wouldn't feature on *Look North*, having been pulled out of burning wreckage by morning commuters on the A696. Surveying the departures hall bustling with excited travellers, I felt a twinge of holiday excitement for the first time in several years. Newcastle Airport is the perfect size for an airport: neither embarrassingly small nor inconveniently large. It also boasts the optimal amount of retail outlets to pass an hour or two and creates opportunities for gloating, as you check out the prices of travel adaptors and immodium while your adaptor and Asda's own brand of meds are smugly stashed away in the hold. I also packed away my hairbrush because I once had it confiscated by the security people, who are always very pleasant. I shouldn't have asked them if anyone had ever been brushed to death on a plane.

You are unlikely to underestimate the journey to the gate at Newcastle, a scenario that can send you into a tailspin. The stress of hearing your name booming round the airport, ringing in your ears as you do the run of shame across the tarmac is enough to make anyone reach for that immodium (note – I must keep some in hand luggage). Despised by passengers and crew alike, you burst through the plane door, a sweaty red-faced mess, to be met with row after row of killer stares. They proceed to heap more guilt on you by announcing that, although everyone *was* prepped to leave, thanks to the selfish late bastards, 'WE HAVE NOW MISSED OUR SLOT!'

For any self-respecting Geordie, by far the most welcome addition to Newcastle Airport in recent years is not a city break direct to New York, nor is it the Christmas market trip to Vienna, Strasbourg or Budapest, but the introduction of a Greggs. It opens at the crack-of (for Krakow) and for all other destinations, thus enabling travellers to savour one last sausage roll or breakfast bun at a price designed to make only your mouth water, not your eyes. It is common knowledge that we, the Geordie nation, were weaned on such staples and we are about to be deprived of them for seven long days.

Anyway, enough of this small talk – Chrystal is an absolute bloody nightmare! My assumptions about her appearance couldn't have been further from the truth, unless a bald male WWF wrestler had appeared before me wearing a pink leopard print dress and matching kitten heels. When I spotted Hilary in the check-in queue, I thought she was chatting to a random person while waiting for Chrystal. My reason was: that woman with the too-tight-too-short shorts, white stilettos, blonde hair with hot-brush curls cascading over the brightest, blousiest blouse ever, cow's-length false lashes, and newly collagen-infused lips, couldn't *possibly* be Chrystal! She must have pulled an all-nighter to be ready in time, though the orangey tanned face would speed up the process. I am not criticising or poking fun, I simply prefer a more natural look – aka 'old fashioned' to younger readers. Or just 'old'?

I was so stunned I can't remember what she said, just that it was incessant drivel punctuated at least ten times by 'EEEH man, it's brill to meet ya!' Does she really sit serenely on a yoga mat twice a week? I'd like to see that. Her screeching voice and matching laugh could be heard from the far end of the arrivals hall. I read the thought bubbles of the other sleep-deprived passengers: *please God, don't let her be on our flight.* Whenever there was a millisecond of silence she would repeat, over and over, 'Ah cannot wait to get there, me.'

To say I'm astounded by Hilary's unusual choice of friend is in no way strong enough. It must be to do with her new life (yes, we're all at it): new experiences, new attitude, new (and totally unlikely) set of friends? It's baffling, particularly as Hilary's only unsavoury character trait is that she is a secret snob. Secret from me, that is, because she knows I can't bear snobbery and occasionally tell her off like a naughty child if it begins to rear its ugly head. I explain to her how unkind she would be if she really held those views and that we couldn't possibly be friends if what she said *wasn't* a joke, until she backtracks and apologises. Perhaps this is the new edition of Hilary. Okay, so I said Chrystal has an irritating voice, that's not snobbery, it's to do with how loud and embarrassing it is for those associated with her. There are many posh people with loud and embarrassing voices too, so you can all stop shaking your heads at me right now.

There was no trace of okay-yah – she's broad Geordie and has been there, done all that, with bells on. Chrystal is the full package: loud and over-the-top embarrassing, and I now know why the pre-holiday rendezvous was never arranged. Every crass remark is followed by, 'Eeeh, worramalike?' For example, at the check-in desk:

Chrystal: Eeh I bet you're dying to get that uniform off when you get home, mind. (emits loud, dirty laugh)

Young man: (smiles in a polite but patronising manner)

And that was before she started on the booze. In no mood for solids, she whisked past Greggs and headed straight for the bar where breakfast was served in the form of a pint and a half of cider. When Hilary couldn't help raising her eyebrows, Chrystal told her not to be so judgemental and pointed out that she couldn't possibly have managed two *whole* pints! Like the young check-in desk man, the new, compassionate Hilary simply smiled politely.

Boisterous people in a public space make me wince. I want them to be happy, to have fun, spread their wings and fly after escaping a controlling relationship; I'd just rather not be there for the maiden voyage. By the time we boarded, every passenger knew it was Chrystal's first holiday as a 'young free and single lass' (followed by a huge laugh) and how much she 'cannot wait, man'. Everyone is also hoping her two dogs or 'me bairns, man' are okay staying in kennels for a week as they've 'only had doggie daycare and never a sleepover'. It was way more humiliating than if we'd turned up late. Chrystal was certainly hovering recklessly close to the edge by ordering another two drinks on the flight. The cabin crew were starting to mutter and kept looking over; she was on their radar but sufficiently buffered by two sober people so as not to pose a threat to the safety of others and cause the aircraft to plummet to the ground.

Finally reached the resort after a long and arduous coach transfer that stopped off at every single hotel on the coast, or so it seemed. Luckily Chrystal snored every kilometre of the way, which was far less embarrassing than her speaking. The apartment is much tinier and shabbier than it looked in my head. I'm renaming madam 'Chrystal Tips' because that's what she does with her stuff, tips it all over the bloody place and we're tripping over it while she has yet another kip! Shouldn't be so harsh, she's reeling from a hellish life running round after Gibs, a lazy and demanding man who she usually refers to as 'That Bastard' – thus we already have common ground. Although, Twat was in no way controlling, just idle. I shall dig deep, switch my mindset control to 'positive' and get on with enjoying the week, unless I CBA.

The resort is pleasant enough: a long stretch of beach with a promenade of bars and restaurants. Fortunately, not popular with the younger generation and too few clubs to attract stags and hens. And there's sun. The warm variety – in February! How fantastic is that? See, I'm getting into the swing already and almost looking forward to the rest of our first day – if I put my headphones in and ignore the mess.

Monday 10 March

8.30 a.m.Awake way before the others. Sunshine always encourages people to drink. I hope every day is not a repeat of yesterday:

11.00 a.m. Bar then lunch with more drinks.

3.00 p.m. Chrystal goes to apartment to sleep off afternoon booze while Hilary and I explore.

5.00 p.m. Return to a loudly snoring Chrystal, crashed out on the sofa bed.

6.00 p.m. Get ready to go out – pre-drinks then bar for more.

8.00 p.m. Restaurant – Chrystal flirts with all male and female bar staff and waiters (such a cliché).

11.00 p.m. Half steer, half support (not an eighties band) a wobbling Chrystal to the apartment for more drinks while I slope off to bed.

11.30 p.m. See above! Today was a carbon copy of yesterday. I need to be assertive and take myself away to rest my weary ears – Chrystal never stops. Her voice is nails-down-a-blackboard type and, when she's talking at full speed, the writing-with-a-squeaky-whiteboard-pen type.

BUT and it's an upper case BUT, she is not in any way mean or nasty. She is harmless, irritating at times, and as mad as a goose. And Hilary assures me that when you peel away the brash exterior, there's a kind, lovable soul inside. I'm still at the unwrapping stage, but I'm sure the soft centre will be revealed soon – that could be the wine talking, of course. What's amazing is, Hilary's really different around her – miles more laid back and, dare I say, almost *fun*. Also, there's a lot less looking down her nose going on. For that, Chrystal, I am eternally grateful.

Tuesday 11 March

An exhausting day managing Chrystal. Went to a market where, much to her delight, they gave away liqueurs ('shots' to the under sixties). Well, madam took three for herself – the archetypal, shameless Brit abroad; cringeworthy to witness. This set off a major flirting spree with the ecstatic stallholders who reciprocated with gusto as the scent of a sale filled their nostrils. She brought home a bag crammed with tat: junk jewellery; a selection of very gaudy wooden animals; matching photo frames and boxes with shells stuck haphazardly to them; five identical scarves; brightly painted plates; dancing figures sculpted in wire and ruined by lumps of plastic stuck to the joints; three belts from the seventies; four cork items that really don't travel well and will be lucky if they see the light of day between suitcase and charity bag.

It would have all been fine and a positive boon for the local economy, had Chrystal *not* demanded a kiss from each of the younger stallholders in exchange for her custom. In the end, she was blind drunk. I did my usual, 'I'm not with her,' keeping a minimum braking distance of two stalls behind every time she stopped. I witnessed the whole excruciating spectacle that ended with an enthusiastic snog, one large arm hooked around the neck of each unfortunate victim who had no means of escape. Halfway around, I realised she had attracted a crowd who trotted after her for sport as she snogged, giggled, and groped her way from stall to stall; a gaggle of tourists – Spanish, British, Irish, all enjoying the free show. They laughed along with her, or *at* her, as she shouted, pointing at more dancing wire sculptures, 'I'll have them sexy ones there. The ones gettn' jiggy with it!' Then she would twirl (I think that's what it was) to the delight of the loyal fan club. Some had phones poised, ready to send the crazy gyrating Geordie lass to the four corners of the internet.

Throughout the horrendous ordeal, I pretended not to have noticed her and dropped at least four stalls back by the end of the show. The Spanish tourists were bewildered, but I could tell by the looks on the faces of the Brits that they were on safari; trophy-hunters digitally capturing a real live Geordie woman in the wild, behaving exactly as they'd seen on those TV documentaries set in the Bigg Market. And they were lapping it up. The humiliation of it – although I'm beginning to see the funny side now that I'm not there in person or watching it go viral on the internet. Honestly, I'm not even tempted to search for it in case poor Hilary's on there. Wait a sec… 'poor' Hilary? There is no 'poor' Hilary. This is all her bloody fault. I need some sleep!

Wednesday 12 March

Okay, I know Chrystal's making up for lost time, but the flirting's getting serious and starting to really irritate me now. She insists on snogging Mario, the waiter from Amigos, our regular (four visits) eatery, every time we leave; full-on snogs involving tongues, taking the name of the restaurant to another level. I can't decide if Mario is encouraging her or acting under duress – and there's certainly been activity under her dress too. Chrystal's insatiable, that's for sure. Her appetite for alcohol is in a similar league. She knocks back two drinks for every one of ours, defensively reminding us that she's taller than we are. Oh no Chrystal, you're just greedier.

I'm aware of sitting po-faced, like a miserable prude. A sitting duck for a, 'Cheer up it might never happen,' from a passing stranger, who'd get a tongue-lashing for their trouble and cause a different yet equally embarrassing scene. Must make more effort tomorrow. Sounds as though I'm writing out lines as a punishment, which is what it feels like here at times. She's dragging Hilary off to a nudist beach tomorrow. According to Chrystal it's a *naturist* beach, not a nudist beach so I don't know what she's expecting – fully clothed people interested in wildlife? It will be full of elderly German people, so at least they might not understand her accent and she could also be the youngest person there, which will please her. Maybe it's inspired by her interest in yoga? The thought of her sitting naked on a beach in the lotus position makes my toes curl.

Got to hand it to Chrystal though, she's coaxed Hilary even further out of her shell and is modelling how to have a whale of a time. I can't quite believe Hilary agreed to go! I'm loving the idea of it, just not the reality. I hope it doesn't end in tears. Think I'll stay a distance of two beaches behind. It's far safer. Anyway, I don't want Chrystal staring at my bits, judging, and suggesting things that people wielding scalpels, bottom hosepipes, or needles full of noxious substances could do to improve it, in the name of 'aesthetics'. It's not in the least bit healthy to talk about having 'work' done. Enjoy this life that you've just got back, girl! Stop fretting about that drivel.

One drawback of sharing an apartment is sharing reading matter; I've accidentally learned about vagacials. Yes, I also shouted, 'WHAT?' Be patient, and I will *enlighten* you, which is another hideous procedure described further down:

Women, you've already been told how to improve your ugly, inadequate face, skin, hair, teeth, lips, nails, and now we're stooping lower still. Whatever's down there can't possibly be fit for purpose in its natural state! That...that thing you have lovingly named your 'foof' for years, must not be seen, touched or, God forbid, tasted by any self-respecting male!

Honestly, that is the message. Isn't there enough for young women to worry about? Seemingly not. A vagacial is basically a fanny facial – a steam clean down below. How bloody ridiculous! Get a grip, women! You must also, 'have your aesthetician...' *(a real job)* 'check out your waxing and make sure you're doing proper maintenance at home.' Eh?! The only maintenance any woman should be doing at home is tidying the front garden and sprucing things up with a lick of anti-mould paint every few years. It all smacks of yet another angle on exploiting women's insecurities:

Hey, you – is yours too dark, hairy, big, small, spotty (from waxing), or smelly, then why not pay us to get it professionally steam cleaned?

I can see it dovetailing perfectly with redundant carpet cleaners:

Hey, you – is business slow? Too many people with easy-to-clean silky-smooth laminate flooring? How about branching out into a new and exciting career? Wave goodbye to dirty carpets and become an aesthetician in the vagacial area. Full training given.

Another 'treatment' (aka violation) is a 'lightening cream' to achieve a 'bright pink vagina, the ultimate makeover for mums,' boast the ads. WHAAAT? Chrystal mentioned it once, but I was eating a cheesy bake at the time and didn't dare ask.

Then there's vaginal jewellery for the pierced clitoris, vulva, and labia. I kid you not! Now, that is a whole new canesten of worms. Needless to say, there's not one damn hair in sight on any of the photos – yes there were photos! I blame the internet. Boys, who now learn about sex from internet porn sites, are exposed to images of women with fully depilated, bleached nether regions. Thus, if they have the misfortune of encountering pubic hair on their sexual travels, they think it's outrageous and take to social media to denounce its owner.

Sam keeps me up to date with the social media scene, though I'm becoming more au fait with it myself and I'm not sure I like what I see. She told me about Caroline Criado-Perez, an author and journalist who campaigned successfully to have fifty-one percent of the population, aka women, represented on just one of the nation's four bank notes. As a 'punishment', she was trolled relentlessly on Twitter. I haven't ventured into that territory yet. No underlying reasons for such disgraceful venom; she's a feminist, not a man-hater. When the trolling escalated to death threats, she involved the police.

Criado-Perez has also written articles about the link between the pornography-fuelled expectations of young men and the obsession with hairless genitalia. It's obvious when you think about it. Sadly, not enough people *do* think about it – they lie back and passively accept it, together with other sexual practices previously confined to the domain of pornography. I'm sounding prudish again – wouldn't be the first time in a woman's life that feminism has been misconstrued as such. I'm not against any form of sexual practice, provided that a woman is not put under pressure to perform it by a boy who assures her that everyone he's ever met (on screen) does it.

Oops – that little rant has fallen onto the page, all because I don't want to go to the nudey beach. Now, there's a place where we will see pubic hair in abundance, which ought to be a good thing, after all my ranting – but that doesn't mean I want it shoved in my face, so to speak. Not on my holidays.

Chrystal's educating us about being ahead of the game. At first, I was mortally embarrassed when it came to securing frontline beach sunbeds i.e. plonking our towels on them early in the morning. It's not polite, it's against the rules and my nature, but I'm saying nothing for two reasons:

1. I'm reaping the benefits.
2. Watching Hilary squirm while she's doing it is priceless.

I'm between the two camps, but everyone is at it so if we don't join in, we're squatting on the sand and I'm way too old for that.

Chrystal singing to Take That *and* One Direction with her headphones in is a boy band too far, so we now poke her the minute she starts up. It's the only time I will ever sympathise with her controlling ex, who stopped her singing in the house. It was when the people on either side of us began pointing at her, saying, 'Please no more,' that we had to silence her, which was great because we could blame them and pretend we didn't mind.

She keeps telling Hilary she's going to get her 'mortal drunk'. It's obvious Hilary's already loosening up nicely. Her wheels have been oiled and the engine is revving. I don't know when, or if, the cocoon will burst and a new, colourful, drunken Hilary will emerge, but I want a ringside seat for that one.

6.00 p.m. A blissfully peaceful day on my own at the beach! Weirdly, Hilary was full of chat about the nudey, sorry, *naturist* beach, suggesting she is a convert to the cause – if indeed it is a cause? I'm struggling to imagine Hilary strutting her stuff naked on a beach. This is a woman who has never set foot in a communal changing room, let alone a naturist beach! Love it. With Chrystal in the shower out of earshot, Hilary told me all about the new friends they'd made and how Chrystal was the darling of the elderly German women! Apparently, they've had countless invitations to naturist camps in Germany. We had a good laugh and Chrystal joined in to embellish the stories. I can picture the scene – not that I particularly want to. She's so enthusiastic about everything, which is very endearing and contagious. I admire her for it. I spent far too bloody long brooding and moaning about my life when I split up with Twat.

11.00 p.m. Bedtime! Evening was more of the same. Too tired for any further details. It'll be good to get home for a rest.

Thursday 13 March

A wild evening! Just back from the karaoke bar with the added bonus of El Toro, the mechanical bull. No dear friends, he didn't have the pleasure of bucking *me* off his back. Coupled with the fact I was wearing a dress and didn't want to reveal what lay beneath to all and sundry, I was far too scared of breaking my neck. Pure heaven for Chrystal, though: two perfect activities for an exhibitionist who's been caning the sangria like it's an Olympic sport. First, we endured a screechy rendition of 'I Will Survive' and a passable version of 'I Got You Babe' – a duet with pint-sized Paulo, another terrified barman she dragged to the stage. I must admit it was great, with everyone joining in and cheering madly at the end. With heaps of pizazz, she knows how to work an audience, does our Chrystal. When she was gently but firmly removed from the stage to make way for other wannabees, her fans booed and chanted 'Chrys-tal, Chrys-tal!' until she disappeared in search of Paulo, who'd legged it as soon as he could. Hilary and I tried to calm her down as she bellowed for him over the music. Smelling trouble, Paulo had sensibly gone to ground. As the post-performance adrenaline subsided, Chrystal wailed, 'Aa've gotta find Paulo-ooo!' Attempting to distract her, Hilary said, 'Ooh look, a mechanical bull!'

You didn't think that one through, did you Hilary? Without blinking, Chrystal leapt onto it like a teenager and began whooping and yee-hah-ing in the style of a seasoned Wild West rodeo pro! El Toro had met his match – this lass wasn't giving up lightly. Several people drifted in to watch and couldn't quite believe how the drunken woman from the karaoke could stay on the bull for so long.

'Whoo-hoo! A've got great thigh grip mind, Toro!' she screamed, as the fan-club egged her on, chanting her name for the second time that night. It was an impressive spectacle while it lasted. Suddenly, the bull operator ramped up the speed a notch or two and Chrystal was flung like a rag doll from the mechanical beast onto the cushioned surface below. I'm *so* relieved she's wearing jeans tonight, otherwise it would have been another type of show altogether. To her absolute delight, Paulo appeared from nowhere. Grinning in admiration, he looked down at the blonde heap on the floor.

'Chrystal! You are very clever riding El Toro like this!'

Hilary and I cringed, wondering what her cheeky retort would be, but to our relief she answered almost like a normal person.

'Ah thanks Paulo, mate. He's knackered us out, mind.'

Understanding the gist of her message, Paulo (barman turned paramedic) bent down then carefully untangled, smoothed, and checked her four limbs for damage. The sangria must have broken her fall.

'All good. Ready?'

Paulo was certainly much stronger than he looked because, with a brief but amusing struggle, he hauled Chrystal up from the mat and tenderly rearranged her hair as she looked down lovingly into his eyes. It was a very touching scene. Without a word, she despatched him with a hug and a friendly peck (no tongues) then headed for the door, through the politely applauding crowd, while we trotted behind her in disbelief.

Friday 14 March

Spent the daylight hours relaxing while solar-powered Chrystal soaked up the sun's rays, converted them into energy, and stored them up for her night of non-stop fun – like that rabbit in the battery adverts. Read on!

Saturday 15 March

Oh my God – have I got a story for you! Can't believe last night was real. It was by far the best holiday craic I've had in my whole life. Honestly can't decide if I'm:

a) appalled
b) angry
c) amused
d) jealous

e) all of the above

In keeping with the last-night-of-a-holiday tradition, i.e. one last chance to party hard, Chrystal excelled herself and broke Hilary in the process. Yes, wrecked her. Hell bent on having a fling and getting Hilary drunk, Chrystal's two missions were conveniently rolled into one and accomplished with flair. Throughout the meal at Amigos, we listened to a tedious stream of sexual banter between Mario and Chrystal. Then Hilary, who had been observing her friend, a graduate in Outrageous Behaviour, joined in! When Mario sat down at the table between the two women who were both intoxicated with alcohol and sheer bliss, I decided enough was enough. As they squashed up beside young Mario, almost smothering him, I beat a hasty retreat to the apartment to pack.

Later, I could hear Chrystal's dulcet tones shattering the peace in the out-of-season resort as she bellowed, 'Luna Bar eleven o'clock!' presumably at Mario waving them off at the door, having been snogged within an inch of his life. At that point, I remember laughing naïvely to myself as I got ready for bed, happy that my old friend and yes, my new *friend*, were enjoying life. Exactly how *much* and what *type* of merriment they would indulge in, is about to be revealed. Are you sitting comfortably in Shady Pines, in your reclining chairs with footstools? Then I'll begin.

My rude awakening began at 3.13 a.m. with Take That (sadly not the band themselves but just as loud) blasting out in the lounge. I'd left the bedroom door open and was about to get up to pointedly slam it shut, when I heard a mixture of high-pitched and suspiciously low-pitched giggling. Had I not witnessed it with my own eyes, I'd never have believed what happened and would assume it was a horrific nightmare. I don't need to scar myself for life by documenting the details or a blow-by-blow account (sorry), suffice to say that I'd NEVER EVER expected Hilary to be involved in a real live, tabloid style three-in-a-bed sex romp! Given what you know of Hilary, my dear Shady Pines friends and younger readers, do you agree, that nothing, *not one thing,* would seem further from the truth? Please address the bench when you answer.

I wonder if she was inspired by the doggers and has harboured a yearning to give it a shot ever since? Or is it more likely she was totally oblivious to everything last night, unaware of what she was doing after downing at least one whole jug of sangria? Whatever the explanation, I'm desperately trying to erase the disturbing scene, along with its accompanying sound effects, from my delicate brain: Chrystal in the throes of passion shouting, 'Howay Mario, pet!' followed by a rousing rendition of 'Relight my Fire'. She moved rhythmically during the Lulu bit, while a topless Hilary kept time, waving her hands from side to side to the music – a bizarre, pornographic backing singer. I could take *that* no longer, so I reached for my earplugs and buried my head deep under the pillow for what was left of the night.

Mario was despatched at 4.23 p.m. I heard him say in a very polite and proper manner, 'Very good, very nice, thank you,' as though he'd just sampled a Victoria sponge at the Women's Institute annual garden party, bless him. The door slammed, followed by 'Jesus Christ,' from an exhausted Chrystal flopping onto the sofa bed, then hippo-like snoring from Hilary. My last thought was, 'They'd better not have broken the bloody sofa bed, or we'll lose our deposit.'

I've left them sleeping it off in the apartment. Now sitting in the sunshine avoiding Amigos, savouring the last drops of warmth and a perfect Spanish coffee. Neither of them has moved a muscle since last night, when they moved every one of them – Mario's included. We'll definitely miss the flight if I don't go and flush them out.

3.00 p.m. Airport. How we ever made it here is a miracle! The driver had to stop the coach twice to let Hilary off to be sick. She flatly refused to use the toilet. At the airport, she rushed off to sample *their* toilets, emerging once to make a brief appearance at the check-in desk and only just managed to survive security. After catching the faintest whiff of duty-free perfume in the air, she hightailed it, hand over mouth, to try the next toilets and is still in there. Poor Hilary, I remember similar occasions in my youth, but never any on this side of forty. Chrystal, on the other hand, is clearly used to drinking gallons and has no trace of a hangover, though she's very subdued. Mind you, they both stank of stale wine this morning. And so did the apartment.

Tentative enquiries were made:

Hilary: Did we wake you up when we got in last night?

Me (smiling sweetly): No. Well, I heard a noise but went straight back to sleep.

Oh no, my girl. I'm saving this one until we're safely ensconced in her flat. If she can ever face alcohol again, I'll loosen her tongue with a few drinks and demand a full debriefing. At the gate, I was beginning to think they weren't going to let us on the plane. Thought Hilary was hiding in the loo out of embarrassment, but she came back looking green with dark circles around her eyes. Thinking I was engrossed in my diary, writing the boring, censored version of the holiday, she flashed Chrystal a knowing smile. Barefaced cheek! I'm sorely tempted to stand up right now in front of the queue for boarding and read out last night's entry because I'm damn sure she's blissfully unaware of what exactly went on. I've got to admit, through the sleep deprivation, I'm starting to see the very funny side of their shared holiday romance!

10.30 p.m. Home safe and sound without further humiliation or fines to pay for Hilary barfing on the plane. Thankfully, she made it to the loo before the charges kicked in and hid it well from Carlos, our chief flight attendant slash prison camp guard who was obviously having a very heavy shift. It was an evening flight, and some people were already tipsy after making the most of their last day. Seeing potential for high jinks among several of the groups: young men; mixed age stags and hens; Chrystal who oozes trouble from every pore, Carlos launched a pre-emptive strike before things (we passengers) got out of hand. Before the safety announcement began, he issued a stern reminder that we were *not* in a bar in Gran Canaria, nor did he wish us to be the subject of a TV airline documentary (he knew his audience). Therefore, if we were going to enjoy the flight (and not be taken out and shot) we must now be silent, pay attention to the safety announcement and 'do no swearing' during the flight. Then, from row eight, a cheeky chappie dared to say, 'Ooooo!' in a 'don't get your knickers in a twist, mate' style. At that point, all one hundred and twenty of us thought we'd be ejected from the plane. Carlos marched down the aisle, fixing the now terrified guy with his evil dictator stare.

'So, you think this is a joke, eh? Is your safety a JOKE? Show some respect or you will NOT be travelling tonight!'

Stunned silence from the travellers while everyone prayed no one was too drunk to disobey the rules. I patted Hilary's leg to comfort her. She looked like death and Carlos wasn't helping. I was convinced he'd run amok with a machete if she dared to heave into the duty-free carrier bag between her legs. Poor Hilary. Oh, how we suffer for our misdemeanours!

Miraculously, the plane took off with an altogether different ambience from when we boarded. There was subdued giggling in some rows, instantly quashed with a glance in their general direction from Carlos. One fearless woman, enjoying the craic by saying to others, 'Eee divvent, man. Carlos'll get yous!' created camaraderie throughout the plane, uniting us against the oppressor. She then took on the seemingly impossible task of taming the wild beast by chatting to him. This was watched by many, who thought it unwise to take their eyes off the snake, should it lash out unexpectedly. But tame him she did, with her genial Geordie patter and, as he pushed his trolley down the aisle, a hint of a smile could be seen on his face.

Minding our p's and q's and grovelling like good pupils desperately trying to get back in Teacher's good books, there wasn't so much as a peep out of any of us, having already pissed Teacher off, big-time.

The holiday ended in a crescendo of craic: an extraordinary last night (winking emoji) and a lively flight home that continued right through passport control where Chrystal attempted to charm the expressionless staff without success – no surprise there. An integral part of their training is to watch episodes of *Fawlty Towers* without being allowed to smile, let alone laugh. Even the Carlos whisperer didn't try her luck with those guys – she had more sense.

Tuesday 18 March

It's taken until today to motivate myself into unpacking and washing. Can't wait to get back to the allotment but I'm struggling to muster up the energy.

I've no idea if the holiday falls into the *good* or *bad* category. When Hilary joins the rest of us in Shady Pines, it'll make a thoroughly juicy story for a rainy afternoon. Sadly, I doubt anyone will believe her. They'll say she's delusional and call a meeting to increase her medication. Okay, I hear you – I'm opting for *good*. I may still be exhausted and in a state of shock, but one thing's for sure – it could never, ever be described as *boring*.

Thursday 20 March

I love it when you think in a certain way, then something happens to change your whole outlook. After our first encounter in the check-in queue, I was convinced Chrystal would be unbearable. Admittedly, I wanted to dive under the table with embarrassment at least five times a night, but now I think, okay – live and let live. She's been in a crap relationship, is thoroughly harmless and despite the wrapping, I agree that what's inside is essentially solid gold. And she's a woman's woman, as proved by kindly sharing her conquest with Hilary. Exactly how much choice Hilary had in the proceedings, is another matter.

I've had my eyes opened to a new facet of life: women my age are entitled to gratuitous sex, and it is not beyond the realms of fantasy (no, not *that* kind of fantasy) to enjoy it. Although I'm still hankering after Lucas and not interested in anyone else yet, he helped me overcome my fear of sleeping with someone other than Twat. After seeing way too much of Chrystal in action, I'm not sure I'd be up to scratch but, if pushed, I might consider taking it up as a hobby and would be willing to learn. Not so keen on the initial process though, all that outrageous flirting. Maybe I should be the third person and find a confident friend to reel them in for me. Now that *is* a joke – I was carried away in the post-holiday moment!

If you'd said to me a week ago, 'Lizzie, you know your friend, the very straight one, a bit stuck-up – do you think she'd be up for a threesome with a girlfriend and a younger bloke?' I'd have asked if you were on drugs. You never know what life has in store (or online) for you.

We're all capable of surprising others. It usually happens through a change of circumstance – from misery to happiness, slavery to liberation, often following an escape from a toxic or stagnant relationship. Perhaps, my Shady Pines friends, it happened to you in your later years? Another such escapee was Lydia. When I finally forgave my fabulous hairdresser Denise for coercing me into an all-over rinse instead of highlights, due to excessive coverage of grey hair, she regaled me with the heart-warming tale of her mum, Lydia – a woman on a mission. Lydia was seventy-four (*not* a typo) when she decided enough was enough, packed her bags and left grumpy old husband of fifty-two years Frank to lead a far happier life alone. Except, she's now rarely alone and never lonely, a far cry from the isolated existence she endured with Frank, who drank far too much and didn't like her leaving the house. With the world at her feet, she now travels with friends or family, abroad, and to every corner of the British Isles accessible by a National Express Coach (and The Divine Comedy). This lady has finally reached paradise without having to:

a) explain her every move and endure endless moaning for having a life

b) wait on someone hand and foot who suffers from a common male affliction: learned helplessness

c) return to an alcoholic harbinger of doom

Like many women of her age, Lydia survived decades of drudgery running the house, cooking, cleaning, shopping, *and* working. When they both retired, nothing changed. Apart from changing the odd lightbulb, Frank continued to be waited on hand and foot. Rather than pummelling him into submission, a fantasy that entered her head on an increasing number of occasions leading up to her departure, Lydia took out her frustrations on the moss that grew between the paving stones on the patio, engaging in hand-to-hand combat with it on a weekly basis. As a consequence, the patio was as pristine as the day it was laid. Confiding in her daughter, Lydia said she found her own thoughts disturbing, particularly the clichéd ones about burying a body under the patio. After all, she had watched every episode of *Brookside* when she was younger. It could be the perfect crime as suspicions would never be aroused, given its permanent moss-free air of freshness.

Don't worry, Frank was spared the Trevor Jordache treatment and is now ably supported by his long-suffering family. I hear you ask, with pity in your voices, 'Did Lydia ever give him a chance to change?' Of course she did – not that he deserved one! When Lydia first left, Frank was ordered by Denise to woo her back, to tell her how he felt and what he would do to make amends. So, when she returned a few weeks later with an open mind, ready to either collect the rest of her belongings or stay and give it another try, she was met with the pitiful extent of Frank's wooing ability:

'Lydia that patio's really missing you, mind.'

Ta-da! Job done, Frank – how could she possibly resist? To be, er… frank, you had the best seat in the Last Chance Saloon, and you totally blew it. Surprising though it may seem, Lydia declined the heavily disguised romantic gesture, brought him a final can of beer, and packed up the rest of her belongings. With a spring

75

in her step and a fleeting glance at the moss-covered patio, she left for good. Lydia, you are indeed a legend.

Saturday 22 March

At last – a brief visit to the allotment! Feels like ages since I was here, but the weather's been foul since the holiday. Walking through the gate felt surprisingly familiar, like coming home, yet exciting at the same time. The perfect blend of peace without boredom. A week of never-ending gluttony has left me lethargic and in need of a good dose of digging. To be fair on myself, watching Chrystal in action is draining; she never stops.

Tuesday 25 March

After a few more days in recovery, I spent today reflecting on the holiday. Yes, that counts as an activity – it's a verb, and a verb is a *doing* word. Hear me out and you'll discover more about Chrystal's life with her ex-partner and the shocking stories she shared as the week unfolded. I hope you'll better understand her holiday antics and won't judge her for them.

With Chrystal released from captivity and Hilary secretly looking to reinvent herself, it was a perfect storm. Both unshackled, shaking off their chains and basking in the company of kind and supportive women, without the controlling men whose default setting was to undermine.

Gibs is a textbook case. Although I don't wish to stereotype, he even looks intimidating. Abusers and survivors come in all shapes and sizes, and gender identities, but I am referring to a male abuser in a heterosexual relationship. Anyone meeting

Chrystal now would be shocked to learn that she'd stayed in an abusive relationship for six long years.

She was initially attracted to his pumped-up body-builder's physique. Not my cup of tea. Works in a garage – an all-male environment with older men for role models. He started off as the perfect partner, then ever-so gradually, the criticism crept in: 'I prefer you in this dress. I don't like those shoes as much as the others. What have you done to your hair? Keep your voice down,' until she would seek his approval for everything and bow to his demands, for a quiet life. It escalated to fully blown control over the years and eventually he stopped her seeing her friends by complaining of feeling 'lonely' if she went out. So, she stopped. Not worth the aggravation.

It is a documented pattern of coercive control in relationships and is not confined to men: grind them down slowly – drip, drip, drip, push, push, push until they are crushed. Then keep them where you want them: underneath your thumb. But keep up the pressure, keep on driving until they feel worthless then no one else will want them. Don't relent, or they may crawl to the door and escape into a world of freedom. But there's little chance of that. Every ounce of confidence has been knocked out of their fragile body. You ripped their guts out, leaving an unrecognisable carcass – as was your plan. A coercive controller is very skilled in their art. They are devious and manipulate the mind of the controlee into feeling pity for them, disguising it as concern or love, 'I'm missing your voice. I'm miserable,' masking their true agenda: malicious intent to control. Such situations creep up on people. Fairy tale turns horror story. Thankfully, there is more awareness now, though for many it's too late, or simply futile. As friends, we feel we're wasting our breath, trying to make them see what they are blind to. But try we must, because one day when it dawns on them that we're right, they will know we support them unconditionally. Chrystal was almost broken, but not quite.

I'm still processing the details of her awful ordeal: the constant phone calls, checking where she was, what she was doing and who exactly she was with, despite running it past him before she was allowed to leave the house. Once, determined to ruin her day out, he hid her credit cards just before she left to meet friends. The cards turned up in a place she'd searched thoroughly – thus gaslighting her with, 'Must be your age, love.' He called her eight times that afternoon. She answered once, fearing the consequences if she ignored him.

I understand if you dear readers prefer to skip the following paragraphs as there are details of violence – they are upsetting.

Whenever she came home, he'd shout and bawl. Why didn't she answer him? What did she have to hide? Who was she *really* with? Seething with jealousy, testosterone oozing from every steroid-filled pore. Accusations flying, Chrystal would placate him, having made the mistake of standing up to him on one occasion, after which he pinned her to a wall, holding her neck in his colossal hand, pressing on her windpipe. Gibs would stalk her, sometimes blatantly, walking past the place where she was trying to enjoy herself. At times he would do it slyly – spying on her – obsessed. God forbid should she be seen exchanging words with another man, including bar staff or waiters. He'd wait in the house, in the dark, then leap out at her when she crept in. One night Chrystal argued and tried to fight back so he grabbed her hair and dragged her to a wall. I can imagine how petrified she felt, I can picture the thug with veins bursting out of his forehead, spitting bile and misogyny into her face. I refuse to repeat his words. The next day there would be the inevitable remorse. The,

'I'm not worthy. How can you ever bring yourself to forgive me?' Promises, promises, and yet more promises. He'd slaver, dripping empty words of faux remorse over her vulnerable, enervated body. Then she'd shower, scrubbing her skin hard to cleanse it of his filth. After that she decided to change tack.

It was easier to refuse invitations. It kept the peace. It's so difficult to think of this effervescent, fun-loving woman acting this way, yet not at all surprising, considering how she was treated. Fragment by fragment, he had chipped away for years at her will and inner strength until she scarcely recognised herself. Just before it was too late, she took stock of the situation. It came after she'd been allowed to meet up with her sister Amber on her birthday. Gibs didn't want to arouse suspicions among the family and needed to perpetuate the myth of the perfect partner. Chrystal left the house as usual, dressed down and without makeup. She would arrive at her venue, dive into the loo and apply lipstick, blusher and eyeshadow, hidden in her bag, then remove it before she left for home. When she was telling us the story, I let out a loud, involuntary gasp because it's impossible to believe Chrystal is capable of *not* wearing makeup. It explains why she trowels it on now, poor love. That life-changing night, Amber caught her frantically cleansing her face, like a teenager with the world's strictest parents. 'Good God are you getting ready for bed?'

Chrystal broke down and told her everything. Two months later, with her sister's support and a meticulously planned operation, she walked out on her abuser. She reported him for the attack, but by then the only bruising that remained was the psychological kind – and that would never disappear. Sadly, it would be her word against his, in the absence of photographic evidence of her injuries. Of course, he stalked her relentlessly at first, sitting outside her flat for hours but because he hadn't physically threatened or called her since she left, Chrystal was unwilling to report him for fear of escalation. A perfect catch-22 for Gibs; emotional torture for Chrystal. She moved twenty miles away, changed her car twice in eight months and moved house again but to no avail; he's always tracked her down. It is becoming less frequent, and she's hopeful he'll give up if she keeps reporting him. She considers herself lucky to have escaped the relationship in time so, despite the persistent stalking, feels relatively free and is certainly making the most of it, especially when she goes anywhere out of his reach.

Sleep well, friends. Please nurture relationships with people who enhance your life, and ditch those who don't.

APRIL

Wednesday 2 April

You can't beat a trip away with girlfriends because you always learn something! During the non-stop chit-chatting, from trivial to profound – the hallmark of a girlie weekend – you invariably pick up a useful tip or two. A bond develops when, away from our normal life, we are holed up together. It's life-affirming; women are great at it.

This holiday was no exception. The potentially life-changing nugget from the week was not *th*e vagacials and Botox, but the delights of HRT. Chrystal swears by it, and I've accidentally seen the results – remarkable, I must admit. Combined with leaving Gibs, she says it's given her back her mojo. It looked, to me, like tenfold with bells on – and good on her! Since learning about the menopause and experiencing higher order madness, I've wondered about taking it myself. Must research it first, though the anecdotal evidence is positive. Chrystal went 'reet off sex'. I can't imagine her doing that but seeing a photo of Gibs helped. Like me, she had difficulty sleeping and sieve-brain (aka brain fog) – forgetting names, words, and just about everything. In Chrystal's case, the fog morphed into a dense, red mist most of the time, like PMS on steroids. Again, as it was mostly directed towards her controlling partner, it's not quite a fair test. Let's not forget aching joints and everything on that list of five million symptoms associated with the menopause. All gone – cured! Feels twenty years younger. I fear that's an exaggeration, but if it's half as good as she claims, I'm in. No one wants to take medication unless it's a last resort, but this one sounds to me like a good punt.

Friday 4 April

Meanwhile back at the allotment…

Warning – power walking in several layers of gardening clothes not only *looks* stupid but makes you sweat like mad. History dictates that tissues (or loo roll) and I have a shockingly dysfunctional relationship: I abuse them, and they always let me down. Hal turned up just in time to see me mopping my damp brow and upper lip with a scratty piece of tissue – not my best look. He'd left some packets of tomato, chilli, pepper, and leek seeds in the greenhouse for me and called by to explain what to do with them. Apparently, (here come the rules) I should have done this weeks ago at home as they have a long growing season, and the greenhouse is still too cold for them. I couldn't have left them while I went on holiday anyway, so it's all worked out well. It's like having pets or kids. Rumour has it, you can't leave them home alone either, unless you're going to make a film about it.

Hal seemed more relaxed than before and listened with great interest to the holiday lowdown, including Chrystal's antics, or most of them. I sense a sharp intake of breath from you at this point, but of course I missed out the last night! I'm not betraying my friends to a man I barely know. When he'd finished laughing at the market visit anecdote, he looked at me for a few seconds too long and said, 'It's good to see you again.' Not sure if it was awkward or pleasant. Probably both.

Sunday 6 April

Arrived at the allotment early this morning. It was freezing cold and windy, so it was deserted. Taking advantage of the situation, I wandered over to the naughty corner. No sign of anyone, or so I thought. When I passed the target's shed, the door opened for a split second then slammed shut. I nearly jumped into the muck heap with fright! Like a frightened rabbit, I dashed home and didn't look back. Rule number one of *An Idiot's Guide to Snooping*: Don't get caught snooping, you idiot.

Hilary rang to apologise for her hangover on the journey home. She's been lying low since the holiday and still has no idea I saw her shenanigans and much, *much* more. When the time is right, I'll tell her. But for now, I'm carrying a guilty secret that could be defined as *voyeurism,* which is deliciously ironic – even though I don't live in Gosforth. She's bound to be mortified, but I'll assure her it's fine and make sure she appreciates how much her friendship with Chrystal enhances her life. Then we'll laugh at her exploits.

Thursday 10 April

Everyone's been calling or texting, demanding the gory details of the holiday so I'm keeping it to a brief, toned down snapshot of Chrystal's exploits only, making sure she sounds fun and not totally bonkers, or that would be unkind. Hilary may still not remember hers so I'm going with the 'What goes on in Gran Canaria, stays in Gran Canaria' rule. Simon's quizzing me about Allotment Man – Ha!

'You fancy him, Moffitt! You come over all coy when you talk about him and you're defensive when anyone else does.'

Told him he's talking garbage, or rubbish, if Americanisms offend you. Truth is – he might be right! Mentioned I might ask Hal on a hot date to a garden centre sometime, only half joking.

'Whaaaat?' was Simon's incredulous response. He knows I hate garden centres and I defended myself by promising not to look at any awful clothing in there. Where else can I buy allotment paraphernalia – Greggs? If I go, I'll stick to the horticultural paths, or I'll get palpitations and that's not a good look either. He launched into a string of double entendre nonsense, channelling 1970s stereotype Larry Grayson, about Hal showing me the best tool for trimming grassy areas and what did he think about melons. I think it'll be useful to go with Hal – I might even enjoy it! Never thought I'd write that in a diary, this side of ninety.

A gang of masked mice have broken into the greenhouse, held a seed-fuelled orgy and left before dawn – how dare they! They didn't scoff the lot, so I planted the remaining tomato, chilli, pepper, and leek seeds in trays in case they come back for round two. Following orders, I took them home, placed them on sunny windowsills and crossed my fingers.

Sunday 13 April

It came to me in the night what our friend in the corner plot is up to – he's a fence! Ironically, not the garden kind – we're talking stolen goods! Yep, I've watched enough police dramas to spot a secret lock-up when I see one. Saw him again today wheeling his 'barra, laden with plastic-covered contraband, backwards and forwards from car to shed. His plot may be a mess, but this plot's thickening neatly, mark my words. Unlike most at the allotment, he never acknowledges anyone he passes. Something that doesn't fit the fence or even burglar stereotype is that he looks far too straight. His clothes are old enough for, ahem, 'gardening', but smack of country gent: small-checked shirts worn with faded red cords, bought from a small shop with a large price tag, in Corbridge, Hexham, Alnwick or somewhere equally rural. Far too clean shaven to fit the profile of thief. However, he'd win the prize for shiftiest fella on the site, that's for sure so I'm sticking with my first instinct. Difficult to age: neat curly grey hair and weather-beaten skin. He mustn't work because he's there off-peak, during the week when it's quiet. An early retiree, perhaps?

I think the police would laugh me out of the station and make a snide remark about watching *The Sweeney* – if they're over fifty or *The Wire* – under fifties. They'd all be wrong; this crime scenario belongs firmly in the *Vera* camp. If I share my theory with Hal, he'll no doubt tell me to keep out of it, so I don't think I'll do that.

Tuesday 15 April

I'm lonely, *really* lonely today. I know I shouldn't be, but I'm missing Lucas, or what he offered me: the intimacy and yes, the sex. Not any old sex, just his. His was the Taste the Difference of sex, not from the bog-standard range. It's not that I need a partner to enjoy life – it would be another component of it; a hobby or interest, an extra-curricular activity but definitely not the be-all and end-all. In an act of masochism, I wasted the day watching films that made me cry. How ridiculous. I need to snap out of it and get myself out tomorrow... or Thursday.

Thursday 17 April

Took my flask and lunch to the allotment – it was great to get out. Miriam came past, already in mid-rant. She'd been drinking and it wasn't much past twelve. I expect she'd argue it was officially the afternoon.

'What a blarsted joke! That bloody committee sent me another effing letter!'

Looking even more dishevelled than usual, she was clearly very upset. Telling me in unnecessary detail what she was going to do to them when she got her effing hands on the unfortunate committee members and *their* members, she was, as my mum would say, 'full of hell'. To comply with the rules, the plot needed tidying up or she'd face eviction from the site. I feel very sorry for Miriam. She mustn't have much in her life. She rejected my offer of help, but I trailed after her as she cursed and swore enough to make Gordon Ramsay blush. As her plot is beside the dodgy guy's, I must confess to an ulterior motive – though I wasn't rewarded with a sighting today. Once there, I told her in a matter-of-fact way that I'd come tomorrow at ten o'clock and dig her plot. She could be there or not, I'd still come. For a split second she very nearly cracked a smile – then turned it into a sneer, saying I could please myself! Don't mention it, Miriam, you're welcome.

Friday 18 April – Good Friday

Ever been had? It certainly was a *good* Friday for someone! Half of it was spent weeding Miriam's plot and barrowing it to the compost heap. I also bagged a load of rubbish from the plot and took it to the skip that had conveniently arrived a few days earlier. She turned up at half past ten and spent the entire time in her shed, poking around and mumbling on a loop that it just wasn't effing fair and how her husband used to help her but now he can't due to his effing back, and how she always volunteers at the annual working party – now *that* I'd like to see! The working party is when the shared areas are tidied: the orchard trees are pruned; the fencing mended; the water troughs cleaned. What I've seen of Miriam's work ethic so far, I'd be surprised if she ever showed up, though I've heard there's a barbecue and the plot holders bring wine and beer – in which case...

When I left it looked great! Because the shed contained her secret stash of booze and presumably a ton of empty bottles, I wasn't allowed in there, so she guarded it by getting not-so-quietly sozzled as I beavered away outside. When I left, she didn't have the awareness to thank me, but I let her off due to the stress she was under. I've only myself to blame so I won't moan about it much, except to point out that my fair share of community service is now complete for the year, and I have credit in the bank.

Once home, I had a bath to ease the aching muscles and an early night.

Saturday 19 April – Easter Saturday

A traumatic day. Barely slept. No, it wasn't the text – it was the bloody menopause yet again. Woke up all hot flushy. I was tired so drove to the allotment, tailgated on Osborne Road by a young guy in a stupid car who FLASHED HIS LIGHTS AT ME to move over! How DARE he! I now admit the driving was slow to the point of dangerous in the style of a much older person, but there is NEVER any need to flash someone out of the way. The red mist descended. I slammed the brakes on, got out of the car and flew over to him just as his window and his mouth were opening. I shouted, almost screamed at him. I think it went something like:

'WHAT ARE YOU FLASHING YOUR BLOODY LIGHTS FOR IN YOUR EIGHTEEN-YEAR-OLD BOY

RACER'S CAR, YOU MACHO GIT....' blah blah blah (delivered in shouty capitals).

At the same time, he was shouting at me to move the car before he called the police, to which the obvious response was, 'GOOD! I'LL TELL THEM ABOUT YOUR AGGRESSIVE AND DANGEROUS DRIVING!' ending in a flourish with my signature comment, 'YOU WOULDN'T DARE DO THAT IF I WAS A MAN!' That shut him up. Maybe because he didn't have a clue why I said it, but I knew it was true and I'm glad I included it in the tirade.

I marched back to the car, pulled over, and shook for a while. Flying into an uncontrollable rage is not good for your health. I've been feeling more and more like this, and anxiety is creeping in with it. I believe they're very typical menopausal symptoms. It's a relentless parade of bloody misery as a woman, or is it unique to me? Last year's depression replaced with the fully blown menopause. I can't think of another explanation because I'm essentially happy with my new life. Needs a bit of tweaking, but it's on track. Hormone replacement therapy, Chrystal? I want to bloody well get rid of them, not replace them; they're nothing but trouble.

Ate three Easter eggs as compensation – feel worse now.

Sunday 20 April – Easter Sunday

To add insult to injury after my charitable works on Friday, I found out that, in keeping with the North East tradition, my potatoes should have been planted on that day! It's a strange one, as Good Friday can vary by a month every year, but who am I to argue?

Instead, I planted them today! It's hard work, digging deep trenches, lined with newspaper for extra protection – a tip from Hal. And *so* satisfying when I'd finished. The early varieties are new potatoes for summer, then there's a maincrop in September – red ones for mashing and baking. I love the look of the high ridges of soil on either side of the trenches – it felt quite creative. My muscles ache again. I'm going to have great biceps after this weekend.

Bit the bullet and texted Hal. Stupidly, it was after a large glass of hard-earned wine. NEVER text someone after a drink unless you know them well. It ought to be illegal, if only to save us from ourselves. Don't drink and text – you know it makes sense. A phone is a lethal weapon that will land you well and truly in it:

Do you fancy coming to Cowell's, then up to the nursery gardens in Alnwick sometime? I could do with your advice for the paths.

Brief, factual. You can't complain about leading anyone on (and up the allotment path?) with that innocuous suggestion. Then panicked about the word 'fancy' and whether he'd think I chose it subliminally because I fancy him! However, you lot might be shocked by my sudden desire to go to any type of garden centre, if you remember my rants on the subject only a matter of months ago. In my defence, Cowell's is a family-run, authentic garden centre, where the focus is (shockingly!) on horticulture. It is not a department store in disguise or somewhere to take toddlers and elderly relatives for the day. And I thought a trip to Alnwick then over to the coast would be nice. A two-garden-centre holiday!

Trying to stay calm. I'm not in a flap because I don't fancy every last bone in his body, like I did Lucas's – only some of them. Now *that's* the wine talking.

Monday 21 April – Bank Holiday

Called Sam who laughed and laughed about my road rage. 'Good for you! Can't stand those boy racer types. And no, they wouldn't do that to another guy because they could end up dead.'

I love my daughter! Told her I need HRT. Her reply was, 'Look, you've always been radgey and I don't want you to stop being you.'

The sentiment was very sweet, and I said it'd take more than a few pills to stop me flying off the handle or having a good rant, but she's not the one waking up at three in the morning in a panicky sweat, forgetting to do two out of every three jobs, and losing two out of every three items. She's calling round tomorrow after work – probably checking up on me. Still no reply from Hal – now regretting the text, which isn't helping my anxiety.

I went to buy a new travel card and had a hot flush in the queue. It's the month of April and it's only just above freezing in the metro station. I felt like a drug addict having cold turkey, and Christmas was months ago.

Wednesday 23 April

Finally a reply: *Sounds good. Just need to sort out a few jobs and I'll get back to you.*

Hmm – he's in no rush, but better than nothing.

Thursday 24 April

GUESS WHAT? Sam's pregnant! I'm going to be a Grandma, or a Granny, Gran, Nanna or someone, in December. She and Ben are over the moon and will be GREAT parents.

How EXCITING! Naturally, I still feel far too young to be a grandmother. Then again, I felt the same about becoming a parent, and once was enough. I don't think grandparents have to be as sensible as parents, mind you. I certainly won't be! And when they realise I forget everything, they won't want to leave me in charge of the baby for long. It's a win-win for me! It's such lovely news and a great positive focus for my yo-yo emotions.

Thinking back, she's looked peaky for the last few weeks. It's not yet on general release, so I mustn't blab – that's going be tricky and I'm bound to forget.

Saturday 26 April

I planted some broad beans on the rougher patch as the raised beds aren't made yet. It's still chilly at night but they don't mind the cold – they are the hard cases of the veggie world. Although, they mustn't be broad Geordie beans because I was advised to put some of that fleece stuff over them that I bought online, and Geordies don't wear fleeces. A complete misnomer, fleece is a very fine manufactured material designed to protect young plants from frost, birds, or the shock of being evicted from their cosy greenhouse just as they were getting used to a life of Riley.

I'm going to bring my grandchild to plant seeds in three years' time. What a heart-warming thought for a chilly day. Enough of that talk.

Sunday 27 April

A date! Not a date, I meant a *day*: *Sorted a free day. Friday 9th?*
He's certainly playing it cool, which is a good thing. Ooh, listen to me! Must stop reading so much into things. Why am I

doing this? I am (quote) 'happily single' after all. Yes, people of the Shadier Pines, I court trouble. Eager to hand over my money and jump back on the rollercoaster where I belong – feeling great one day, guilty towards Lucas the next – why? I don't really deserve it – do I? Occasionally, I'm like a turbo-charged Chrystal but usually I'm in confirmed celibate mode. Life would be far less complicated if I chose the second option – how boring would that be? Certainly wouldn't be in keeping with a 'grabbing life by the horns' (or anywhere else for that matter) attitude.

Besides, it's all talk. since Lucas left, coupled with my ever-increasing list of menopausal symptoms, I've not thought about sex much and I'm only interested in Hal for his horticultural knowledge. I fantasise about compost bins and trailing lobelia. And no – that's not something to discuss with your 'aesthetician'.

However, I'd be lying if I said I'm not massively excited!

Monday 28 April

It's taken months, but I've finally finished digging, and learned that you can have too much of a good thing – another great excuse for a celebration! What do you mean, 'It's only Monday'? I'm retired and can please myself. Opened wine *and* chocolates I'd kept since Christmas as a reward for all the hard graft and the news about Sam.

MAY

Thursday 1 May

A very strange encounter this morning. I've watched a mother and son walk past the plot several times in the last few weeks. Their names are Scott and Sandy – Hal aka Radio Allotment told me. Scott must be in his thirties and they're always together. Sandy's a lioness with a wild, unkempt mane and an all-over rinse of golden hair. Okay, so that's a male lion. Don't be pedantic and cut me some slack. I've tried to catch her eye as they pass, but I'm blanked every time. Scott's a bit starey. Maybe it's because he'd like to stop and talk but isn't allowed. She's usually berating the poor lad for something or another. Perhaps I'm being unfair, and it's justified, or bad timing and it's usually the other way round – but I don't think so. They always argue on the plot and her voice is often raised. Maybe they have an issue to work through and come to the allotment to thrash it out, something they can't do at home for some reason. Aren't people intriguing? It concerns me, because he's tall and broad – a sturdy lion cub who could do considerable damage should he ever lash out.

Today Scott came on his own, off the leash. He even stopped and spoke, 'Looks like a different plot.' Then shyly answered my questions with 'yes' or 'no'. Apparently, Sandy had a hospital appointment. His voice was gentle, and I noticed for the first time that he was an attractive young man. In the presence of his mother, this asset is heavily disguised. Still, it was progress. Not one for small-talk or eye contact, but it was nice to talk to him without the scrutiny from mamma who'd taken her paws off his tail and let him run free for the afternoon. How liberating it must have been for him.

Around 3.00 p.m., with dusk looming, threatening to curtail the fun, Sandy came crashing through the gate. Giving me a sideways glance and ignoring my greeting, she dashed down the path with great urgency. Then it started – the usual scrapping, but this time it was Scott's voice that was raised, 'YOU'RE NOT SUPPOSED TO BE HERE!' followed by a high-pitched roar from Sandy, protesting about it. 'DON'T YOU blah blah blah…' and an 'OW!' from Scott, at which point I thought about intervening. Then it went quiet.

I waited a while then wheeled some imaginary rubbish to the skip to check both parties were still alive. Like wild cats after a spat, each had retreated to opposite ends of the plot, Sandy – face twisted into a snarl, keeping one eye on her son. Scott – head bowed and hunched over his spade, digging furiously, channelling his anger, burying it deep into the soil.

Mother has returned to maintain the status quo. When they were leaving, Sandy ushered her son on ahead as he passed my plot. He turned around as he walked, staring nervously at the two of us, unsure of what was going to be said behind his back.

She spoke gruffly, 'I'm Sandy and that's Scott, me son. Excuse him, he's a bit shy,' as though he were six. My first thought was, 'have you ever afforded him the opportunity to prove himself otherwise?' She explained she's had an allotment since her husband left twenty years ago and how it's also good for Scott – though there was no reason given for that statement. I suspect he just CBA to leave home (likely), or perhaps he's recently broken up with a partner (unlikely) or had mental health issues (highly likely with a mother like that) – STOP! Then she dropped it:

'Anyroad, I see you've met Hal. He's great with greenhouses and everything you want to know about growing stuff. Can turn his hand to anything, that one.'

I could detect a softening of her voice as Hal crept into her thoughts. Snapping out of it, she fired the question:

'Are you married? Boyfriend? Girlfriend? Partner?'

Where on earth did that spring from? I nearly said, 'To save time and energy you can use one word: 'single' and anyway, what business is it of yours?'

But as usual I chickened out. Told her I'm 'happily single'. Made me proud to say it because it's true. And it's a huge contrast to a year ago, when I was *un*happily single, which was a result of many things, least of all my relationship status. Or was I being defensive? Sandy likes Hal and she's checking out my availability. Please don't view me as competition. I'm a woman's woman; I'm on your side. Still, I get the feeling I'd better watch myself.

I don't think he's interested in me – not in the boyfriend-girlfriend-partner sort of way. He didn't reply straight away to my text, so there you have it.

Saturday 3 May

The allotment working party is tomorrow. I'm really looking forward to it. We've been asked to bring homemade cakes so I'm off to buy some from the corner shop and take the wrappers off.

Sunday 4 May

Working party! A day of camaraderie, a chance to meet plot holders I never knew existed, those on a different shift pattern to mine. Think street party for gardeners. You may live two plots away from some people, but your woodchipped paths never cross. Newbies like me are eager to impress and do the same jobs as the men (of course) so I volunteered to clean out all the slimy baths where everyone dunks their muddy watering cans during the growing season. After a few months the water turns black and murky, as if frogspawn could appear on the surface at any time or a green clawed hand might grab you and pull you under, never to be seen again.

Everyone is in good spirits, smiling and joking with strangers, bonding over the jobs in hand. Hal took on the macho stuff like fence-mending and hedge-trimming using a chainsaw. Scott was there and Sandy put in an appearance, if only to chat to Hal and weed her own plot, which is *not* at all community minded. As predicted, even lower down that scale was Miriam, who walked past when we were discussing the tasks and laughed out loud, right in our faces, sending a hot flush whooshing around my body. Scott helped me empty the baths by hand. Then, in the absence of harmful cleaning products or a brush, I invented a body scrub for baths. Sadly, this product is extraordinarily niche and will not be shortlisted for my next business venture, but I discovered it by leaving the muddy silt deposits on the bottom (where the zombie hand and frogs live). I scooped it onto a soft, unassuming sponge and used it to scrub off the slime from the sides of the bath. I must confess that I'm very pleased with myself – slime scrub? Why not, when there are dead sea scrubs and mud masks? Perhaps not, though some people eat placentas – it's all natural after all.

Scott was an ideal partner, being so quiet, and we just got stuck into the job. How satisfying the results were: a sparkling pool of clear water to dip our cans into. I've decided anyone who abuses the water by washing plant pots or tools will be rewarded with a slap – no first warning, straight into a rage followed swiftly by physical violence. And if that doesn't work, I'll put an electric fence round each one.

For lunch, we were treated to a delicious fry-up of bacon, sausage, and veggie burgers – courtesy of a super-efficient family team. Everyone contributed *homemade* cake and I slipped my corner shop offering onto the table when the coast was clear. There was a vast array of drinks including wine and *homemade* cider, both of which I abstained from in case I was tempted to have a go with Hal's chainsaw later. When no one was listening, I arranged to meet him at the gate at ten on Friday.

A lady with perfect skin (bath scrub?) was giving away some amazing hand thrown 'reject' pots, all far superior to anything I could ever muster up; how generous of her.

Suddenly Miriam honed into view. Like a bloodhound, she'd sniffed out the wine and proceeded to neck it. Some kind people tried to chat to her, but she was too far gone and simply stared back at them menacingly. It was quite uncomfortable as the others kept glancing over at the ticking time bomb. Suddenly, with a loud, 'GET LOST, the lot of you!' she whisked the remainder of the wine away to her lair. Could have been worse I suppose. A collective sigh of relief was heard, and knowing looks were exchanged. These are good, caring people who recognise a sad lost soul, and some will think to themselves, 'If my life had taken a different turn, that could have been me.'

Full to bursting with community spirit, Scott and I carried on for round two of bath cleaning, leaving the others debating the no-dig versus dig method of gardening as they sipped their wine in the sunshine.

Exhausted after a hugely rewarding, physical day; I'm in a state of total relaxation, warm and glowing with love for my allotment, the people in it, and for life in general. I resisted wine this evening because I feel as wholesome as a brown bap with extra pumpkin seeds.

Thursday 8 May

Sam came round to discuss the 'date' at the garden centre tomorrow – two things that will never again appear in the same sentence – it's laughable! Before you Shady Pines lot get over-excited, my tongue is very firmly in my cheek – and it won't be straying anywhere else, while we're on the subject. For obvious reasons, I've kept it quiet but in the interests of safety I told Sam, who is over-enthusiastic as she's always hated the thought of her mother living alone. The fact that, apart from the odd wobble, the mother is generally quite happy living alone, thank you very much, doesn't seem to register with daughter. More role reversal.

Daughter: You're driving him there in your car, aren't you?

Mother (rolling eyes and sighing): Yes.

Daughter: Ring me as *soon* as you're home.

Mother (rolling eyes and sighing): Okay.

Also in the interests of safety, I ended the conversation there.

Friday 9 May

The big day out!

Before I met Hal, I took another look in corner non grata and clocked something out of the ordinary, as we detectives say: the shed has four air vents on its back wall. Bingo – I'm a sleuth of the first order of sleuths! It stands to reason that a shed doesn't need a vent, unless there are goods in there that need to be kept dry, fresh and not smelling of compost, or your customers will complain. I wanted to run around the allotment punching the air. No one wants to buy stinky swag, even at a bargain price. I'm a genius. Couldn't wait to tell Hal, who dismissed my perfect theory as 'far-fetched'. He reckons it could be home brew in there and thinks he might be flogging off the excess too. I argued that two secret drinkers in the same corner of an allotment site was a highly unlikely scenario.

Hal failed to see the funny side, which highlighted just how exciting Lucas was, despite his desperate circumstances as a refugee. Hal is a more serious man by far. Life is serious enough without others constantly reminding us of that fact. We thrive on laughter, and Lucas certainly filled mine with vast quantities of the stuff. STOP thinking about him and making comparisons with this innocent bloke who is just a friend!

Instead, I'm writing this and admiring my handiwork: a clear, weed and rubbish-free plot, pristine and ready for wood chip paths and a brand-new greenhouse. All wildly exciting. Even looking forward to the garden centre trip, provided it doesn't sell any excess nonsense or have a clothing section. Hal's sworn it hasn't.

10.00 p.m. Had a brilliant time! Feeling very upbeat about life and weed suppressant fabric. Cowell's – now, *that's* what I call a garden centre: plants; seeds; tools; garden essentials; a few aggregates (look it up); fencing. It's a perfect size, without even a sniff of a beige acrylic jumper or a kitchen utensil. It smelled of rich compost, every inch of it transporting me back to my childhood and the gardening slash hardware shop on Chillingham Road. Dark and mesmerising. Stepping through the door felt like entering the bowels of the Earth. My dad often took me there after school to buy seeds or gardening tools, and to visit the beautiful ginger – or 'Gingerbread Man' cat as I called it – who permanently lay on a pile of hessian sacks, curled up tight, fast asleep. I adored that shop. Perhaps my love of gardening has always been there, lying dormant, like the Gingerbread Man cat.

Hal appeared more at ease than he ever is at the allotment, although I had to use a teacher voice after he made the mistake of trying to tell me which turn-off to take. We chatted all the way to Alnwick about where we were taken as kids and our favourite haunts of Northumberland: Seaton Sluice was my family's beach of choice, and Bamburgh for a special occasion. Equipped with the essential sturdy windbreaker to put up in the dunes, we enjoyed hundreds of picnics there – egg sandwiches with salad cream and varying amounts of sand, depending on the direction of the wind that day. There are photos of me paddling, wearing a swimming costume and a thick home-knit cardi in every one of them! It was lovely to reminisce about the magic of ever-changing rock pools, the distinctive smell of seaweed and the *never*-changing sub-zero temperature of the North Sea. Hal was taken to Newbiggin-by-the-Sea, very close to where he was brought up, in the mining town of Ashington. His special occasion beach was Whitley Bay and the amusement arcade or, for a rare treat, the Spanish City – a mini fairground. I called him 'jammy' because I didn't go until I was seventeen! There's a diary entry somewhere – I'll find it another time.

His dad was a pitman but sadly not one of the painting crowd, who also hail from Ashington. That's just as well, or I'd have been far too interested. I'm a sucker for a celebrity, however minor, or miner they may be. Hal was in his early twenties when the pits closed so he moved away in search of work. Here's a man who would have gone to university, but it wasn't an option for most at the time. Despite the grants, money was tight, so he was encouraged to leave school and start earning; the family had experienced severe hardship during the strike. Only the 'gifted' pupils from his school were destined for university. His parents were understandably terrified of him taking a step into the unknown world of higher education because it carried with it the risk of unemployment at the end. From his tone, it was clear he would have been interested in going to university – I felt quite sorry for him but didn't let it show. Tired of the constant arguments over his future career path, Hal left home for a job selling cameras in Dixons, in the metropolis of Newcastle, where he shared a flat with three other young men. Later, he moved south to become a 'travelling salesman' as they were known. Very 1970s!

Told myself on no account must I ask if he has a partner or has ever been married as it would make him think I'm interested in more than just his gardening prowess. We were scarcely approaching the A1 when:

Me: Do you live on your own?

BUFFOON!

He's been married once, no children. Hal moved around with the sales-repping job – very unsettling for his wife, who wanted to stay in one place. Strange, I can't see him as a sales rep: too much driving and talking, not enough *doing* or *making* for Hal. Maybe that's why he left the job early. I'm forgiving my flappy mouth because I was concerned there may be someone at home wondering who he was swanning around Northumberland with.

Expertise is attractive, provided the expert doesn't turn 'know-all'. Hal is quite the Alan Titchmarsh, or preferably Monty Don (sorry Alan). I fell for his extensive knowledge of bark chippings, though I had to argue the toss environmentally against plastic weed suppressant in favour of fabric – he's not great in that department. Scintillating conversation – you poor diary readers will be desperately trying not to fall asleep, if you're not already.

At the garden centre I was predictably side-tracked by the alluring rows of colourful seed packets which reminded me that it may already be too late in the season for some, like the gorgeous orange peppers I had my eye on. Came out with an armful of seeds, three bags of woodchip for the paths and wobbly legs from the shock of paying for it all. Warning: do not, under any circumstances, assume that growing your own produce is a cheap alternative to the supermarket! It was short-lived and I bounced back up to high doh by the time we got to the car and suggested we have lunch at Craster.

It's a truly romantic place. NO not in the lovey-dovey sense – I'm talking historical, olde-worlde, picturesque. An old fishing village on the coast, just north of Alnwick. It epitomises the Northumberland coast: characterful and rugged – not a chocolate box affair. The harbour is dotted with small fishing boats – not a tourist boat in sight, a clear sign of an authentic working fishing village. A smokery selling the famous (if you're a Geordie) Craster Kippers emits the most delicious smell of woodsmoke – and fish! Of course, we had to buy a pair to take back to the city as a souvenir. Thought of Debs who hates fish and refuses to go to Craster, or 'that fishy hellhole', which is tantamount to blasphemy.

'Willocks? Cockles?' Hal shouted, before we left the smokery. It was out of character for him, and we had a laugh in there. 'Willocks', the Geordie word for whelks, are traditionally eaten in many a seaside town by kids, using a pin (health and safety?)

to wheedle them out of the shell. Remember when they sold them in pubs in town? Every Friday night, a poor lad would hawk the basket of fishy delights around the pubs, including The County where Debs, after several ciders, would involuntarily retch and make a scene, screaming, 'No, no take it away!' at the top of her voice as if he'd produced a boa constrictor. I told Hal the story and he laughed politely, but you need to know Debs to really appreciate the embarrassment factor to its fullest extent. You also need a stupid, immature sense of humour, which Hal doesn't have. Lucas, on the other hand…. oh no, that just slipped out – I haven't been thinking of him nearly as much lately. I had to spoil it.

Ate at the fabulous Jolly Fisherman pub that has maintained its unique character, even after a makeover. Its signature crab soup and sandwiches both sit comfortably in the category of 'unrivalled'. Conscious that I've lapsed into restaurant reviewer mode, before I stop, I need to tell you that at one time the menu was pretty much thus:

Crab sandwich
Cheese sandwich
Ham sandwich
Cheese and ham sandwich

Then the eighties happened with a toasted option for each of the above – positively avant-garde!

One of the luxuries of retirement is a weekday lunch in a popular place like this. The dining area has three sides of glass overlooking the free live show that is the North Sea. I've spent many hours in that room with binoculars, spotting the various sea and wading birds in winter: cormorant, shag (yes, it *is* a bird), eider duck, guillemot, oyster catcher and gulls galore, picking them out among the wilderness of water and rocks. Hal chatted about his fishing expeditions with his grandad who had a boat in Amble, further down the coast. Living away from home for so long, he's lost a lot of his accent, which is a great pity. However, his Northumbrian, baritone drawl resurfaced when he reminisced, and I spotted it straight away when I first met him. The vowels are very different from Geordie – it's *bairg* for bag, *baird* for bed, *durg* for dog, *curb* for cub – riddle me that! He included too much detail about the various boats and their features, but I was intrigued by the names of the fish they used to catch: c*ur*d, h*air*ddock, h*air*gfish, (have you guessed them yet?) ling, pollack, and wolf fish! It's a shame we don't have so many now due to environmental pollution.

After lunch, we walked a little way along the clifftop path then back to the Mick Oxley gallery so I could get my own back for the boat conversation. The space is filled with amazing, dramatic, atmospheric paintings by the brilliant artist who lives there. I could have bought every single one of them. The subject matter suited Hal perfectly – the sea and Northumbrian countryside brilliantly depicted, brought to life on canvas.

Craster is on everyone's itinerary when you have visitors from the south to entertain. With it comes the weight of your fellow Northerners, bearing down on your shoulders, compelling you to show off the hidden gems of Northumberland. Afterwards, you wish you hadn't, because they go home and tell everyone how mind-blowing the North East coast is, and they saw no coal mines, mills (there were never any), dirty factories, or whippets. The issue being, we don't want it to become swamped with too many tourists – just the optimal amount, if you please. By all means, come and visit, but if you could get together, coordinate your movements, and allocate time slots, that'd be very much appreciated, thank you.

Rounded off what had been a perfect day with a short walk to Dunstanburgh Castle. It is perfectly ruined: not too decrepit, but photogenic and thoroughly aesthetically pleasing – an artist's dream. Dating back to 1313, it is the opposite of its more famous neighbour, Bamburgh, which is a complete *and* inhabited castle. Indeed, Bamburgh is the poster girl/boy/non-binary castle of castles. No one bothered to renovate poor Dunstanburgh, but that distinctive shape gives it charm and uniqueness. Together with hundreds, if not thousands of local artists throughout the ages, J.M.W. Turner appreciated this beauty and saw fit to capture it not just once but many times from different angles, in delicate watercolour, oil, and ink. Dunstanburgh is erratic, spiky, random, and looks spectacular from a distance – I can relate to it.

Along with my favourite Turner painting, *Norham Castle, Sunrise,* another Northumbrian relic, they were all bequeathed by the artist to the National Gallery and are mostly found hanging around in the Tate, down in That London.

Bed after a sensible amount of wine and feeling great: skin is tingling from the wind (unless I'm having a stroke) and I'm pleasantly tired; fulfilled not exhausted. Hal is very easy company.

Saturday 10 May

The seedlings have all come through now! I'm so excited at seeing their tiny green heads popping up through the compost, demanding to see the sun. The leeks are like miniature blades of grass. They are so cute! I mustn't treat them like goldfish and overwater them, not that you can overwater goldfish, but people kill them with kindness by overfeeding. The trays are now the focal point of the lounge – who needs TV?

Sam called demanding to know if I'd made a GP's appointment to ask for HRT. Feeling negative after another poor night's sleep, I told her they'll probably say it's risky and won't give it to me. Typical of my exceedingly thorough daughter, she's read a few articles that suggest the risks are not nearly as high as first thought, and if I actually bothered to read the statistics, according to Sam, I'd realise I'm fine to take them – whatever that all means. Anyway, she now thinks it's a good idea. I think the GP is better placed to decide that. I'll ask for an appointment with a woman. There's nothing quite like personal experience to evoke true empathy. I don't want a thirtysomething man nodding sympathetically as I explain the evils of brain-fog, night sweats, and road rage. I want someone who was once drowning in it and will throw a high-spec life jacket for me to reach the other side in one piece.

To shut her up, I promised Sam I'd request an appointment after my smear test on Monday – ugh!

Monday 12 May

Apart from it being a life-saving measure, the entire concept of a smear test or a 'ride on the silver willy' as Debs used to call it, is pretty vile.

Nowadays, it's even more foul after my menopausal tsunami struck, dragging with it all manner of unpleasantness in the nether regions – and I'm not talking Pacifics here, I mean much further south. I know I'm fairly wimpy compared to many of my friends, but it made my eyes water. The nurse told me there's cream available for it. Cream? Does it come in gallons? I need the fire brigade not bloody cream! The silver willy was bigger than I remembered it (not in a good way) and the world's supply of lubricant or similar was not going to help a jot – no siree, Bob.

As a result, my mind was made up there and then – I'm fast-tracking straight to HRT without fannying around with petroleum jelly and its messy derivatives.

I asked for an appointment with 'any woman doctor' which sounds strange, but better than 'female', which sounds like you're referring to an animal. Anything's better than 'lady doctor'. That belongs firmly in the 1950s, as Jodie Whittaker will agree. It's a few weeks away on June 13th – one thing I'm *not* likely to forget.

Friday 16 May

There's a wide variation in allotment styles, often reflecting the personality traits of their owners. Some are immaculate; everything is in equally distanced rows, not a weed in sight. Those people may be retired or perhaps have OCD, and you can verify the latter by taking a sneaky look at how tidy their greenhouse is. The windows are kept clean and glistening, there's no junk lying around inside. Plant pots neatly sorted or out of sight in a box. Canes are tied in neat bundles according to size. They may or may not have wooden signs or other decorative items bought from a craft fair as proof of how cherished it is. Their garden furniture is carefully oiled, waxed, or painted each season to keep it as good as new.

At the other end of the spectrum are the agents of chaos, like me. We struggle to keep it tidy. I haven't the excuse of work, just haplessness. Storage areas are made from old wooden pallets in a hotchpotch of colours: green, brown, bamboo yellow, and blue. Our greenhouses are full to the brim of *stuff* no one can bring themselves to bin. The hoarders can barely move inside theirs. Garden furniture is an assortment of oddments scavenged from skips in the back lane. We prefer to call them 'recycled'; some are already rusting. But the one thing that unites us is love for our allotments. There are many people who would give anything to own one, but haven't enough time for it, or have mobility, sensory, or health issues that make it impossible. I realise how privileged I am to be the custodian of something so special – it's a mindfulness thing.

Monday 19 May

I heard something on the radio that I hope is outdated by the time I pick this diary out of the box in Shady Pines: there are more people named Steve heading up a company in the FTSE 100, than the *total* number of women or people from an ethnic minority group in the same role. Just digest that for a moment...

I was so shocked, I treated myself to peanut butter on toast before bed. The sort that doesn't contain orangutans.

Wednesday 21 May

Up early and ate my breakfast at the allotment. It was an oasis of calm, with birds tweeting in the morning sun, and the rush hour traffic could just be heard faintly beyond the trees – commuters, school runners, the outside world. A strange juxtaposition, reminding me how lucky I was to be on the inside of the fence. In a squawking flurry, a gawky gang of young jackdaws arrived to patrol around the plot, picking at pieces of grass and pulling at the soil for anything of interest – the bored teenagers of the area. They were so engrossed they didn't even notice me. It was very entertaining!

Saturday 24 May

9.00 a.m. Shattered after too much wine. My idea of 'sensible' must be 'stupid', in reality. I just can't take my alcohol these days. I've read that the wretched menopausal body doesn't have as much water sloshing around inside as it did in its youth, rendering the alcohol stronger and less diluted as it courses through your veins. This could be seen as the only positive side effect because it's much cheaper, but it's also annoying because you tend to forget, and I am incapable of drinking slowly. It's just not in my nature. Be warned, it can be very embarrassing as you peak much earlier than your younger drinking partners and are liable to be hustled into a taxi before nine o'clock.

Meeting Hal to take measurements for the beds – *allotment* beds – I know how your minds work. Hal is making them, so you can lower your eyebrows immediately. I'm paying the man for a service, that's all. Oh, grow up, you lot – it's a business transaction. No more, no less! The low, bottomless wooden boxes dug into the ground are great for controlling weeds and soil quality. You must fill them with compost, manure and decent topsoil and I've seen them on *Gardener's World*, apparently.

10.00 a.m. Hal measured up and left. But does he measure up to the job? Must stop being so childish. He'll cut the wood at home then bring it to the allotment to assemble, like an Ikea purchase. Otherwise, he wouldn't get it in the car, like those people who build an aeroplane in their loft then can't squeeze it through the window to fly solo round the world. Except, this is the reverse scenario.

When he'd gone, I sat in the greenhouse looking at the allotment accessories, planning out what should be grown where: brassicas (cabbage, broccoli, sprouts and cauliflower) the alliums (onions and garlic), legumes (peas and beans), potatoes, salad leaves, sweetcorn, and root veg. During such an absorbing activity, darkness crept in unnoticed. I was about to leave when I heard a squeaking noise outside – a bird? No – too rhythmic. It grew closer. A large shape trundled past the greenhouse. I sat perfectly still and watched as Barrow Man (not to be confused with affable multi-talented *John* Barrowman) pushed his trusty one-wheeled vehicle down the path towards his plot. Well, there you have it: proof of 'gear' being hidden in there. Why else would you sneak in, under the protection of near dark, away from prying eyes – or so he thinks.

Monday 26 May

An older guy with a mop of white hair and an unsteady gait stopped by the plot while I was planting parsnips and beetroot. I was so absorbed in spacing them exactly as directed on the seed packet, in perfectly straight lines, that I jumped when he spoke.

'Hallo! Aam Billy. Are you new here? You've got the face of an angel and ya hair's beautiful. Aam gonna enjoy walking past here from now on.'

My heart sank. I'd come for peace and quiet, not a spot of casual objectification. He was wearing a Save the Whale tee shirt, so was half sound, but clearly hadn't heard of the Me Too movement. So, I did it. Nipped it in the bud with, 'I'm Lizzie. Nice to meet you, Billy. Now, if we're going to hit it off, I need you *not* to pass comment on my looks. It's not nineteen seventy-five and I've had enough of that sort of thing.' Stopped short of saying 'crap'. He looked offended, 'Aa was just being friendly,'

In my 'nice teacher' voice I cooed, 'It's okay, Billy. I appreciate that but I'm just not comfortable with it.'

Billy stood looking puzzled, but I channelled Deborah Frances-White and stopped myself apologising to him. Instead, I complimented him on his tee shirt and he sauntered off with a cheery, 'Thanks sweetheart!'

Okay, so I'm not going to turn him into a feminist overnight. You can't undo seventy years of conditioning in thirty seconds. He means well and at least he didn't sulk and stomp off.

Tuesday 27 May

There is a curious plot at the site, loved and cherished by a cute elderly couple who are always there together. Although meticulously tidy, it's also peculiar because they have a stone animal fetish going on there, interspersed with the odd gnome. It's as if they cultivate vegetables around the animals, as a sideline, when what they really wanted was somewhere to show off their scary concrete jungle. It reminded me of a horror story from my teenage years, prompting a delve into the diary box as soon as I got home.

Mum and Dad had been to the Scottish Borders – Jedburgh, Kelso, and Melrose, where the scenery is rugged and the buildings glow in the sunset, adding to the magnificence of the red sandstone. They returned with a story they could hardly tell us for laughing. On the way home, they'd visited a small garden, open to the public and packed with concrete statues created by Murdo, a remarkable ninety-year-old man. Unfortunately, each one was painted in garish colours and in need of varying degrees of repair, ranging from 'a little TLC' to 'smash it up and start again'. Luckily, Polaroid photographic evidence taken to bring the story to life, was now stuck (with Gloy) firmly into the diary. This included a wild-eyed Lawrence of Arabia sporting a pair of false teeth shoved between red concrete lips to form a terrifying skeletal grin! Poor old Lawrence's once-flowing white robes now hung from him in tatters.

'It's them bloody thieving bastard birds!' explained Scotland's answer to Henry Moore, in his wonderful singsong Borders accent, during the guided tour of the collection.

A resourceful man, Murdo had scalped a doll and stuck it over the concrete head of a small child sculpture. Two small (and much too bright) blue eyes stared out maniacally from the face, creating something far more chilling than your average horror movie doll.

'They've ruined little Shirley Temple,' he announced, sadly.

Feathering their nests, the said thieving birds had filched most of Shirley Temple's curls of black hair from her grotesque rubber-capped head, leaving her bald, save for a few pathetic whisps sprouting through the holes. Mum had to take deep breaths to stop herself laughing then made a mad dash for the portaloo (nice) so she could let it all out without offending their creator.

My parents were the kind of people who often found themselves roped into sticky situations. So, when Murdo casually mentioned he was too young to pack up the plinths just yet, and that his next project was a Jacob sheep, Mum offered to take him some horns from a friend who bred them. This latest gesture was borne out of guilt for laughing at his lifetime's work.

Flicked forward to the school holidays and an afternoon I don't need or want to be reminded of. Home alone with Debs, dancing to loud music, having drunk one whole can of forbidden cider *each*, the doorbell rang. There stood a man in overalls holding out a binbag.

'The sheep's horns for your mam.'

He made it sound like a daily occurrence. Perplexed (and slightly squiffy), I took the heavy bag from him and promptly dropped it. How many were in there? The entire flock's? Stupidly, we peeped inside the bag and leapt back in horror. Aaaagh! The horns were STILL ATTACHED TO THE HEAD! A sheep had died, and this man, a pound shop *Godfather,* had granted Mum's mad request by decapitating it, gift-wrapping it in a binbag and delivering it personally to the door. Five stars for customer service but the aftercare was non-existent. We shrieked, cried, drank more cider, and giggled, leaving the bag of death in the garden, its contents spilling out onto the lawn like a scene from *Quatermass and the Pit.* Luckily, urban foxes hadn't been invented in those days, so we left it where it was and went to bed before the parents could see we were extremely, though justifiably, drunk.

Thursday 29 May

My precious seedling babies are ready to flee the nest to their new home in the greenhouse. For most, it's a halfway house en route to adulthood outside, or for tomatoes, a grow bag of their own. If they are to flourish, choosing the right week for the big move is crucial: if it's too cold they'll die, and I will be devastated. I'm always trawling the internet for advice. Everyone has a conflicting opinion, but somehow you machete your way through the information jungle and arrive at your own conclusion, teasing out the common denominators in the arguments. The brassicas are the hardier characters in the veggie family. I love them because they have all done as they were told and even I, with my novice ways, couldn't kill them off. Leeks are exquisitely delicate creatures who enter the seedling world resembling a blade of grass, their perfect white roots thickening as the weeks pass. They demand careful handling. The tomatoes aren't great. They've had too much heat, not enough light and are thin, spindly things. Classic newbie error, apparently. Exactly how much heat and light do you want – just tell me! They are the children who look sickly and don't eat much but are tough and turn out fine in the end.

Hal couldn't resist commenting on how leggy they looked, so I leapt to their defence in true parent style. Told him I'm going to bury them deep when I repot them, and they'll be fine. That shut him up. Still, I sneaked them into the greenhouse when no one was there, ashamed of their appearance. Unlike the golden children, the brassicas, who were paraded down the main path on a particularly busy day so I could lap up the comments, 'Ooh thank you. It's beginners' luck, I'm sure.' I wish I could stop being such a stereotypical woman and just take the compliments when I reply – and *own my awesome* as Sara would say.

JUNE

Sunday 1 June

A milestone has been reached down at the ranch: the raised beds are in! Sense of personal achievement is at a new high. Okay I didn't make the beds (or I'd have to lie in them) but over the past few weeks I've transformed that plot with its neglected mounds of earth, ridden with rampant couch grass, weeds, stones, and glass. Now, six fabulous, raised beds stand on clean, flat earth, their natural wooden sides still pristine. The area is soon to be delineated with paths covered in bright, freshly chipped wood. I can't wait to do that! Hal is a great craftsman – I know I've said that before, but it really is worth another mention. He doesn't want to chat when working – concentrates on the job in hand and is super-organised. Nor was he too proud to ask for help in turning over the unwieldy structures ready to be secured into the soil. I loved being able to contribute and it was a break from levelling out the area outside the greenhouse so I, yes me, myself, *I*, can lay a small patio. I've looked it up and I know how to do it.

We paused for lunch and a brief chat about spacing, paths and layout, but other than that, Hal never took a break. He's got stamina for a man of his age – it's tiring just watching him!

I saved the other news until the end, to prove my life does not revolve around men: Hal has invited me out for a pizza. No, no, NO! Not a 'date'. We are friends and he wants to pay me back for the Craster lunch and to share his earnings from the raised beds job – he joked. We argued about who should pay for the pizza because I'm embarrassed that he won't take anything for all his time and effort spent making the beds. How generous of him, unlike Twat, who was mean with money until he left me, then began flashing the cash he supposedly didn't have. That was when we were settling the divorce. I haven't thought about him in a long while, which is great. Stop! I refuse to let the past ruin a lovely day. Though it's good to be reminded of what an odious wretch he was – and no doubt still is.

Texted Sara about my invitation – a mistake as she's now overexcited about it. I refuse point blank to call it a 'date'. Sadly, she says he has 'old man humour' as I mistakenly told her his anecdote about the fish and chip shop in Wallsend that caught fire and ended with 'the whole place was gutted.'

Monday 2 June

Hal keeps mithering me about making a brassica cage, to protect them from evil butterflies who like to lay their eggs in their tasty leaves. I think it's a cage with net, not bars or they'd just fly through them.

5.00 p.m. Ta-da! I have made my own brassica cage – a makeshift one using three thick plastic pipes bent into an arc, with each end stuck in the ground, straddling the raised bed. Not strictly a cage. Stretched over the top is a large net with minute holes to keep out those pesky butterflies, and everyone else. I researched how to make it, then noticed Billy had the blue plastic pipes necessary *and* kindly gave me a net! How lovely of him. He was fantastic – no silly remarks, just a matey, 'There ya go, now,' when he presented it to me. Wouldn't take any money for it either. Lovely! He's beginning to see the light. I planted the baby brassicas from the greenhouse straight into it without 'hardening them off' i.e. getting them used to being outside, because I'm so impatient. Cabbages, sprouts and broccoli. Also popped some kale in there too. Brassicas are pretty resilient and don't need mollycoddling, but as kids they have poor spatial awareness and need plenty of room to grow.

Wednesday 4 June

The doc's appointment can't come soon enough. That's how desperate I am. I need help. It's crept up on me and now it's an enormous snowball, gathering momentum down Cow Hill. Just to prove it, today I surpassed myself and won gold in the Idiocy Olympics. My best achievement yet in the Preparing to Leave the House category. Granted, there's always so much gear to take to the allotment: flask, lunch, reading glasses, keys, phone, food waste for compost bin (nice), and the inevitable 'stuff' I can't resist when passing a shop with a gardening section. Eager to get on with my new project, I always forget at least one item from the above list. After all, there be paaaths that need a-laying – I have the voice of a West Country farmer in my head for all matters allotment because, well I suppose it's all about the laaand. Now I'm rambling – sorry.

As per usual I'd dumped everything on the floor, packed it up and put my coat on. Then the usual frantic keys search ensued. One hundred percent sure I'd put them in the pile, bag is emptied once – no, twice – still no, house is re-searched – no. Now I'm unable to trust my memory as far as I can throw it, I assume keys were never there in the first instance and are lost, decide to tackle it later and get the spares. Forty minutes later, I leave the house.

Enjoyed laying the weed suppressant out for the paths. It's an activity to suit those of an impetuous nature as the edges don't have to be cut perfectly straight, though perfectionists out there would disagree. Wonky edges can be disguised, squeezed under the sides of the raised beds, a most satisfying job. I'm straying off-piste again. The main point of this anecdote of menopausal madness is that all the time I was working, I could hear a muffled tinkling noise. Thought it was the neighbour's windchime but it sounded closer.

When Hal came, bearing gifts of home-made chocolate cake and weed suppressant pins, the heavens opened. As we made a dash for the greenhouse, I put up my oversized fur-lined hood and something whizzed past my ear and landed at my feet. Hal asked me if I always kept keys in my hood. I was ecstatic because I knew I'd put them ready to go and I wasn't going bonkers hearing jangly things. Hal loved the ridiculousness, and I chose not to mention the menopause as it's rather too much information for someone I don't know well. He'd only stare at the floor anyway.

I didn't have him down as a baker. Thought he'd be too macho – but again it's always good to be surprised. We should never pigeon-hole a person. Anyone who bakes and/or cooks (two things I avoid) deserves serious consideration and a place on the reserve list, if not given the job on probation.

Thursday 5 June

Quiet couple of days. Bought some sourdough bread from the bougie bakery round the corner. Went up to allotment just to sit and take it all in. The peace and inner calm I feel sitting here listening to the birds chirping is simply beautiful. Every time I'm here I marvel at the vibrancy of the surrounding shades of green and the small but constant changes to the fruit and vegetables as they grow. My home garden is a disgrace in comparison and practically devoid of greenery. It could be an equally rewarding space, but I neglect it because I'm enjoying being outdoors and seeing other people – okay then, *most* of them, *some* of the time.

Friday 6 June

Sara's blabbed about tomorrow's pizza event thing or whatever it is – now known as 'pizzagate' as I have been accused of being secretive. Simon and Hilary have since been badgering me for details of my new 'fella'. This isn't good and I'm blanking them. In fact, I'm having second thoughts about it. I like him, he's quite attractive I suppose, but he's too serious and I'm not looking for anyone now – it's far too early. Listen to me getting ahead of myself. I'm sure he's only asked me because he doesn't want to feel indebted after the Craster lunch – which smacks of sexism. Also, I've now decided against sleeping with people as a new hobby option – it's really not *me*. I'm not ruling out having a special friend, whatever that means, either with or *on* benefits – I'm no snob – but I don't think anyone could compete with Lucas and how utterly gorgeous he was/*is* (he's still alive).

Typical of me to overthink everything. JUST GET ON AND ENJOY IT! I am boring the pants off myself, so God help you lot. Seriously, I'm looking forward to it. I couldn't take Lucas anywhere in case we were discovered. It'll be a treat. Eating with Twat was an altogether pointless affair. Why go out to sit silently at a table in a public display of disaffection? Why would we put ourselves through that and pay for it to boot? It's so long ago since I went out with a male friend other than Simon.

I feel quite fluttery in the stomach department – though it could be down to the multi-bean casserole ready meal I had tonight. Night-time sends me way too giddy. I must check the fullness of the moon because I am definitely influenced by it. A full moon sends me vampy, wild, delirious – everything that spells trouble.

Surprise surprise – I haven't a clue what to wear for it so now I'll be awake half the night thinking about that and be even more of a wreck tomorrow. Update – moon is full.

Sunday 8 June

Hungover – badly. Miserable and wretched. Oh my God and bloody hells bells. What have I done? Woke up this morning in a panic, with no clothes on next to a man in my bed who's wearing pale blue Y-fronts. Wondered if I'd been drugged as I still have no memory of coming to bed – though it used to happen many a time after a heavy night in the old days. I'm clutching at straws. What did I do?

1. Nearly died of shock.
2. Felt sick.
3. Was sick.

The fact that said man was still wearing his pale blue Y-fronts, was comforting on two other fronts:

1. Hopefully, they stayed on all night.
2. I may not have had sex with a man who wears Y-fronts after all.

Have you never slept with someone by accident? 'What do you mean, BY ACCIDENT?' I hear you shout from Shady Pines. And don't give me any of your outdated, sexist attitude towards women and sex. Get with the twenty-first century! I need your support.

Crept out of bed, grabbed a dressing gown, and rushed to the downstairs loo in an effort to be sick quietly – always a pointless exercise. Stayed there for ages, freezing, trying to piece together the events of last night and what the hell I was going to do about it. Looking like a ghoul who'd been caught in a tornado, I crawled back upstairs to face the music. Hal was already dressed and sporting a big grin. A bad sign.

'Did…did we…?' I stuttered.

'No. Though you were determined to have a go!'

AAAAGH! My stomach heaved, accompanied by a vile image of what a drunken me 'having a go' might look like. And I'm telling you, it wasn't pretty. Perhaps I was channelling Chrystal? Hal was surprisingly relaxed about the whole escapade, but he wasn't the one who'd humiliated himself, was he? Being there this morning smacks of keenness – he wasn't frightened off. He didn't make a fuss or say he wanted to make sure I wasn't sick and choked to death. Before he left the scene of the crime, I apologised twenty times, blaming a combination of mixing my drinks and the rich food – yes, that old chestnut. He didn't flinch. Seemed like he was happy to be here. I fear I may have a situation on my hands. Jesus H. Christ, here we go again.

Post-mortem:

Okay you were right – every last one of you, and I was wrong: Hal thought he was on a fully blown date. He turned up with flowers for starters – no not the edible sort. It was cringey. I tried joking that it wasn't my birthday, but an awkward silence followed. Hal missed out on the feminist education most of my male friends had in the eighties, and didn't move with the times as far as women were concerned. Smartly turned out in a shirt and tie, bless him, it felt like an episode of *First Dates* – the oldies' bit. I'm not suggesting for a minute that a feminist must not be given flowers, just that it was OTT for this occasion: two friends having an early doors cheap meal out. And the *blazer* – put me right off. He'd morphed into someone's dad.

At first, the conversation was stilted as I was taken aback by the chivalry and his dress. I think I'd have preferred him in a dress, but soon the conversation flowed, as did the evil wine with its hidden agenda of malice.

Roma is a timeless gem of a family-run restaurant near the allotment. Unique and welcoming, the décor reminds me of my first taste of eating out as a teenager in Newcastle, except the clientele are well behaved, not drunk and riotous as we were then. Alas, no disco to dance away the wait between courses as we would in the old days of La Stalla in town, but the background music spanning the decades proved an ideal conversation piece to fill any gaps. The food was delicious: whitebait then home-made pasta in a creamy salmon sauce – Debs would not have approved. Sounding like a reviewer yet again – though I realise I often talk about food now I'm older. I know you want nitty gritty. And again, I'm putting it off – for a different reason than when I wrote about my first night with Lucas. Back then, I wanted to prolong every moment, savour it, eke it out until the last minute because I was in love with him from the outset. This time it's painful and excruciating. I'm ashamed to admit I was worried in case any of my friends saw me with this very smart, but too-formal-for-my-liking guy. What an uncharitable thought, from the horrible, drunken wildebeest that I am. Poor Hal – now I'm being patronising. You should not pity your date.

My toes are curling as I write this, but by the time we'd walked back to my house, the cold air made me feel not only dizzy, but even more drunk, and stupid with it. We were having a good laugh by then. I should have reined it all in but was caught up in the moment, donning wine goggles instead of waving goodbye like any normal person would have done, and I kissed him – a full on proper snog which I now bitterly regret, even more than that time I snogged Upside-Down-Face man from the pub when I was nineteen. I insisted Hal came in for coffee, which turned into wine (a miracle) and more.

I vaguely remember putting on music and forcing him to dance. Although he'd removed the blazer, I was onto a loser; this man is no dancer. My last clear memory is spinning around the room (or was it the other way around?) alone, then collapsing onto the sofa in a giggling heap. How could I behave so irresponsibly towards such a nice man who'll certainly take it as a green light and think his luck is in – and who could blame him? Or will he? Perhaps he'll be avoiding *me* for the foreseeable. Oh God, why do I get myself into such scrapes just when everything starts going my way? I'm a living, breathing bin icon. Ooh that's going well, so select *delete*, click – bin it. Feeling good about life, so select *delete*, click – bin that too. You see how IT savvy I am now? What shall I do? Options:

a) avoid – I've watched that *Snog, Marry, Avoid* – and I'm not marrying him

b) act like nothing happened

c) pursue a relationship with him out of moral duty, as a punishment for being obscenely drunk and making an arse of myself

While a) is very tempting, I feel b) is the only practical solution to this unholy mess. I'm out of control and blaming it all on the menopause for screwing up my alcohol intake.

Monday 9 June

Now I've spent a day in rehab, there's only one thing for it: get stuck in at the allotment. *Dreading* seeing Hal but can't spend my life in hiding, like poor old Salman Rushdie. Seeing how well the seedlings are growing gave me a welcome boost of positivity – I need to be proactive, grow up, and smooth things over with Hal. Or perhaps they need unsmoothing? Either way – they require immediate attention.

Noticed Scott and Sandy on their plot. I was completely on edge. Scott came over and made me jump. My first thought was, 'Oh my God, Sandy knows! Hal's told her we slept together and we're now an item.' Heart pounding, I waited for the death threat.

'Me mam says have you got a fork she can lend?' I resisted the teacherish temptation to say 'No, but I've got one she can borrow. Does she want to stab me with it?' He didn't make eye contact, but was sweet and actually said, 'Yours is looking good now,' which surprised me. I looked over to see Sandy waving cheerily. Phew! She must have moved on already...

To distract me from the drama I'd become embroiled in, I set to work on the paths. Luckily there wasn't ground much left to cover before I moved on to the *pièce de resistance*: scattering the woodchip! It was a sensory delight to smell and handle the fragrant bark chippings, every armful building a carpet of springy loveliness. Their cream, orange, and brown tones, enhanced by the setting sun, illuminated the entire plot. Straight lines of the beds and paths juxtaposed with random smatterings of colours and textures in the bark – gorgeous. One of the most rewarding, aesthetically pleasing activities I have ever experienced! I sat in the greenhouse drinking lukewarm tea and admired my work.

A familiar voice shattered my blissful period of guilt-free contemplation. I knew Hal would come, eventually. I blushed and had a real fluster plus a hot flush – double whammy. Hardly surprising, when the last time he saw me I was naked, paralytic and attempting to do sex on him – ugh! I channelled Sara and Deborah Frances-White (again) – both willing me to say nothing about the other night and definitely not to apologise for the umpteenth time. The awkward silence was filled by Hal.

'Great night, mind. Have to do it again sometime.'

More AAAAGH! Instead of clearing up the mess there and then and telling him the whole debacle was a terrible, wine-fuelled error of judgement, I mumbled, 'Yeah,' in a way which said, 'NOT ON YOUR LIFE!' but as I didn't say the actual words, could be interpreted by a keen person as, 'OOH YES PLEASE!'

I am an utter turkey with only myself to blame. In all probability, I *will* come crying to you at a future date – don't mention dates! Like Dick Whittington, my stomach has turned again just thinking of it. At least that's over with. I've seen him now and can stop dreading it. Still going to avoid him though. However, I think I just made things worse for myself – which wasn't quite the idea at all.

Shitsville!

Wednesday 11 June

As if by magic, just before I plead my case for HRT, a spot of ideal admissible evidence pops up to support my defence. Property developers have crept into my street over the years, encroaching on the traditional domain of families by creating student housing. Cramming in six bedrooms where there were two, they are a lucrative proposition. Many of us were students once, and it's not their fault, BUT they keep a different schedule to other residents. Now that the clubs are open all night, no self-respecting party animal is going to roll home before three or four o'clock, having lost all sense of neighbourly awareness and volume control they had when they left the house.

Last night, I mistakenly told a neighbour how quiet the students in our street have been, then I was woken at 3.30 a.m. by shrieks of laughter and slamming of taxi doors, followed by BANG, BANG, BANG on their front door as they pointlessly attempted to rouse their housemates. With perfect timing, I threw up the sash window just as one did the same to their lager, and without a thought for *my* neighbours, screamed, 'OI – KEEP THE BLOODY NOISE DOWN WILL YOU? IT'S HALF PAST THREE IN THE SODDING MORNING!' Then I slammed the window down with a gratifying flourish, making sure everyone in the street who hadn't heard the students was now wide awake. No, I *didn't* think it through, before you ask.

Met Sara and Simon before my appointment, in one of our favourite cafes, The Butterfly Cabinet, in Heaton. Needless to say, they loved the yelling-out-of-window story and were relieved I hadn't lost my touch as a world class ranter. It was unanimously agreed I may be operating in hair trigger mode, and for my own sanity and that of my neighbours, it would be a very wise move to try and blag a load of HRT. I threw them the bare bones of the Hal situation, careful not to flesh out the entire story as I couldn't bring myself to relive it, nor did I want the whole of Newcastle to know. We're dealing with gossipy Simon, here. They suggested doing nothing at all, which I was ecstatic about, and made me promise not to be driven off my beloved allotment by a ludicrous, self-imposed ban. If he asks me out again, I will politely decline.

Sorted! A problem is certainly halved when it is shared, and other related clichés.

Friends are such a tonic! Could do with more of that, and less of the gin – it only lands me in trouble.

Friday 13 June – a lucky day

At 11.25 a.m. I became the proud owner of an HRT prescription. I'm euphoric! I knew someone who was once refused it and prescribed antidepressants instead so it feels like it's contraband. Now I'm scared in case it has no effect or, worse, *side* effects e.g. putting on two stone or hallucinating, not that I've read about the side effects yet. What sort of idiot doesn't bother to read about possible side effects? Yes, I investigated increasing the risk of serious stuff but didn't consider the less life-threatening, potentially annoying ones. They're patches. I've never looked forward to taking any medication before, but I'm actually excited, which is a sad indictment of my middle-aged status. It's temporarily stopped me worrying about Hal and how I'll have to let him down gently but firmly and wheedle out of this predicament. With the help of my little patchy friends, I expect to feel like a new woman, one who would never lose her purse, put keys in her hood, or seduce anyone when out of their tree – well, maybe not the last one.

Update: you could paper two walls with the list of side effects.

Sunday 15 June

Sam came to the allotment today armed with a bombshell to drop: Twat had the audacity to make sure I know that he and his partner (aka the other woman) are splitting up 'in case I'm interested'! WHAAT!? Out of pure spite, I'm delighted she's leaving him! Even better, it's to be with a woman, which will annoy him intensely. Exactly how pathetic does he think I am? Yes, he meant *interested* – I checked. Does he think I've been sitting here for two and a half years waiting for this moment to arrive, like a dream come true! I'm burning with anger, and this time IT'S NOT A HOT FLUSH! It's a genuine, perfectly rational rage. Poor Sam was on the receiving end of my wrath and it's so difficult when it's her father, who still showers her with gifts in exchange for her affections. I don't want her to feel awkward, but on this occasion, I need the messenger to be in no doubt of my true feelings, at the risk of her being slightly injured in the crossfire.

Bloody furious he's treating our daughter as a go-between. He's the lowest of the low. As if I don't have enough to worry about without wondering if that arsehole's going to come a-knocking. I'd love to see him try. Some of us have a life waiting to be lived, without these men crawling out of the woodwork and getting in the way. Anyway, he's taken to wearing a hat: Twat in a hat – perfect! What's he hiding under there? His baldness of course – he's so vain. And breathe. Reluctantly, I have his number – we share a daughter after all. During my low period last year there were times when my fingers itched, desperate to call and give him both barrels. I just couldn't shake off the resentment. I stopped myself several times by picturing his perfectly slappable face and thrashing seven bells out of the nearest cushion.

Fortunately, Sam seemed to be expecting the negative response from me so, having fulfilled her duty, she was keen to change the subject so we could move on with our lives.

Impressed with the progress on the allotment, she singled out Hal's raised beds for praise and teased me about 'that bloke who obviously fancies you'. Instant red face ensued so had to tell her I was not blushing, but flushing, which soon shut her up as she felt guilty. And, after her announcement about Twat I just couldn't face the ordeal of repeating the whole story. Well, not the *whole* story, obviously. Glad he didn't drop by when she was there.

Monday 16 June

Who knew you could be emotional about seedlings? Need that HRT to kick in. I now have a reason to jump out of bed early (before ten) in the morning: I must open the blinds to let the sunshine smile on my little babies, giving them the best start in life. Except, there isn't much of the hot stuff about; it's usually cloudy.

The latest crisis: my Facebook account is proving to be a dangerous weapon in the wrong hands. We also have an allotment Facebook group. Naturally I joined at the start and have found it a mine of information. I've learned an enormous amount and now cringe at some of my early posts and questions. I enjoy walking around the plots, spotting the real-life people who have chosen a profile picture of themselves instead of their dog or holiday to Malta. Occasionally I've introduced myself and thanked them for their help with a query; it's a good way of getting to know people, but it depends on my question and its naivety rating as to whether I reveal my identity or pull up my hood and walk by. However, nothing I've asked so far compares to my social media faux pas today:

In all innocence, I was scrolling through old posts on the subject of cucumber growing, to avoid the embarrassment of asking another stupid question. Anyway, I was about to send a private message to Jenny, an ace gardener who I met a couple of times, asking for advice. But for some unfathomable reason I'd created a group containing Tommy McTaggart, Cockney Darren (never met him), and Billy, who all received the question, 'How are your cucumbers so huge?' OH MY GOD! No, it's *not* funny sending men I hardly know a private message containing a double entendre. My only hope is that a) they're all literal types or b) have no sense of humour! Aaaagh! I wrestled for ages with the best course of action and instead of messaging an apology, I panicked and immediately changed the carefully selected profile picture of me in dim lighting, to an anonymous sunflower. When I returned to delete the group, cheeky Cockney Darren who clearly has nothing better to do with his life, replied, 'Drop by the greenhouse one day and I'll show you mine!'

Now, without the exclamation mark, it's most likely innocent. *With* the exclamation mark, it's downright bloody suggestive. I've been cringing ever since and am hoping not to have attracted another garden visitor. That's the last thing I need. What if he'd already recognised my profile picture and knows where my plot is? I'm so useless and am going to delete that group or superglue my fingers together so they will never stray across another screen to create havoc.

Wednesday 18 June

Measured up for paving stones for the patio. Infinitely more thrilling than measuring up for curtains. Ground is neatly levelled and raked obsessively after each visit, so I need to get my skates on and get it laid. Scott and Sandy trudged down the path. I waved and he smiled. Sandy ignored me but (oddly) sent Scott back to ask if I needed any help! How did I know she'd sent him? Because his words were, 'Me mam says, do you want any help?'

Very thoughtful of Sandy – no one can accuse that funny fish of being predictable. Maybe it was because of the fork-lending/borrowing thing. Taken aback by the gesture, it was only polite to accept. Scott was surprisingly helpful and knew about sizes of paving stones, or 'flags' as we in the trade call them. Turns out he wanted to enrol on a Horticultural course at Kirkley College but struggled with the English and Maths required. Instead, he became a labourer and loved it until sadly he was made redundant, which knocked his confidence further.

That's all I found out – except that he's thirty-seven. I suspect he's going through a rough patch mental health-wise. It's very sad. I suggested setting up as handyman or gardener. 'Do you really think I could?' was his response. Launching into teacher mode, I buoyed him up. Told him he clearly knows what he's doing and must have lots of skills to deploy from his labouring experience. Judging by his lack of self-esteem, I suspect he doesn't hear much positivity from Sandy. We had quite a chat. He hated school and was bullied. It breaks my heart to hear such stories. After decades of anti-bullying education, kids and adults are still suffering. His friends are all 'online mates', which I also found very sad, but it beats having no friends at all. Anyway, I'm optimistic I might have raised his self-esteem by letting him help and praising his work. We decided he'll act as consultant and labourer when I lay the patio. He understands I want to do it myself, but I could do with his expertise and a hand lifting the flags into place. Hal would take over in that situation and wouldn't be happy to stand back and watch me, I know his type. That is, if he ever wants to speak to me again (stomach churns).

As usual, I didn't notice how late it was as I was too busy investigating the price of the flags (I know how to enjoy myself).

Barrow Man walked past, not leaving but arriving – after nine o'clock at night! With bagsful of swag to stash in the shed – at a guess. I held my breath and stayed still – he gives me the creeps, but I'm determined to find out more. Could be the 'No. 2 Ladies' Detective Agency' (thank you Alexander McCall Smith), except it sounds like the strapline should be 'Constipation Investigation'. It needs a rethink.

Friday 20 June

An uplifting afternoon in the greenhouse. The shelves are now filled with tomatoes, chillies, peppers, peas, beans and sweetcorn. Each is a well-proportioned miniature plant, apart from the gangly teenage tomatoes, who tower above the rest. Looks like they're all getting on well together – no fighting yet.

They're now wallowing in luxurious sunlight and are shooting up, not in the heroin addict sense of the word, though I am fast becoming an allotment junkie. Everyone should have one, but they demand time and dedication. I've squeezed a chair into a corner and am in my element, writing the diary and drinking coffee from a flask and plastic cup – bliss! I prefer my old-fashioned flask to the hi-tech versions that keep it warm for twenty-four hours. Where's the fun in that? Reminds me of beach picnics with Sam and her father, before he became a fully blown Twat. This fresh air malarkey is brilliant for quality sleep. In fact, it's almost as effective as rhubarb gin – only not as delicious. Maybe it's down to the HRT – that's a joke. I know it takes weeks to kick in. To spoil it all, I still have that feeling of impending doom, worrying about the Hal situation. Checked HRT patch – still there so feel happier.

Saturday 21 June

Slept well. Could be the placebo effect of HRT. Met Hilary and Chrystal for lunch and impromptu drinks on Grey Street. Cheered me up no end, watching revellers, hellbent on partying, wend their merry way down the street with its spectacular backdrop of neoclassical architecture. In various guises, through changes in fashion and building trends, people have played out this scene for hundreds of years. Hilary's been on a few dates from her app, 'Linda' or something. Mentor Chrystal is actively encouraging her to meet people under a strict code of 'getting a few meals out of them if they're a pain in the arse, or sleeping with them just the once if you fancy them'. This mercenary attitude is in keeping with Chrystal's mission of making up for lost time *plus* seeking revenge on the patriarchy. Hilary is her protégé but says she hasn't slept with any yet because 'you don't know where they've been' (Gosforth Park?). At which point Beelzebub rolls her eyes in despair at the Mother Theresa attitude, remembering their last night in Gran Canaria, and regales us with tales of her most recent young conquests and their vital statistics.

High on life and cocktails, Chrystal set about arranging to meet another unsuspecting twenty-nine-year-old victim (who looked more like twenty) from her app. When she emerged from the toilet with half a loo roll wrapped round her ankle, we frogmarched her to the nearest taxi and bundled her in. It was great to see them, and Hilary laughed and laughed at my Hal story. Not quite the desired effect, but I saw the funny side for a few seconds, which is progress. Didn't dare tell Chrystal or she'd sign me up as a new recruit for her sex crusade.

Hilary says I'm not to worry and no, I don't owe him 'an explanation or the time of day', which is a harsh but refreshing attitude from my ex-conventional friend. She has listened well to her mistress – who is still proving herself a good influence. In an effort to engage my friends in healthier pursuits, I've invited them to the allotment in the next couple of weeks, when there's more to see.

Feeling much happier so I'm having a very early night before I ruin it.

Sunday 22 June

Planted out the lovely peas and beans. It involved playing around with bamboo canes for the plants to cling onto and netting them to keep the greedy birds from scoffing the lot, thus ruining all your hard work over the past few weeks. All great fun. I'm using bamboo arches for the climbing French and runner beans – they might look good when they're fully grown and different from the usual straight ones.

Tuesday 24 June

Today was TT Day – tomato transplant day! I bought two grow bags, each the weight of a two-year-old child (though less wriggly) and wrestled them into the greenhouse. Another surprise benefit of gardening is the amount of problem solving required. It keeps the brain on its toes with issues such as: how the hell do I fit that into there? What can I do to stop those bloody pigeons breaking through the new Fort Knox arrangement of canes and nets to demolish the peas? How in God's name can I stop the sticks poking through the blasted net? It all involves a sizeable but necessary amount of swearing. However, once achieved, the job satisfaction rate is high. I hope Shady Pines has a garden for you, and future me, to enjoy, even if it's from a distance, through a window. Green is soothing for the soul.

Saturday 28 June – Plate Day

As you may remember, The Northumberland Plate is the grand finale of Race Week that used to be held on the Town Moor. However, a middle finger is raised in defiance against our temperance-promoting ancestors as it is not only a gambling fest but also a day to enjoy a drink with friends. The only day of the year you will not be able to find a taxi in Newcastle is Plate Day, unless you are going to or from Gosforth Park Racecourse, and even then, someone else will have nabbed it before you. I'm creating the wrong impression here, we're not some sleepy backwater where Bob's taxi firm serves the whole city – quite the reverse; there are hundreds of taxis! Equally, there are hundreds of people heading to the biggest race meeting of the year, all dressed up to the nines, most wearing high heels – thus ruling out walking, driving, or catching a bus. Akin to a wedding, outfits are planned months in advance, sales of false tan rocket, and the embarrassing cousin of the hat – the fascinator – is stuck awkwardly to the side of many a coiffed head for the day.

Men's interview/wedding/funeral/court appearance suits are dragged from the back of the wardrobe, their horrified owners wailing, 'Do I *have* to wear one?' and their female partners shouting, 'FFS. For the last bloody time, YES!'

There are strict rules for the end of Plate Day. You *must*:

- have great difficulty finding your taxi and getting the whole party into it

- spend ages dissecting each other's betting wins and losses of the day
- adjourn to a bar for round two of downing wedding-like quantities of alcohol in keeping with your attire
- have at least one woman in your party barefoot by 7 p.m. at the very latest
- have someone in your party embarrass themselves e.g. fighting, arguing, being sick, crying

Luckily, our merry band of revellers included Chrystal, so as a group we stood a good chance from the outset of ticking all the boxes in terms of rules. Hilary, Sara, Simon, Chrystal, and I had a brilliant day, though it wasn't without its hairy moments – as you can imagine. It began with Chrystal insisting on pre-drinks at Hilary's, setting the tone for the day. I clocked Hilary looking on with fear in her eyes, so I reassured her that all would be well, though my fingers were crossed behind my back when I said it.

I loved every single one of the magnificent horses – all highly toned athletes, muscles rippling, coats shining in the sunlight, meticulously turned out and ready for action. The jockeys are either tiny, skinny, or both. I don't know how they manage to control such powerful animals and steer them skilfully around a course, carried along by the roar of the crowd, giving their all to be first past the winning post. There were some exciting neck and neck finishes, with Chrystal cheering them on at the top of her voice, getting louder and more screechy as the day wore on. Striking lucky with a few of her bets, she convinced herself this marks the beginning of a lucrative new career as a professional gambler. Simon tried in vain to tell her that each win was a mere fluke as she knew nothing about the sport. I had to tell him to stop winding her up – for all our sakes. After a quiet period spent sussing out Chrystal and acclimatising to the sheer volume of her personality, Sara joined in with the fun. By the end of the day, Hilary and I took on the mantle of 'responsible adults' with the three others verging on a handful.

As predicted, they insisted on going to Jesmond for more drinks. Of course they did, they were in full flow. We managed to herd the cats into a taxi, with Chrystal shouting, 'Eeh me FEET!' at the top of her voice, and us promising she could take her shoes off at the bar, but not before. It was like sharing a cab with toddlers as Sara and Simon felt carsick and complained endlessly about the stop-start journey as we snaked through the traffic towards the city centre. Out of frustration, I resorted to mindfulness, chanting, 'This too shall pass,' forcing myself to think of the lovely day we'd had up till then.

On Osborne Road, every hotel and bar was packed with racegoers, many sitting outside, catching precious rays. Predictably, Chrystal fell getting out of the taxi and knelt on the pavement giggling. It took three of us to help her up then hide her from the door staff who would have sent us packing had they seen what trouble we were about to unleash on their afternoon. We managed to find a corner of the garden away from the entrance, but realised too late that Chrystal had access to passers-by on the street and was soon courting male attention from several angles, egged on by Simon. A cattle prod would have been useful to fend them off and put a stop to the banter. We had a few minutes of peace when Chrystal and Sara went to the loo, then Sara returned saying she'd left Chrystal talking to a guy inside. I stomped in to find her leaning against the men's toilet door, snogging the face off an equally drunken man who was wearing her fascinator. To my horror, I heard her mumbling something to him about a hotel room but before I could intervene, someone came out of the loos, thrusting the lovebirds forwards, causing them to land in a tangled mess on the floor. Instinctively, I grabbed Chrystal's dress and pulled it back down over her exposed knickers, which made her yell, 'OI! PACK IT IN YOU! I'LL GET THE BOUNCERS, MIND!' while lashing out at the bemused, thoroughly squashed man underneath her. The door staff arrived in a flash and were less than amused. I intervened before madam made it worse, apologising for my friend and doing my level best to haul her up and usher her out of the building, signalling in desperation to the others outside.

People laughed as Chrystal was cajoled into leaving, which prompted that famous saying, 'What dy'a think you're lookin' at, eh?' from our furious, barefoot friend. The taxi was quite an ordeal. As soon as we were on our way, breathing a premature sigh of relief, Chrystal burst into tears for the entire journey, wailing, 'Me fascinator! He's got me fascinator!' Never having been a frequenter of bars or clubs full of drunk people, poor Hilary was in a state of shock and stroked Chrystal's unruly hair in a motherly fashion while the rest of us blocked our ears.

I'm proud to say that the rules of Plate Day were well and truly adhered to.

JULY

Tuesday 1 July

Now seriously worried. While laying out string for the patio boundaries, I had an unfathomable exchange with Hal, who arrived with more presents in the form of several packets of seeds. I thanked him but didn't tell him I'd ordered plenty already. As predicted, he offered to help with the patio and when I told him about Scott, he fell silent and looked away. I could see he was upset. After the tumbleweed stopped blowing around the plot, he said, 'Oh, right. Okay then.' His words were clipped, his tone brusque. How dare he be angry! I started gabbling about how the poor lad doesn't have much of a life, always seems down, could be depressed and blah blah and more blah. Now I'm hormonally furious! I got rid of one miserable, quietly controlling twat who I wasted far too many years with, and I refuse to be answerable to another. He stomped off mumbling, 'I'm away to water me beans,' and I just managed to stop myself from shouting, 'WHATEVAH!' like a petulant teenager, after realising I simply CBA. He can bloody well sling his macho hook. I'm not allowing him or 'the incident' spoil my enjoyment of the allotment. That would be a tragedy. Anyway, I'm needed here – I have fishy business to expose in the top corner.

Two questions:

1. Why isn't life straightforward by now?
2. Why am I such a muppet?

Wednesday 2 July

I fear I may have lost the few remaining marbles that were rattling round in my head. Evidence: I've invited Simon for a snoop in the corner plot. He's even more excited than me. I may live to regret this. Blabbermouth Simon is not exactly the go-to guy for the position of sleuth's accomplice. Although he's an utter wimp and frightened of his own shadow, he looks the part and I'm not going alone. For half a nanosecond it crossed my mind to invite Hal.

Drawbacks:

a) I'm avoiding him
b) he wouldn't play ball anyway

Simon, on the other hand, is in his element. Yes, Simon, it's 'just like the telly but real' and yes, you have to be sensible because it's potentially dangerous – therefore not 'like the telly' at all. He swore on his (latest-in-a-never-ending-line-of-boyfriends) boyfriend Jamie's life that he'd be discreet. Hmmm.

Friday 4 July

A productive day! I single-handedly collected, transported, and scattered bags and bags of compost and topsoil for the raised beds. I'm elated and exhausted in equal measures. They're beautiful: rich, dark, fertile. Just the finishing touch of manure to add and they will be perfectly ripe for sowing. There was a queue at the muck heap earlier, the lure of manure. The best of it's at the bottom anyway – black gold. Even Hal, emerging from his huff, had to congratulate me when he walked past the beds, resplendent with fresh earth. Annoyed with myself for feeling the need to tell him it was all my own work, but a quiet life trumps principles at times.

Only the contentious matter of laying the patio remains. Hope I can make a good job of it. Sara reckons I'll 'smash it', which isn't the intention at all. If the Hal thing gets too complicated, I can always bury him under it – must stop thinking like that about patios! Speaking of my little minx of a friend: a young guy, escorted by Scott who'd let him in, came to the plot. Scott pointed unceremoniously at me, grunting, 'Lizzie', and deposited him at my feet. He was very sweet.

'Hi, I'm Adam, is Sara here?' he asked, looking confused. Resisted the obvious reply, 'yes, she's hiding in the compost bin,' and told a lie, pretending she'd mentioned coming then didn't. Dejected, the poor lad thanked me and walked away. Just wait till I see her – she's definitely cheating on him. She's so lucky I can think on my feet in these situations, or she'd be busted!

I can't help myself. I'd had a Hal-free day but couldn't resist courting danger. Maybe I'm one of those adrenaline junkies? I hardly think so – can't handle the stress. Had a walk to the corner. I could smell something odd in the air as I neared the shed. At first, I thought he was burning plastic in there, but it was more pungent and chemical-like. Eureka – alcohol! He's moonshining.

I'm over the moonshine. I've cracked it. I looked it up: according to a guy in South Carolina it's pure, free of chemicals, and has a nice smell – could have fooled me! Oh yes and it's hangover-free. Now I'm interested – not really. Wow, the plot thickens, and I'm not talking topsoil. I need to be in that shed.

Walking home, I called Sara to tell her she'd been rumbled by Adam. Let her panic for a minute, then told her it was a lie – but I'm telling no more of those to her innocent victims about where she is or isn't.

Looking forward to seeing Hilary and Chrystal plus dogs tomorrow.

Saturday 5 July

I wouldn't be at all surprised if there's already an eviction notice from the allotment committee winging its way through the ether to the letterbox on my computer after today's antics.

Hilary and Chrystal arrived, along with two enormous, psychopathic dogs. When she talked about them on holiday, I pictured her with two cutesie Chihuahuas peeping out from a designer handbag or matching white toy poodles sporting diamanté collars – one pink, one pale blue. Instead, a giant black greyhound named Pickle and an ever-so-slightly smaller grey lurcher, Cheesy, dragged a yelling Chrystal along the main path, hell-bent on finding trouble and sandwiches. Cheesy immediately leapt up and plonked two filthy paws on my shoulders while I ducked and dived to avoid his tongue flicking into my mouth. Meanwhile, from the other end of the lead, the ineffectual owner shouted, 'Down, Cheesy boy!' which sounded bizarre in itself. Taken aback, I laughed politely, as non-dog owners do. Pickle began rummaging round in my bag, and after more chaos, Chrystal finally tamed the over-exuberant beasties by diverting their attention to treats. Not sure if those TV personal doggy trainers would approve of reinforcing bad behaviour in this way, but it was an emergency short-term solution.

After a brief tour, the humans made all the right noises at the 'before' photos, as though genuinely impressed by the makeover. It felt like showing off a new house I'd spent months renovating. We sat on camping chairs drinking coffee and biscuits in the sunshine, enjoying the serenity of the place. For ten blissful minutes, even Chrystal was calm – until hell, and the dogs, were unleashed: from the other end of the site came a high-pitched whistle and loud shouting; two sounds irresistible to nosey dogs. Leaping into action, canine Starsky and Hutch flew off to investigate. Frantically, the three of us gave chase as they bounded straight over the plots at full speed, emitting screeches of sheer doggy joy that translated as, 'This is the BEST day of our lives! She's brought us to an adventure playground!' Everyone knows dogs are grateful creatures and say that type of stuff all the time. Sadly, what dogs fail to understand is the equally common phrase used by dog owners, 'Get back here NOW!'

Cheesy paused momentarily, cocking an ear towards his irate owner, before ripping up a whole sprout plant and running around awkwardly with it, while Pickle tried to steal it. Seconds later, Cheesy dropped the plant so he could hurtle around even faster, with all the grace of a camel, pulling wheelies in the woodchip which rained down over newly-raked beds. He dug a hole in Scott and Sandy's prepped and manured raised bed then darted off before anyone could grab the lead and spoil his entertainment. Remembering his racing days and delighted to have found a new human friend, Pickle also sped around in circles, sending earth flying and Scott tearing after him. What a fantastic game! Then came a sound I'd never heard before – Scott laughing. In fact, he was in hysterics after Chrystal threw herself on top of Cheesy's lead and emerged from someone's brassica patch covered in mud and broccoli leaves. The shy young man who rarely cracked a smile, was at last having *fun*. Luckily, Billy was the only other person around – it made his day too.

I failed to see the funny side until much later, when the vandals were recaptured, and all damage rectified. Despite their stereotypically hangdog expressions and tails between legs, I had to ban them from further visits before an 'it's you or the dogs' situation arose. Chrystal apologised profusely for their behaviour, which is hypocritical when I think back to Gran Canaria. As she coaxed the crestfallen, ungainly animals into the car, she asked, 'Who's your mate, the man of few words? He's lovely – and a dog person.' Aaaagh poor, innocent Scott! NO Chrystal, you are not going there, or anywhere near, for that matter. It would be tantamount to abuse. Remember – I must face these people on a regular basis.

Sunday 6 July

Needed a day to myself after the shock of yesterday so I got up early and walked through Jesmond Dene and Heaton Park. It was gloriously sunny and very peaceful. I always look out for kingfishers whizzing along the Ouseburn, after seeing one a while ago.

Tuesday 8 July

Awake early and jittery about tonight. After telling him about the smell, Simon thinks the 'poor guy' is making a few vats of home brew and won't entertain my theory of a wholesale moonshine operation, or anything equally sinister. Says he'll be wheeling it away at night because it'll be strictly against the 'ten thousand commandments' as he calls the allotment rules. My dad made home brew and it didn't stink like that stuff – I told him. He was having none of it. We shall see.

11.00 p.m. Head is well and truly spinning after tonight. In Simon's car, incognito in pitch-dark. Fully undercover. It was even more exciting than *The Tracking of Malcolm*. Sounds ripe for a crime drama, until you realise it stars *Dogging* Malcolm then it becomes an entirely different movie genre. Of course, it's thrilling because Dogging Malcolm isn't a potentially dangerous criminal. Simon laughed at the mention of Malcolm and will never let Hilary live it down. Not ever.

I led Simon down the path by torchlight to wait in my greenhouse, hiding among the gravel, low on the ground – not easy at my age. People in glass houses should not only refrain from throwing stones, but also hiding. Should have paid more attention in science at school, instead of jiggling the gas taps. It was excruciatingly painful, but more impossible was trying to keep Simon quiet. Just before I seized up permanently, we heard the unmistakeable squeak of a wheelbarrow.

Giving him a few minutes to get busy in the shed, we broke cover. Next stop: behind Hal's shed, nearing the target. I guided Simon, making, tentative baby steps through the dark. It was easier for me as I know the paths. A tiny thread of light was visible above the shed door. Target in position. It felt like a real mission, and we were both nervous. For once, Simon didn't laugh or attempt a wisecrack. Our cover story, should we be caught, was that we were worried about Hal who wasn't answering his phone. Perfectly feasible.

Simon couldn't smell anything so we moved away from Hal's shed where he could sniff the air, like a bloodhound. At that moment, the target's shed door was flung open. Instinctively I gripped Simon's arm as he jumped back into the dark. Moonshine Man emerged for a few seconds, hauling a large metal box across the floor. After a brief struggle, he loaded it onto the wheelbarrow and covered it with rustling plastic as we stared into Aladdin's cave. We caught a brief glimpse of bottles, tubing, pans, and gas canisters, all crammed into a wall of shelving before MM went back inside and slammed the door shut.

'That'll be the moonshine in the barrow,' I whispered to Simon, terrified.

'That's not moonshine, it's meth,' he replied, 'It's a freaking meth lab!'

'What?'

'*Like Breaking Bad*, – crystal meth? Methamphetamine. It's a Class A drug, Lizzie.'

While I froze, taking it all in, he added in a voice I didn't recognise as his, 'We need to leave – *now*.'

Never, in the history of knowing Simon, has he spoken with any degree of gravitas. I don't know how we got out of there without Moonshine Man hearing my heart thumping through my jacket. Pure adrenaline carried us out of the allotment to safety. Simon explained the massively popular TV series that had passed me by while I wrestled with Freeview. I digress – if he's right then this is an extremely serious crime. When asked what he thought we should do, he told me, 'If we have any sense at all, then we'll do nothing.' Apparently, ever since this *Breaking Bad* thing there's been a spate of copycat 'cookers' in houses, lockups, and garages all over the world. However, surely *the world* doesn't extend to a little allotment site in Jesmond. It's hardly The Bronx, is it? I just don't believe there's a *real* drugs lab in that shed – it's too far-fetched.

11.30 p.m. Simon texted telling me not to breathe a word to anyone, which is completely out of character for him, given his penchant for gossip. My friend was almost unrecognisable tonight. If he's right, can I really stand back and pretend I'm not privy to a serious offence taking place at my beloved allotments? The committee wouldn't stand for it. I sniggered at the thought of the members' faces as *Breaking Bad* was explained to them. It's absurd! Class A drugs are *not* rolling off the production line in one of our allotment sheds. It *must* be moonshine, or alcohol of some description. Vodka made from potato peelings is a possibility. Maybe other plot holders supply him – there could be a whole network on the site. Or is it beer after all? I'm going to have to sleep on this one, though I need a medicinal brandy to stop my head spinning.

Wednesday 9 July

Up early, pacing the floor, mind racing with the stress of the discovery. My first thought was to tell Hal. Then I came to my senses, realising that would be an act of idiocy, on a par with whoever suggested politics as a viable career option for Boris Johnson. I'm also trying to distance myself from Hal. He'll be furious about us going against his sage advice to stay away from Moonshine Man and will also be jealous of Simon (note - must plant sage). I didn't like his reaction when I told him about Scott helping me with the patio. I'm saying nothing.

Friday 11 July

Been reading up on carrots, as a diversion. For a traditional native vegetable, grown in their millions, they are surprisingly fussy: the child who is never happy, for whom the watering can is always half empty, the soil browner on the other side. Their natural enemy is the carrot fly – the most useless type of fly ever. It's even afraid of heights above one metre – an airborne version of Viz's Pathetic Sharks who wore rubber rings and were terrified of everything. Unlike their aquatic friends, the carrot fly can wreak havoc. As soon as the ground is disturbed, they smell carrot blood a mile off and swoop, stuffing their faces and laying their eggs in your precious veg, destroying it. Carrots need very soft soil. While everyone else puts up with less than perfect conditions, the carrot child will moan and refuse to cooperate until it's all sorted. Bloody hell, it's not as if we're asking much of you, all you need to do is sit there and grow. It's hardly brain surgery.

You'll never catch a carrot fly in the act. They are so tiny and sail through life under the radar, because to venture any higher gives them vertigo. As a pest, they're very effective – the Olympic silver medallists of garden pests, with gold going to Team Slug every time.

I don't hold out much for my first carrot brood – but you never know.

Sunday 13 July

Text from Hal: *Hello stranger x*

Two words plus kiss. No invitation so no danger of rejection. Very clever. I've always hated that expression. It's a passive aggressive euphemism for, 'You've been avoiding me, haven't you?' By way of reply, my barometer stomach lurched. Not a good sign. This is my own doing, so I must deal with it. On that fateful night I was indeed drunk, but never gave the impression I was about to spend the rest of my life with him. One night, perhaps, but even two would be open to discussion. I suppose he could be forgiven for thinking I fancied him after my outrageous behaviour – stomach lurches on cue again and head shakes involuntarily – that's a new one.

Despite the risk of encouraging him, I'm dying to tell him about the shed discovery. Just thinking – perhaps he already knows? Has he looked inside the shed himself one dark evening. Or is he involved in the enterprise – their plots are very close to each other after all? Is he the potato peelings supplier? That's a job you won't see advertised. He's shirty whenever I mention it.

Here's the other dilemma: do I reply to the text or ignore it? I can hear you all shouting a cacophony of advice from Shady Pines. Trouble is, it's all conflicting, so I'm forced to go it alone this time, and blame half of you later. A list is called for.

For replying:
- Keeps things civil.
- He'll text-bomb me if I don't.

Against replying:
- He'll think I'm still interested – not that I ever was, for more than a day or two…

Now I have Tom Jones singing, 'Text bomb, text bomb, you're my text bomb,' in my ear. It's a short list and whatever I do, it must NOT spoil my enjoyment of the allotment.

I'm a greedy, reckless fool. Still feel hyper after last night. So much so that, against my better nature and sensible side of brain, I'm off to get a Filet (that should be double 'l', Ronald, you junk-food-pushing clown) o' Fish Meal from the dealers in town. I'm discombobulated, but more cheerful now that I've written that stupendous word for the first time in my life. A chocolate milkshake may well be in order as an extra comfort blanket.

5.30 p.m. Not only was it a wild goose chase, but also a total fiasco. Went to the drive-through near Gosforth Park (yes, there). Spent ages in the huge queue with mouth watering and cheeks aching in anticipation as I inched closer, only to find the well of chocolate milkshake had run dry. You MUST be joking! WHAT DO YOU MEAN, 'NO CHOCOLATE MILKSHAKE?' Might demand a refund on that HRT. Then, slightly calmer, sensing the poor young lad reaching for the panic button, 'No I do NOT want strawberry or sodding banana. And I don't want the fish thing either, THANK you.' Then I was stuck, more inching ensued, past each window, explaining through gritted teeth not just that I hadn't ordered anything, but the petulant reason *why* I hadn't ordered anything – as if they were remotely interested. The look of disbelief on their faces said it all: *who, in their right mind, goes window shopping at a drive-through?* To cap it all off perfectly, I turned right instead of left and was trapped in the queue for the pigging drive-through AGAIN! Nearly crying, I was so mortified by the thought of facing the same people and having the same conversation with them, I ordered a coke and poured it into the gutter as soon as I could. Why? Not because I don't like coke, but my stupid brain forced me to panic and make a mad choice. Drove home and looked at the clock: just after five – great I can legally open wine! After all it's an emergency.

Careful not to apologise, and after excessive deliberation, I texted Hal: *Been a bit busy. Stop by the greenhouse when you're passing.*

That, my friends, was forty minutes of my life I'll never get back.

Monday 14 July

Still feel uneasy and need to avoid the allotment, so I took the metro to Whitley Bay. What a pure tonic it was. The entire seafront has been revamped, restoring the area to its Victorian level of popularity, wooing back many tourists from Scotland

and Yorkshire who flock to the small hotels, boating lake, crazy, mini, and dinosaur golf – who knew there were so many golf permutations? This wonderful seaside town is heaped with character. There's even a cinema run by volunteers. As well as the annual carnivals, the thriving group of artists hold an 'open house' exhibition where you can have a nosey inside people's homes, and their art exhibits of course! This can feel rather weird and intrusive but is a great event loaded with community spirit. It's how society should be – rather than closing doors to keep everyone else out. The whole place emits a warm, welcoming glow, although a friend who took part admitted she felt like a monkey in a zoo.

Down by the sea is The Dome, once known as the Spanish City, when it housed the exciting mini fairground – Hal's favourite day out and special summer holiday outing for several generations of Geordie kids. It wasn't Spanish or a real city but was so named for its Moorish, white-walled exterior complete with splendid dome. It now hosts, among other carefully selected outlets, a world-renowned fish and chip shop. Okay, perhaps that's an exaggeration, like the diner in *Elf* with the 'world's best cup of coffee' reputation. When I caught sight of it through the sea mist, I laughed out loud remembering the fateful day Debs and I went with two very attractive boys who we were determined to impress: Davey and Jonno. I've checked out the diary entry for more detail and can now indulge you with the truth, and not a hazy, rose-tinted specs version.

For once, we were successful in securing a date where nobody was punching above their weight. It was a match made in Hebburn, over the river, where the boys lived. We met them when we were forced to go and support Debs' brother's football team, which turned out surprisingly well, as we bagged two of the opposition at half time. One week later, they travelled all the way to North Shields on the passenger ferry and walked to Whitley Bay where we whisked them away for an afternoon of fairground fun – or that's what we all thought. En route to the Spanish City, each couple shared a bag of chips to enhance the romantic atmosphere of the occasion. It was all going swimmingly with the boys laughing at our jokes and a great deal of foreplay to foreplay – the pushing, shoving and slapping that teenagers engage in as an excuse to touch each other. Once there, we headed straight for the turbo-charged waltzer and screamed our way around and around and around, not because we wanted to go faster, but because we were genuinely terrified and wanted it to stop. Of course, the boys hated it too, but weren't allowed to scream in the seventies.

After what felt like twelve hours on a stormy sea, the ordeal ended, and we staggered away with our jelly legs, clinging to the boys for support in silly girlie style. Debs glanced over, looking desperate – she was as green as I felt. Covering our mouths, we ran full pelt to the nearest bin where we were violently sick in full view of the boys. For ages. We'd blown it. In one fell swoop they went from totally devoted, to totally revolted – a sad departure from Olivia Newton John. When we finally managed to lift our shameful, vomitty faces out of the bin, our potential life-partners had scarpered. Distraught, we dragged our sorry selves to the bus stop via Boots, to freshen up with the free makeup testers.

Before returning from my trip down memory lane, I called into For the Love of the North, a wonderful shop created to promote the beauty of the North East through the eyes of local artists. I love it in there. The owners are a fantastic couple, hugely dedicated to the business and its ethos. Few workplaces in Britain boast a sea view and it's a pleasure to support this enterprise – a treasure trove of exquisite Northumbrian and Geordie themed gifts. Inhaling the medicinal sea air, I strolled along the magnificent promenade to Cullercoats, with its perfectly formed bay – a favourite with early morning swimmers of the intrepid variety, surfers, paddle boarders (any time of day), and all manner of vessels in the boat category. The sea put on its best performance, from delicate white horses to galloping rollers – the full monty – showing off its skills to an appreciative audience. My befuddled head and frayed nerves were soothed by the swooshing sea and smell of comfort food.

I avoided looking at my phone all day. When I got into bed, I saw there was a text from Hal, sent at 2.20 p.m.: *That'd be great. See you soon xxx*

Oh nooooooo – three kisses? Hint not taken on the no x front. One thing I've learned over the years: men are impervious to hints.

Wednesday 16 July

Arrived at the allotment to find a whole tray of cauliflower seedlings upturned on the ground. Yesterday they were growing in the greenhouse. I'd kept them back as spares in case the first batch became slug food.

At first, I thought it was the wind or a particularly angry bird, but they'd been taken outside and strewn over the path. My eyes were burning as I picked them up, and a knot tightened around my stomach. Scott wandered past soon afterwards.

'Do you want a hand?' he asked, shyly. Apparently, there are occasional spates of vandalism from local kids. With a plot close to the main gate, I'm an easy target for them. Still, I feel very aggrieved, and angry of course.

Scott was very kind, taking my mind off it by asking after 'them crackers', aka the dogs! Before long I was laughing hysterically as he reminded me of the arc of soil, a mud rainbow that showered everyone in its path as they rampaged around, having the best day of their lives dodging our attempts to bring their excitement to an end.

'Aye, canny hilarious,' he declared, summing it up perfectly. Feeling relaxed after the dose of laughter, I persuaded myself not to take this personally and together we tidied the mess.

Suddenly, Sandy's dulcet tones torpedoed through the atmosphere of calm, as she yelled for her son, 'Scooooooooot – get here NOW!' With a sneaky eyeroll in my direction, Scott jumped up and headed back to their plot. I could hear her berating him for ignoring her and disappearing. Another row ensued as he tried to explain; she soured his sweet gesture yet again.

Throughout the morning I asked passers-by if they'd seen any strangers around last night. They all offered sympathy (and cauliflowers – better than tea). People are essentially good, and this special community more than makes up for the few saboteurs out there. Even Miriam was outraged, and I enjoyed her over-the top sweary reaction which was well-meaning and hurled in an appropriate direction for a change. No sign of Hal.

Now that I'm home I can't stop thinking about it. Why would anyone commit such mindless acts? I suppose it's the nature of vandalism – or am I being targeted?

Thursday 17 July

Hilary called. Chrystal's having more problems with Gibs. He parks opposite her house almost every day, up to two hours at a time, watching her from his car – an ancient BMW with stupid wheels. It used to be silver but now it's grey, having lost its shine many years ago. Partner turned stalker. She *must* report him, or it could escalate as history has proved. Her logic is they'll warn him, and he'll know it's upsetting her, whereas she says she'd rather give the impression she 'couldn't give a toss'. It's such a hard call. Personally, I'd go with report, report, report, every time. Deterring a stalker requires the sledge-hammer treatment, not kid gloves. Don't leave anything to chance or assume they've got the message, or that message will be manipulated, twisted to suit their own agenda. Poor Chrystal. This is dreadful news. Just as she's repairing her life and making up for lost time, up pops the ugly head of her miserable past in subhuman form.

Visited the allotment with a degree of trepidation, as you do when your house has been burgled, wondering if more vandalism had occurred. Luckily there was none, and I spent time watering and planting out sweetcorn seedlings. It was heavenly. Not a soul around, not even Hal. I mustn't decide that my life is imploding because of a few blips, or I will slide back into the dark place in which I found myself last year. I'm telling myself these are temporary and insignificant setbacks.

Met Sam at the Tyneside Cinema café. She lifted my spirits chatting about the baby's room. I'm excited and need positive things to pull me up, though I feel neither qualified nor responsible enough for the job of grandmother! With her analytical, scientific brain in top gear, she launched into a detailed account of what was going on in her body week by week. This was in addition to the complicated logistics of what would happen if Ben isn't around when she goes into labour. I think I'm included in that scenario, but I'd glazed over by then and didn't dare admit to it. When I was pregnant with her, I had one book and a few leaflets from the hospital. To me, computers were things we reluctantly had to teach the kids about once a week. The internet was yet to be rolled out to all except for those creatures known as 'boffins' who spent all day and night dismantling and building the wretched machines in their bedroom instead of going to the pub with their mates. And That Bill Gates of course – he was one of them.

Sam dismissed the vandalism instantly as the work of kids, 'bored youth' as she jokingly described them, *à la* older generation. She doesn't know about my list of suspects though:

Hal – disgruntled
Moonshine Man – irritated
Sandy – jealous (ironically of me and Hal)
Imagination is raging out of control.

Saturday 19 July

My good fortune ran out – Hal came by. You can run but you can't hide in a greenhouse. He was really supportive about the vandalism and although I was almost sick when I first saw him, it was all very amicable. I've removed him from the list of suspects, though the cynic in me wondered if he was overreacting to disguise his guilt. When he told me I should have called him immediately, alarm bells rang for a second, but I silenced them sharpish. You'd have to be pretty damaged to do something like that, and for me to think like this is just plain nasty, when all he's done is help.

In my defence, he definitely has a jealous streak; he didn't like the fact Scott helped clear up the mess. Jealousy is not an attractive trait, as well we know.

Hilary and Chrystal, with dogs safely confined to the car, called in to announce that Chrystal has applied for an allotment.

She has visions of sharing it with Hilary. However, what she doesn't realise is Hilary doesn't like getting her hands dirty. Er… slight problem on an allotment which is basically made of dirt. I can't see Chrystal risking breaking a nail either – or wearing sensible clothes and what about the two loveable but wild beasties masquerading as pets? I tactfully explained that they'd have to agree to canine community service as a punishment followed by intensive doggy rehab before being allowed anywhere near the site. Think I successfully put her off the idea – CBA with the responsibility of it all!

Speaking of rehab, Miriam shuffled past, head down.

'There's a drinker's face if ever there was one,' remarked Chrystal, loudly. She was given a stern telling off from Hilary, who saved me the trouble.

'Shush, Chrystal! She looks like she could turn at any minute,' then we all giggled, which wasn't kind (or safe) but *very* funny.

Scott's eyes lit up when he noticed Chrystal sitting on the patio. He stopped to ask how the dogs were and if he could help take them for a walk one day. Chrystal being Chrystal, immediately replied, 'Monday's good,' way too enthusiastically for my liking. Now he thinks it's a date – a doggy play date – let's not go there again. Also, she's much older than she looks – not that I'm ageist – it's the experience gap I'm worried about. We can only hope he doesn't suggest Gosforth Park as a meeting place.

When I warned Chrystal to be very careful, she was horrified and screeched, 'Lizzie, MAN!' as though I was completely out of order, adding, 'I'll not be drinking so he'll be safe as houses, bless him.' After I lectured her like a child about giving him the wrong impression, she laughed hysterically. I was left feeling like a killjoy, but it was good craic at the same time.

When they'd all left, I lost myself in the beauty of the allotment. The tomatoes have fruited – shiny green beads, each surrounded by protective soft spikes. They are thirsty plants and fussy eaters, requiring a special diet. To cajole them into growing, we use liquid seaweed. Their smell screams organic – so deliciously unique, even the best shop-bought vine tomatoes can't mimic it.

Someone I haven't seen for ages is Moonshine Man. He's reached number one in the suspect charts.

Monday 21 July

Was dying to ask Hilary how the dog-walking had gone. I was surprised Sandy allowed Scott to have some freedom, though it's unfair to assume she wouldn't. Beforehand, Chrystal was very firm with Hilary and acknowledged that, while she'd been attracted to Scott at first, she now 'appreciates his vulnerability and would act appropriately'. Methinks Hilary was summarising this as I don't, for one minute, think Chrystal will have used those words. She'd ended the indignant retort with, 'I'm not a flamin' savage, man!' Now that, I can believe, is a genuine quote.

They met at the allotments and walked on the Town Moor – good plan. Poor Chrystal. She must have felt she was well and truly under the microscope and consequently (to serve us damn right) told Hilary there was 'nothing to report'. Either that, or it could mean she's in shock after the worrying element of the story: Gibs appeared when they returned to the car. He pulled up and parked across the road. I could feel my heart racing. He knows she comes to the allotment. He's now seen Scott *with* Chrystal. This is alarming news. He'll jump to conclusions. After pressure from Scott and Hilary, Chrystal reported him but thinks it's a waste of time. I'm now worried for Scott, and terrified for Chrystal.

Wednesday 23 July

Why do I feel so foul? No energy this week. The HRT is definitely kicking in – I won't have a word said against it. My brain fog has begun to lift, I'm less forgetful, and I *was* calmer until recently. I'm brooding about the vandalism but it's also the Hal situation, due to my own crass stupidity and getting carried away as though I was in my late teens, not late fiftysomethings. I'm missing Lucas. Like any recovering addict, I'm on a rocky road: chugging along fine most of the time, then ambushed by a craving – out of nowhere. I'm an idiot. This needs to STOP! Perhaps a day out with Chrystal will help – or maybe not. She's kindly bought tickets for Hilary and me to see Noel Gallagher in Exhibition Park on Sunday. I'm hoping Chrystal may be more guarded when she's on home soil. I doubt it as a gig involves alcohol, which invites trouble and induces more misery the next morning with low mood. So, it could all end in tears. As my old school reports will tell you, dearest Shady Pines people, I am 'easily led'.

Thursday 24 July

Made a good choice today. Forced myself out of bed for a drop of cultural medicine and walked into town to the Lichtenstein exhibition at the Hatton Gallery. Art invigorates the soul, mine anyway. I appreciate it's not for everyone, but I'm lucky to live somewhere with free entertainment on the doorstep. The Hatton Gallery belongs to Newcastle University and occupies a small but perfectly formed space within its grounds. Roy Lichtenstein was famous for his sixties pop-art taken from cartoons, but there were three breathtaking pieces based on Monet's *Water Lilies* I had no idea existed: screen prints *on* enamel *on* stainless steel. As if that's not complex enough, the steel had hundreds of tiny swirls etched into it in the same pattern as the metal dashboards in the American cars of the 1920s; each individually pressed onto the surface using a metal drill suspended from the ceiling. Incredible! A video portrayed the artist as a happy, fun-loving, pleasant character *but* I was disappointed to see prints of naked figures, with an explanation of 'contrasting geometric lines with the curves and undulations of their bodies'. Have you guessed the sex of the models yet? Hmmm. Highly predictable – using any limp art-related excuse to include the female form.

His widow said he 'adored' women. This expression smacks of something way back in time, the *very* old days. What they usually mean is, they adored *looking* at women, even deigning to talk to the attractive ones before objectifying them through their art. Of course, Lichtenstein was in his heyday when the women's movement was in its infancy, when a woman's place was in the kitchen and bedroom, but it still winds me up. I'm trying very hard to focus on your waterlilies, Roy.

Watched a few groups of newly graduated students celebrating with their proud parents. It was very uplifting. I hope they made lifelong friends and precious memories here and haven't been annoying around the shops or bawled at by the neighbours for screaming when they fell out of the taxi at four in the morning. No, not *those* memories!

Sunday 27 July

A brilliant day! Noel may not be on everyone's list of top ten celebrities but when you get to my age without seeing Oasis live, you ought to make the effort when he has the decency to rock up within walking distance from your house. It'd be madness not to (sadly they weren't on the line-up). However, there were more items banned from being taken into the park than there are on any Kardashian wedding present list. No umbrellas (it poured) – or chairs (what about we oldies?) Bags were to be 'no bigger than A4'. Now, correct me if I'm wrong, but if this is about security, how likely is a terrorist to say, 'Oh no. I was going to pop the explosives in my A3 bag. Now I'll have to leave the whole kit and caboodle in the house.' Riddle me those, dear readers.

When the day arrived, I'd forgiven the council for their crazy rules and, apart from the weather, we had the time of our lives. Chrystal told Hilary she was allowed one moan about the cost of the drinks and another about the food. They're getting to know each other well! Wouldn't be surprised if Hilary's last gig was The Nolans, forty years ago. Anyway, she used up both allowances within ten minutes of arriving and was forced to make do with inward seething. The atmosphere as Glasvegas, Editors, (or *The* Editors as you Shady Pines folk no doubt call them) Ride, and The Vaccines (yes, it's *The* Vaccines) warmed us up after the North East rain lashed down upon the umbrella-less crowd in an attempt to spoil our fun. We were having none of it! A young steward kindly gave us each a festival poncho aka plastic with holes and a hood. We looked like pixies – especially Chrystal whose rosy cheeks exaggerated the look. The rain kept her out of mischief too; she behaved impeccably.

As the afternoon turned to evening, the volume of the crowd in full voice grew and we all bonded, including some poor young guy from Sunderland who couldn't find his friends. He latched on to a group of Newcastle supporters who showed off the allegiance by chanting, 'We hate Sunderland!' and ended up singing, 'We love Sunderland!' Now that is a rarity among the warring footie fraternity. Noel came on stage with his Manchester City shield behind him – ever the provocateur. He swore a lot but charmed the entire crowd with perfect renditions of 'Wonderwall' and 'Don't look Back in Anger'. Courtesy of the hard-core Noel fans, there was a modicum of singing along to his own, recent tracks, with the other ninety five percent interested only in Oasis classics.

More Manchester tunes from the Stone Roses, Inspiral Carpets, and Happy Mondays were blasted out for the dispersing crowd – a sea of revellers, euphoric with nostalgia. We all sang at the tops of our voices; even Hilary joined in. A drummer appeared in the subway, causing a jam of pedestrian traffic as further spontaneous dancing took place. He wouldn't have squeezed *that* into the A4 bag. It was one of those emotional moments I'll remember always. Communal singing is a very powerful, spiritual experience that induces happy crying in older women. I just managed to hold it together but was well aware of my moist eyes and ridiculous expression, exactly like Paul Whitehouse's Chris the Crafty Cockney burglar as he stared through the window in the Christmas edition of *The Fast Show*.

Monday 28 July

My first salad leaves are ready! The lettuce, spinach, and rocket planted only a few weeks ago are absolutely delicious. I didn't realise raw spinach could taste creamy! A gem from Billy today. We were chatting about holidays, and he said, 'Aa went round the world once. Didn't like it.' There's no answer to that!

Took photo of a large mouth ulcer to send to my doctor – yes, she requested it. It was horrific. If you ever need to deter someone who's interested in you, send them a picture of the inside of your mouth and pretend it's an accident. Might send it to Hal.

Wednesday 30 July

Digging up potatoes is like digging for treasure! You never know how many you're going to find on each plant – one of mine had ten perfect new babies – but each dip is a lucky one. All that from one single seed potato. It's the first time I've ever eaten potatoes on their own for lunch – gorgeous!

Simon called with a theory about Hal's reaction to the vandalism: he did it, wanting to play the hero afterwards by helping me clear up, but Scott beat him to it. What was his job before 'sales'? Am I sure of that? Told him that his imagination is too fertile for his own good. Hal's just kind and wants to help – end of story. Not everyone has an ulterior motive – some people are just kind and selfless. On reflection, I've never felt entirely at ease with Hal. Didn't want to get involved with him and put it down to his lack of spark and being rather too straight for me. I didn't say 'boring' – you did!

Not sure what to believe.

AUGUST

Friday 1 August

Lately, I've turned into a hybrid of both parents, watching *Gardeners' World* and listening to *Gardeners' Question Time* in the past three days. How the hell did that happen? The most worrying aspect of this shameful confession is … I enjoyed every minute of it! Age, or horticulture, comes to us all.

Unfortunately, technology joined us several steps ago on life's journey, overtook us on the first bend and is now a dot on the horizon, leaving many, including me, trailing in its wake. I'm doing my best to catch up though – in fact I'm developing a rare condition: an addiction to allotment-related Facebook groups. Just joined 'Allotmenteers', a countrywide group and I'm obsessed with it. Must monitor my intake and keep it under control. This one isn't fluffy and friendly like our group. As it turns out, there *is* such a thing as 'a stupid question' – who'd have thought? In my defence, the answers are often contradictory, resulting in posters arguing over the peat content of supermarket compost or telling someone that if they don't grow peas in guttering, they should hand themselves in at the nearest police station. On the plus side, you'll find the answers to every possible gardening-related query there. I use the plural wisely – there is never one definitive answer in the land where allotmenteers dwell. Invariably, there are several, all contradicting each other. You sift through to find something approaching a consensus, but it's comforting to know there are a few options on offer and that success is not always an exact science. Like choosing a life partner, everyone has different advice that you either follow or ignore. They didn't have social media when I met Twat. Otherwise, from germination to fruition, everyone would have told me to block him.

Saturday 2 August

The allotment is constantly evolving, busily working behind the scenes, preparing gifts to surprise you with when you next lift a leaf and look closer. It's like a child, secretly drawing or making a model because they love to see the joy on your face when they present it to you. Today's offering was from the sprout family. Baby sprouts are as cute as cute can be – the shape of little Galaxians from the eighties arcade and pub game – lined up on the stalk, looking forward to being fattened up for Christmas. Similarly, the embryo of a chilli, cucumber, or courgette, peeping out from the remains of a doting parent flower is beyond exciting – the fruits of your labours.

How I'll contain myself when the sweetcorn arrives, I've no idea. Expect I'll tear around like Cheesy and Pickle, pulling wheelies and yelping with joy.

Monday 4 August

9.30 a.m. I've been targeted again. This time it's sinister. The perpetrator has sent a clear message in the form of decapitated flowers: they know where I live. Ten carnation heads on the doorstep. I'm certain they're from my plot and are my favourite flowers. Seriously worrying and ratcheted up another level. I called Simon who tried to make light of it, 'Carnation carnage? Hardly a mafia job, Lizzie. It'll be kids, or some random idiot chucking them at the door. It's just a coincidence and nothing to do with the allotment. They'll have nicked them from someone else's garden.'

Hmm…could be. Then again, I'm not convinced. They're the same colour as mine. First the allotment, now this.

11.00 p.m. Desperate to get out of the house and away from my head, so had a walk round the park before tea to distract myself. Afterwards, it wasn't even dusk, but I put the chain firmly on the door, put all the blinds down and locked the windows. Feel more spooked than ever and like I'm being watched. Didn't call Sam or she'd have dashed over in a panic – a human ball of stress. Was on the verge of texting Hal but instead I called Hilary whose words of comfort were, 'Woman up, Moffitt.' To my utter surprise, it worked. And that's what I'm doing right now. I think the wine has also helped.

Tuesday 5 August

Lulled into a false sense of security by an uneventful night, i.e. I hadn't been murdered in my bed, I arrived at the allotment to find ten bare carnation stems where a display of delicate shades of pink once stood. I'd tried to convince myself that Simon would be right, and they would be nothing to do with me, but my worst fears were confirmed. They want me to know they're watching me *and* they've followed me. The police won't be interested and say it's kids. I'm not wasting my time, or theirs. Anyway, what could they do? Dust the petals for fingerprints? Hardly the crime of the century, though I can see it making page two of the Chronicle because it's August and there's no other news.

Hal came by. It was nice to see a friendly face. When I told him the latest, he looked concerned and asked if I'd like to go for a coffee. Moonshine Man trundled his barrowful of garden tools past and gave me a hard stare. My God, I'm surrounded by them. Or am I being paranoid yet again? No, because Hal also noticed, and asked if I'd been nosing about. Told him not to be stupid and asked if he thought we should report the vandalism and MM's weird barrowing activities (not giving anything else away!) to the committee – his turn to snap, 'Do *not* even think about it, Lizzie! You don't know it was him and you just don't know who we're dealing with here. What if he found out it was you? You're best out of it. It's not a crime to ferry stuff up and down to your shed, you know.'

Hmm – is it Hal, then? Offering comfort in the shape of a coffee. I'm so suspicious of his, and anyone else's, motives. Age brings wisdom but also cynicism. The trick is to balance them in equal measures that aren't going to spoil your life and freak you out.

Picked a few baby beetroot. They are alive with colour – determined to leave their signature deep pink juice on your hands, screaming, 'We are *not* red!' They were delicious roasted with honey too – extra sugar for energy, which is low these days. That's my excuse anyway.

Wednesday 6 August

Slept well after more medicinal wine. Must drink loads more water before bed!

Yesterday I pumped Hal (not literally) for information about his past. He was extremely vague – evasive. No details of companies he'd sales repped for, and when pressed on what exactly he was selling, he replied with, 'All sorts.' Okay I really don't know what to make of him. He was dismissive of Simon's theory that the cauliflower and carnation incidents are unrelated to the extent where I'm now feeling more nervous than ever. He's convinced someone is targeting me and says he'll keep a close eye out. Now I'm even more suspicious of him – Hal to the rescue, saving the day. Not good. Though I hate myself for being so distrustful, that's just how it is, and I can't help it.

Must remember not to say 'Moonshine Man' in front of Hal.

Saturday 9 August

Hilary's stressing about Chrystal's safety. Gibs is still following her, despite his warning from the police. He's clever and denies it every time. I'm more worried about Scott in case he's the target after they were seen dog walking together. When they came to the allotment, the unruly creatures were instructed to stay quietly in the car as their owner falsely claimed she'd 'not be long'. I'm convinced all dogs must know that translates as, 'I'll be ages,' and therefore a cue to wreck the place out of spite!

Scott and Sandy arrived at the same time and started to chat. Sandy was being unusually pleasant, perhaps thinking Scott was a potential partner for her, rather than a lamb to the slaughter which would be the reality of that unnerving scenario. They arranged another Town Moor dog walk. It suits Chrystal as they are a handful. I do love her – she hasn't grasped the concept of suitable allotment clothing yet, i.e. *not* your brand new white jeans and matching wedged sandals, Chrystal.

They were dying to check out Hal – have a nosey, a 'deek' as Chrystal put it. He obliged with an appearance and a cheery, 'Hello ladies. Everything okay?'

I don't need a bloody minder, nor someone who's bloody-minded – that's me. The two friends giggled stupidly, even the usually serious Hilary. Consequently, when he finally left to mind his own business, they raved about how lovely he was.

'He's a hunk, mind,' was Chrystal's verdict.

I don't want a hunk. He's way too macho for me, and boring. Hilary was well and truly charmed. She'd have really appreciated his formal dress on that fatal 'date' night – perhaps I'll try and steer him her way, though I think she's already veering in that direction. Okay, now I've lost my mind and am grasping at very fragile straws. I stupidly shared my suspicions about him committing the weird crimes. I was accused of paranoia and Chrystal said it was more likely to be 'that fella with the hooch farm'. Had to tell them off for shouting about it in public. The one thing Hal and I agree on is there's something unsavoury going on in the corner of this site. Where we disagree is, what to do about it.

Monday 11 August

Though I still have my paranoiac security regime at home, thankfully I have no more incidents to report. At the allotment, however, I have three uninvited guests in one bed. When I was younger, that would have been a result of a good night out clubbing and bringing home a few strangers who I couldn't remember asking. These days, I'm referring to two tomato plants and a potato. Technically they're squatters, and squatters have rights. Unlike weeds, who have none and must be immediately evicted. Weeds are the lodgers who forced their way into your life when your guard was down, the friends you offered your spare room to and now they've spread all over the house, along with their family and friends. In contrast, the three strays are legitimate plants who've wandered into someone else's patch, in this case the salad bed.

Perhaps the tomato seeds were buried deep in the homemade rich, black compost kindly donated by Hal. A rogue potato may have escaped the harvesting and is in the process of making babies of its own, having reached potato puberty – who knows where they came from? Such are the mysteries of nature. I'm allowing them to stay and earn their keep and if they bear no fruit (or veg) they'll suffer the fate of their poor relations, the weeds, and be turfed out.

Tuesday 12 August

The peas are growing fast, filling out in their pods, which are starting to bulge. I must be patient, or they'll be disappointingly small, and it'll be a whole year to wait for another batch. Though I hate any sniff of bad weather in summer, the rain is great to swell the fruit and veg. The redeeming feature of our climate is we don't often have to irrigate our crops. Baby leeks with cheese sauce for tea – they were amazing! Leeks are the children who sail through life doing all the right things. Unless they're being cultivated for a competition, they require very little maintenance. They do everything you ask of them; they grow in lovely straight lines and require no training. Sometimes leeks suffer from pesky little creatures called the allium leaf miners, who aren't real miners as they do nothing useful. Otherwise, like your easy-going kids, they come up with the goods at the end.

Thursday 14 August

Sandy's twice asked me if I've seen Hal lately, with a lame excuse e.g. 'I want to borrow his secateurs,' or, 'He's going to get me some blood, fish, and bone,' tagged on the end. The first time I heard her say 'blood, fish, and bone' I was repulsed and stared, thinking they must be members of a devil-worshipping cult until she explained that it's a fertiliser. I'm learning all the time. Now, I'm a woman's woman and hate myself for thinking this, but I'm sure she's fishing ('scuse the pun) to see how often I see him. I think it's out of interest, or nosiness, to be blunt. I recoiled in shame thinking about pizzagate.

Haven't seen MM for a few days, which suits me. I'm keeping away as don't want to court trouble, but doing nothing is driving me mad. It's extra-bad for my health too as I drink to make sure I sleep well. I'm sick of the earplugs and they tend to fall out. Okay, I'm rumbled – it's more fun to have wine.

Saturday 16 August

Awake early, worrying. Met Simon in Exhibition Park, outdoors so we couldn't be overheard, to talk through the options. He still thinks he's right about MM, that it's this meth stuff, but I'm certain he's wrong. We've agreed to differ because the dilemma is still the same – to snitch or not to snitch? Simon's argument against it is that MM is already suspicious of me, could even be in cahoots with Hal, and the vandalism was a warning. He's concerned about what could happen next. I suggested that if he's so certain about the drugs, it's morally right to report it to the police, even anonymously. Again, he won't because of the possible repercussions for me. Another idea of mine was telling Hal about our discovery and see how he reacts. That was also rejected just in case he's right and Hal is involved with them. Aaaagh! So, we're back to square one. Just keep out of it – it's none of our business. It's infuriating – and wrong.

Monday 18 August

After watering the allotment and picking my first courgettes for ratatouille (for tea, not the Disney rat), I had a day of nostalgia. It began with a lovely email from Debs, who asked if I ever went to The County these days. It set me on a diary entry hunt for a night when several life lessons were learned the hard way.

The County Hotel on Gosforth High Street is the pub where Debs and I cut our alcohol teeth. Debs' brother Terry was (and still is) six years older and a regular customer there. By association, we would not only be served underage but also enjoyed many a lock-in too. Lock-ins were (and still are) *the* most exciting things ever; there's nothing tastier than forbidden fruit, and we were party to a veritable cornucopia of the stuff. There was a distinctly cavalier attitude towards alcohol in those days when the extent of its risk to health was unknown. At The County, our contraband cup of alcohol, cigarettes, and older boys to snog, overflowed. We wore invisible signs saying, 'WARNING, Terry's sister and mate. Keep clear.' This warded off any unwanted attention, transforming a potential lion's den into a welcoming, safe space for two naïve teenage girls. The landlord's sons were eighteen and nineteen – ideal boyfriend material: super-trendy and studying at art college. We were truly, madly, deeply, head over heels in love with them.

After a long search, I found the fateful night. It was recorded very briefly in the actual diary, due to the rawness of the event and my state of turmoil, but I remember it perfectly to this day; such is the power of the emotional brain. It creates traumatic memories, some of which may be character forming, embedding them firmly as you tread gingerly along the treacherous path of adolescence. Occasionally you slip into the ravine below, taking a while to scramble back up to where you left off, but each time you are stronger as you gather more nuggets of knowledge while down at rock bottom.

One balmy summer evening, we were talking, flirting, trying to impress the brothers as per usual in The County bar. Intoxicated by life and halves of lager and lime, showing off with our smoking ability too, we had a special ploy to make each other appear interesting and hilarious: both pretend to be engrossed in conversation then take it in turns to laugh uproariously at the other. Simple – and probably ineffective. We'll never know for sure, but that night the brothers sauntered past and invited us to a club with them. Time for a dash to the pub phone to make frantic calls and pleas to respective parents, claiming we were going to each other's houses, and not off to town for fun with the older boys who we fancied most in the whole wide world.

Inside the Casablanca Club in the Haymarket, I remembered I'd padded my bra with loo roll to enhance my almost flat chest. Realising this, I panicked but was comforted by the fact that, unlike the ear variety, the paper usually stayed put. Throwing caution to the wind, I danced the night away to ska and reggae, high as a kite on pure adrenaline. I made plans for our next 'date', wondering which exciting places I would explore with my new boyfriend. A generous helping of snogging took place in the seclusion of a red velvet-seated booth, at which point I thought life could never be any better and the delicious brother would probably ask me to marry him. Then his hand strayed southwards to my chest. In my dreamy, drunken state it was too late to stop him. I felt a vague grope of his hand as it explored the top few layers of paper. Sadly, there was no pleasant surprise beneath this wrapping – instead, almost nothing! He withdrew it damn quick with a knowing smirk.

Gripped by a wave of horror-stricken nausea, I headed for the toilets, dragging Debs with me, and cried hormonal lager and lime tears at the complete embarrassment. She reassured me that he wouldn't have been bothered in the least, so we re-applied the makeup and returned to the boys for round two. To our disbelief, there they were, both snogging slightly older, much prettier girls with properly developed breasts. The absolute brass neck of them!

I refer to the two-timing boys, of course. Devastated, I yanked some tissue paper out of my bra, wiped the tears away with it, and threw it into the booth at the cheating pair. Looking back, they will have thought that comical and not intimidating in the least. At that point, I hadn't reached the 'angry' stage and was still in the 'upset' phase of the unexpected break-up, so I ran back to the toilets sobbing uncontrollably, pulling at the rest of the bra padding, and blowing my nose as I went.

Debs calmed me down for long enough to persuade me to leave the building with my head held high and we stomped purposefully across the dance floor where Debs' (now ex) boyfriend was attempting a smooch with his new-found 'older woman'. Debs, crept up behind him, took a step back and screamed, 'BASTARD!' before launching a perfectly aimed kick at his unsuspecting buttocks. He was thrust forwards and fell in an embarrassing heap on top of the new girlfriend, leaving her gasping for air underneath him, while he nursed a bleeding nose from the face plant. Now, *that* cheered me up for long enough to be shoved into a taxi and we laughed all the way home.

In the days that followed, I dragged myself back up from the abyss and reflected on my well-earned gems of wisdom, gleaned from the fateful evening:

- boys are fickle
- boys are only interested in one thing
- boys can be fooled by loo roll, but don't put it to the test
- girls – don't drink too much lager and lime when your bra is full of loo roll

For months afterwards, we refused to go into The County unless it had been swept for brothers.

Tuesday 19 August

Walking back from the shops, I was faced with a dilemma: is it appropriate to tell a fully grown man that his shoelaces are untied?

Risks incurred:

a) he is well aware of it, will choose to do nothing about it and you'll be the one left feeling embarrassed, ending up apologising because you're a woman

b) you will appear granny-like, a busybody instead of a helpful citizen – you'll be snubbed, regret it, and seethe

I watched him walk for at least five minutes and his errant lace came oh so close to being trodden on causing sharp intakes of breath on my part but at the same time making the walk more interesting. Decided against telling him because he had the walk of a man with too much testosterone on board: feet spread apart, almost splayed to the sides. If he were a donkey, you wouldn't buy him. But his alpha gait saved him from face planting, SPLAT in front of several giggling students, and me.

Question – at what age does 'falling over' become 'having a fall'?

Wednesday 20 August

There is something very relaxing about rhythmically stabbing at the ground with a good hoe. No need for simultaneous breakage of the back and knees, you simply attack the blighters from the other end of a long stick with great gusto. Use leverage, it's what it was invented for – and I don't mean you need to influence people in high places, that's the other sort. Job satisfaction is high: a clear patch of earth around your precious vegetables is payment enough for your labour of love. People stress about weeds; they quickly take over and another pops up each time you turn your back. Then it all spirals out of control, so you have a hissy fit, a radge, and rip each one of them out in one fell swoop – a hay-down, hoe-down showdown of a row. A resilient little bunch; they're thick-skinned out of necessity. They soon bounce back, but you keep on top of them and don't let them get out of hand. You have learnt your lesson the hard way. Now they are ousted the minute their little heads pop through the door before their feet become firmly rooted under the table.

It's a very eco-friendly place – devoid of evil slug pellets or dangerous weedkiller. There are our very welcome residents to consider: birds and hedgehogs. Ooh yes – Billy told me that 'them spiky little beggars,' aka hedgehogs, have been seen around the site lately. Great news!

Thursday 21 August

As if by magic, A baby hedgehog has appeared on the path next to my plot! I'm over the moon. She's an absolute gem, with her two black beady eyes and matching nose. Her name's Florence. I consulted my hedgehog expert friend Gwen, who overwinters the gentle beasties in her garage. Some people go to Spain or Gran Canaria, hedgehogs prefer a garage in Ashington. Each to their own – everyone is blissfully happy between October and May, or whenever the warmer weather arrives – unless the hotel isn't up to scratch, then the customers can become somewhat prickly. After seeing photos of Florence, who has already achieved celebrity status on the site, Gwen confirmed she's large enough to be out alone, even in daylight, despite the internet telling me to scoop her up and whisk her immediately to a sanctuary. If Gwen says she'll be fine, then Florence will be fine.

However, I couldn't resist interfering with nature by plonking down a freshly dug worm in front of her and tempting her with water, but she was far too interested in exploring once she'd uncurled from an adorably cute ball and waddled on her way. Like a doting parent, I videoed her snuffling and tearing up the grass by the roots to dislodge the unsuspecting insects – doubt they'd be as juicy as my rejected worm, who was grateful to wiggle another day, happily rehomed in the comforting darkness of the compost bin.

The whole thing was as exhilarating to me as a child seeing a unicorn (impossible) or dolphin (a smidgen more likely). A daytime hedgehog is an elusive creature and close encounters of the spiky kind are very rare – unless any of you readers have worked in a porcupine sanctuary or a cactus shop, both of which count as cheating.

Saturday 23 August

I adore summer at its peak, just before harvesting starts in the fields, when the gardens are heavy with fruit, veg, flowers and leaves. It always reminds me of Tess of the D'Urbervilles and Thomas Hardy's description of the Dorset countryside, *before* something terrible happens, of course.

It's perfect here. I'm writing the diary on the allotment patio, watching the birds busily flitting from tree to tree, feeding in the late afternoon sun. The swallows are out in force, swooping close by without fear, making the most of the clouds of midges who are oblivious to their fate. There's no one else around.

It's been a glorious summer's day! The sort where people moan about it being too hot. I rushed up here this morning, fully expecting Florence to be waiting to greet me, but sadly she'd beetled off. I was crushed, but it means she's found her independence and is making her own way in the world. Instead, I lost myself in Beanworld, a mini theme park on one of the beds. The bamboo cane arches for the climbing beans are a hit! They're resplendent in bright green leaves, covering the curved tops and cascading down each side. I'd planted them in a square, so I stuck my head right into the middle – it was divine. A green haze with the snake-like beans dangling from fine stalks, surrounded by spiralling tendrils. It was incredibly cool and calming, and I intend to return to that happy place in my head next time I'm in the dentist's chair.

Monday 25 August

Up early again on this rare occasion – a sunny Bank Holiday. I'm so happy for all the families who can enjoy a day of less expensive entertainment by going to a beach or park. The allotment needs regular watering in this weather, or all your hard work will be wasted. I love to see the plants thriving, enjoying the care you've lavished on them. They have already shown their gratitude by producing delicious food for you. The tomatoes are starting to ripen. Hurry up you lot – I can't wait to sample those little gifts!

9.00 p.m. When I left the site this afternoon, Gibs' nasty BMW was parked a little way down the road. I felt instantly sick. What was he doing? Waiting for Scott, or for me? He may have followed Chrystal here and spied on me, or is he spying on Scott? I'm worried. Scott was there today; he came for a chat.

He's gradually coming out of his shell and always asks if I've seen Chrystal, which is also a worry. He ought to be careful.

I called Chrystal to check she'd reported the incidents. Good news: the police will speak to Gibs. He's a dangerous man. Speaking to him will make not one iota of difference. People like that can't be reasoned with. Too many women have been murdered by their ex turned stalker. He needs more than a good talking to.

Tuesday 26 August

Feeling the need to be around people, I walked into town. This season, the shops are crammed with seventies style frills and pleats – highly fashionable, highly foul items but the buskers in a sunny Northumberland Street remain brilliant: reggae guitar man, young woman with a far superior voice to any *X Factor* winner. Great to see the crowds giving them money. The sun always brings the feel-good factor to town and even the man who can't play the accordion did well today. I always give to him because I feel sorry for him. I suspect he's a refugee, possibly a member of the Roma community from the Czech Republic. They are persecuted by extremist groups in many Eastern European countries. I'd like to know his story – or maybe I wouldn't. The lively music distracted me from the goings on closer to home, but then I thought of the Refugee Centre and spent the rest of the day moping about Lucas – typical. I *had* to spoil it for myself.

Been racking my brain trying to recall the name of a harmless but irritating woman I taught with who would moan about her packed lunch she made herself every single day! She'd carefully examine the sandwich as if she'd never seen one before in her life and say, 'Ughh, *cheese*!' Now then, I have a radical suggestion:

why not give us all a break and make yourself something you actually want to eat?

I've just remembered her name: Dinah.

Wednesday 27 August

The sunshine didn't last long, and we've had a lot of rain. It's attracted the nemeses of the gardener – slugs. As in life, some people have to spoil it – the garden is not always a bed of roses. Slugs remind me of Gibs or that guy in the corner, creeping around unnoticed, causing damage when your back is turned. They stalk you and destroy your hard work. You nurture the young plants, and they demolish them, leaving their calling card as a killer might, at the scene of a murder: a tell-tale trail of silvery slime, a clue with which to taunt us.

They mount the ground offensive, while the pigeons attack from the air. It's a war. Each battle won against them feels like the greatest victory ever, but they'll seek their revenge when your defences are down, and you must never be fooled into thinking they've given up. They'll return with night vision equipment or lie in wait until you're packed up for the day and resume the attack when you've scarcely reached the main gate.

Friday 29 August

OH MY GOD. Don't know what to make of this. If ever there was a day to use the word *discombobulated* for a second time, then it is today. I opened Hal's shed to borrow the strimmer. It was predictably tidy. Once inside, I clocked some interesting gardening books on the high shelves. I removed one to see how to plant carrots – that's not snooping – and beside it was an old-fashioned scrap book, begging to be opened. A scrap book is always interesting – even if it's about trains – because it gives an insight into its owner. This one was no exception. Instead of newspaper clippings about 'Best in Show Cabbages' – there were photos of a slightly younger Hal … in the army! One was captioned 'Helmand 2011'. Hal was a serving soldier in Afghanistan. Unless he was flogging weaponry and camouflage jackets, this was no sales job. Why didn't he tell me this? Nervous of what I might discover next, I reluctantly turned the page for yet another shock – Hal in a flak jacket, standing outside a mansion. Next to the photo was a business card: James H. Trewitt – Private Security. Perhaps H is for Halford – or Harry, or 'having us on'. I don't know. Could be anything. He could be anyone. My stomach hit the roof of the shed and I had to take deep breaths to stop my heart bursting through my chest. BOOM-BOOM, BOOM-BOOM – the sound of gunfire. WHO IS THIS MAN?

I could scarcely replace the scrap book for my trembling, guilty hands. I can think of several reasons why 'James' hasn't come clean about his past:

a) on the run from someone – dodgy employer, SAS, a foreign government?

b) had shady dealings with organised or disorganised criminals

c) has PTSD from a terrible experience in the army or private security job

d) wants a perfectly innocent fresh start

Which of the above is his true motive? Now I know I was right not to get involved. This man isn't who he claims to be. He has a past. How can I ever trust anything that comes out of his mouth in future. I'll never find out the truth. Yes Hal, or rather,

Neil, James, Jim, Jimmy-boy or whoever you really are, what's all this army and private security malarkey? While I was rummaging around in your private belongings (or was that your rank and name?) I discovered your secret past.

'Yes, I can imagine that,' was Simon's response. How come? He met him once in the street.

'There's a coldness about him; he was one hundred percent sussing me out. And all the stuff about how practical he is, tidy, meticulous, smart – old fashioned.'

'What's that got to do with it?'

'Well if he worked abroad for a long time, in private security or as a mercenary away from cultural trends in habits or clothes, he'd have no idea, which he hasn't.'

'A *mercenary*?'

'Well, you never know. Could've been. He'd have been out of touch with women's stuff here.'

'*Women's* stuff?'

'You know, all that chivalry and dressing up you told me about for the pizza place. And, says he's been divorced ages but no partner on the scene – good looking guy like that? Alarm bells, Elizabeth!'

Simon has a point and he's set my mind whirring. As for our friend Mr Moonshine, Hal sussed him out straight away, warning me not to go near. On the other hand, anyone can see that guy's dodgy from his 'back off' demeanour. Oh God I'm *so* confused.

Saturday 30 August

10.30 a.m. Hardly slept a wink. Simon – ex chief gossip, now absolute sage, must be maturing and advised me not to tell anyone else. Having churned it over and over, my head feels like a compost bin – one of those flash ones with a handle. I'm obsessing about not replacing the books in the shed in their correct order. A man with Hal's background, his attention to detail and neatness, would be bound to notice. What shall I do? Some busybody might see me going in and out and drop me in it. Sounds absurd I know but I'm going to have to act innocent, like I *haven't* been unearthing secrets about his past. And his name, which in all fairness might not be a secret at all. In fact, if I ask, he may tell me it's Trewitt.

Is this man my stalker? I'm hurtling towards that conclusion after yesterday's revelation. Is Simon right after all? Did Hal create this situation in order to be the shoulder to cry on – my rock, after the event. Moonshine Man, conversely, has a good line in death stares to keep me away. I can't envisage him doing that, it's beneath him and he's always pissing around with a barrow.

I shared my stalker theory with Sara. Although chaotic in her love-life, she's actually level-headed and can be relied on to give a suitably objective opinion. I didn't share the latest information about his past life either, just in case it slips out in conversation – she's not *that* level-headed.

'Hell yes!' came the immediate reply.

She thinks he's a control freak with his perfectionism, from what I've told her – maybe I've skewed her judgement. Has she been talking to Simon? Also, he'll have witnessed all manner of horrors in his army life, which will have damaged his mental health. It's a huge worry. Serves me right for being bloody nosey. I now feel sorry for poor Hal. Aaaaaghh! I'm opening wine to de-stress.

Why, oh why can't life be simple? Sam's always telling me that simple equals boring – and yes, my relationship with Lucas caused me countless sleepless nights, due to the stress and secrecy, not the other obvious cause, you cheeky Shady Pines lot out there. Goodnight!

Sunday 31 August

Hungover. Checked phone – oh no! Why, oh why didn't I reach for the old diary box instead of the wine in my time of need – then I wouldn't have texted Lucas! I'm a ridiculous specimen. Can hardly bear to read the message I sent. The demon drink. Those temperance lot from the Hoppings of old were onto something – it always lands you in a heap of trouble. On this occasion, to my great relief, it was harmless.

Me: *How are you doing?*

Him: *Hi Lizzie! Great to hear from you. I'm good, thank you. Missing you of course. London is too big for a single person. Are you okay?* (clearly suspicious of a late-night text)

Me: *Yes, just saying hi. Sorry it's late. Goodnight.*

Phew – could have been one hell of a lot worse! Still, it's unfair to lead him on, though I was surprised at my self-restraint, particularly post-wine. I held back on the true feelings front. Let's face it – I could do without actively seeking more trauma in my life. Verdict: stupid, not disastrous.

Obviously, I have no idea what to think or do about the Hal situation. I could confront him or act ignorant. If I say nothing, then I'll never be able to believe another word he tells me, unless it's about gardening, and he could be making it all up – how would I know?

Forced myself out to the allotment which helped, though I'm back to feeling nervous in the house.

SEPTEMBER

Monday 1 September

Texted Sam who immediately knew I was feeling low. I confessed to thinking about Lucas a lot lately. No way was I telling her what I'd been up to in Hal's shed! She reminded me I'm supposed to be living my best life and channelling my younger spirit, pre-Twat and the boring, sensible years, when I was the quietly rebellious teen. She's spot on. I have fond memories of the past – a mixture of embarrassing and fun experiences, but one made me realise I was more rebellious than I gave myself credit for. And it was risky. Had to delve down to the bottom of the box for my diary of a sixteen-year-old but there it was. Just what the doctor ordered – a trip back in time to calm my troubled brain. Having deciphered the secret codes of initials and anacronyms to hide the truth from the parents, I relived the potentially dangerous escapade at Haggerston Castle. As well as being unable to send late night drunken texts, there were several other advantages of growing up in the pre-mobile phone era; read on for details!

Carol Donovan lived with her very liberal mum, Lindy. They were more like friends than mother and daughter. Carol was allowed to swear *and* smoke in the house and drink Thunderbird wine at parties; a wild child and I was highly envious of her. Lindy's mum owned a caravan at Haggerston Castle near Berwick and one unbearably freezing January weekend, she allowed the two of us to stay there. If I'd told my parents we were going to stay alone in a caravan on a site with a clubhouse, a bar, and a weekly disco that attracted local boys (hooray!), then the trip would become a pipe dream. Knowing full well they'd never buy the 'horse riding' excuse, there was nothing else for it but to pretend Lindy would be responsibly parenting us from beginning to end.

Expertly, we smuggled our forbidden fruits onto the back seat of the X15 bus at the Haymarket then coughed our way up the A1 through half a packet of Embassy Regal, washed down with woodpecker cider swigged from a very large bottle – all to show how grown-up we were. Admittedly, we looked at least two years older after we'd slapped a ton of Miners sparkling turquoise cream eye shadow on and added way too much blusher to our young rosy cheeks, in the comfort of the bus station toilets. I could hardly contain my excitement.

Friday evening was spent in the clubhouse bar, drinking, smoking and generally pretending to be much older. We weren't fooling anyone, but business was slow at that time of year and false ID was for professional fraudsters only as they were the people with access to a thing called a photocopier. Carol was small but super-confident. She'd been drinking in town since she was fourteen and no one ever questioned her age. All you needed was a strong personality at the ready to front it out at the bar. I was on a high, knowing I was safe in my deceit and my parents wouldn't be fretting – win-win.

The caravan was sub-zero with arctic *and* brass monkeys everywhere. It felt like sleeping in a giant tin of coke. Do you want ice with that? Yes please, inside the windows, preferably. The roof leaked, allowing the ferocious Northumberland wind to deposit icy droplets directly onto my face in the middle of the night. Heating, or to be accurate, *defrosting,* was in the form of a very smelly portable gas fire. Despite being young and reckless, we were smart enough not to have it on all night when we realised it caused rivers of condensation to pour down the windows and walls and saturate our bedding. It was hideous! Sleeping in our clothes and huddling together, we were still freezing.

On Saturday afternoon we were typical sixteen-year-olds – scoffing burgers and chips, playing pool, and trying to beat the boys at darts. At night we dressed up again in Oxford Bags (yes, those unfeasibly wide trousers with patch pockets) and checked shirts with another barrowload of makeup trowelled on. Heavy on the purple mascara and red lippy, we were dressed to impress! We boogied on down at the disco and chatted up two older guys who Carol knew: not boys but real men – Gary (twenty-one) and Kev (twenty-two). The weekend was getting better by the minute! Kev's family owned a caravan there; one far superior to Carol's as we were to discover. Gary was his friend. One each. Perfect. We flirted with them, invited ourselves back to their caravan and were bowled over by the luxury of it. It was warm! Posh heating and even a flushing toilet – the works. To this day, I can't believe we actually stayed with two strange(ish) men – in their beds! We'd set out the ground rules – snogging only – inviting ourselves was a huge risk to take as we were technically old enough to give consent. Luckily, they were two decent young men who were no doubt terrified of Lindy. Still, we skated on dangerously thin ice that night despite the heat in their caravan. And my parents were none the wiser.

The morning after, we were ecstatic when our new boyfriends cooked us delicious bacon sandwiches, so Carol suggested we make plans for the evening. Sadly, the upstanding citizens had other ideas and made it perfectly clear there would be no more hanky panky or B&B. Like an inverted version of Stockholm Syndrome, I'd fallen madly in love with my reluctant hero, Gary, and suggested we meet up sometime later instead – funnily enough he changed the subject and wouldn't commit. Those poor guys probably suspected they were a few ropes short of being imprisoned in their own caravan and forced to entertain two irritating young girls for another night. We hung around until forcibly ejected, back to the icy tin on wheels where the condensation had frozen again. With heavy hearts, we packed up and caught the X15 home, leaving freedom and the love of my life behind.

Gary had made the mistake of telling me his address, in Heaton, so I'd bribe Debs with cider, makeup, and records to pace up and down the street for weeks afterwards, in the faint hope of catching a glimpse. Carol was miles too cool for that sort of pathetic behaviour. Later, Carol found out Gary actually lived over in Fenham, on the opposite side of the city. Such is life – it was very wise of him to lie!

Some of you Shady Pines ladies will be shocked at this deception. The level of danger was potentially high – I agree. Although, as it turned out it was worth it to get out of the freezer – even if it was into the fire.

Thursday 4 September

I've been lying low and, yet again, avoiding Hal. Been nipping up to water the allotment later in the evenings, which brings its own hazards in the shape of MM. I've managed to miss him so far this week. Had a more fulfilling day today and am now The Queen of Jam-making! A voluntary domestic duty is a rarity for me.

Along with strawberries and redcurrants, blackcurrants are the crown jewels of fruit, as far as birds are concerned. It's been a cat and mouse game, netting them just in time as they turn from green to black. Pigeons try and land on top of the net while the cheeky blackbirds scuttle underneath as though on an army training exercise. Points of weakness must be blocked using net pins and heavy stones to fox the little blighters. I'd hate to trap them, but they seem capable of finding their way out after gorging themselves silly on my blackcurrants. Black diamonds, bursting with juice, skins ready to split, hang provocatively in shiny clusters, waiting to be plucked free.

I made perfect jam – not too sweet, with a touch of lemon to add sharpness and draw out the flavour of the homegrown fruit. I used a recipe from my Gran's handwritten cookbooks, previously unused by me, from her days in domestic service. Mostly, they are read-only documents containing rather too much war food (or *wor* food for we Geordies), but there are a few treasures in there which can be adapted for our century. I love to picture her writing them in beautiful cursive script, sitting at a long kitchen table. She was a wonderful woman.

I hope my grandchild will enjoy baking with me as much as I did with Gran. Better get practising – haven't done any for fifty years and the day's fast approaching!

Sunday 7 September

Chrystal called after an afternoon walk with Scott and the dogs in Jesmond Dene. On the walk, Scott had opened up about the home situation. His dad left when he was a teenager, which was a relief as the constant rowing with Sandy was very distressing. It appears she is the needy one of the pair. Sadly, she struggles with her mental health but refuses to take her meds. Scott and his dad are close, but Sandy's never forgiven him for leaving and won't have his name mentioned in her presence; it's very awkward. Nothing is how it appears from the outside – Scott is very capable and runs the house. He's actually Sandy's official carer, with secret financial support from his dad. At times she becomes paranoid about Scott leaving, but he's assured her he won't go while she's still ill. He's quite remarkable.

We are all quick to make assumptions about others and their situations, but appearances can be very deceptive.

In the interests of preserving my own sanity, I've decided to try and stop thinking about Hal and his past career. There'll be a reason why he didn't mention it. And, though it pains me to admit, it's none of my business.

Monday 8 September

Cauliflowers are the children for whom you must set your sights low, then they will surprise you. They require firm foundations and infinite patience. For weeks and weeks there is nothing but leaves, leaves and more leaves – satisfying only to a point. I'd peer expectantly into the middle, willing it to be white, but nothing. Overnight, the late developer blossoms, and a tiny white heart appears. The very cutest baby of the brassica world. You must act fast and swaddle it in leaves for protection, or it will turn yellow. Once it is fully grown, it will repay your care and attention with the best cauliflower cheese you've ever tasted. I now know that from experience.

Wednesday 10 September

The need for fresh air of a different kind took me through the lovely Ouseburn, past the artists' studios and city farm. Taking the path that follows the burn down to the Quayside, I wondered if the swans and ducks realise their raison d'être is to create a picturesque view for the residents of the new flats. Gentrification: the smell of 'hand crafted' vegan burgers and locally brewed real ale has replaced smoke from welding, coal fired furnaces, and steam from wrought iron used by the blacksmiths of old. The area may have changed its personality, but at least it still has one, and it is very much alive and kicking.

Saturday 13 September

Allotment in the afternoon. Sandy was quizzing me again, not about Hal this time, but Chrystal, and her intentions towards Scott! Apparently, there are more dog walks afoot – or apaw. Could Sandy be the stalker? She's certainly rather controlling when it comes to her son. In spite of Chrystal's earlier assurances, and being told, 'I'm 'not daft, man,' I'm still worried Scott gets the wrong idea about this new friendship – and he's not the only one. Gibs is a ticking time bomb if he gets wind of a new man on the scene. That monster is well versed in the art of stalking. He'll have seen Chrystal in my house before; the lounge is visible from the road. And he's seen her at the allotment, probably with Scott and the dogs. He'll blame me for it. I can picture his ugly face, spitefully tearing up the caulis and carnations. Enough of him. I'm much less scatty than I was before HRT but it's not a miracle cure, so I have to pop back later to collect the rasps and veg I picked and left in the greenhouse this afternoon!

10.15 p.m. More proof of Moonshine Man's criminality! It was almost dark when I arrived and he was loading boxes into a large white van driven by a huge hulk of a man. Perhaps he's bottled up the hooch and his mate's taking it away to flog around the pubs. Can't see MM doing that himself – far too posh. They drove off sharpish after I saw them. I think they saw me, but I pretended not to notice. Thank God he wasn't wheeling it past the greenhouse, or he could have turned nasty. I'm still feeling very jittery.

I double-locked the doors again *and* have moved a side table loaded up with pans in front of each one. At least I'll wake up if they break in. There are now three or four reasons for doing this, and to open wine afterwards – though moderation is called for after the other night and my mischievous fingers. Must keep phone well out of harm's way.

Sunday 14 September

8.10 a.m. Text from Hal: *Do NOT go to the allotments. Police everywhere. It's a crime scene. A serious incident. No more info yet.*

Has someone dumped rubbish in the bonfire area or taken four barrows of woodchip instead of three? Perhaps there's an illegal pile of weeds where no weed pile should be? All of these are serious incidents in the eyes of the committee. I can't help joking about it – I'm one of those annoying children who laughs when they're told off. It's infuriating, and the very best way to wind up a teacher.

Thoughts (serious) in no particular order:

- Moonshine Man caught selling his wares – I really hope so – he's creeping me out
- widespread act of vandalism involving all our greenhouses and sheds – I'm praying to the God of Allotmenteers that it's not this
- someone has collapsed digging their plot – please don't let it be anyone I know

The last one's the worst and I'm worrying about poor Miriam who's unsteady on her feet at the best of times. And she's an early bird, up at the crack of dawn to feed her addiction. Feeling a bit sick now.

12.15 p.m. Against my better judgement, I rang Hal. Couldn't wait any longer. He reckons Miriam was seen talking to the police. Yay – she's alive! How coherent that conversation went, is anyone's guess. Perhaps she toned down the language for the occasion – on second thoughts, probably didn't. Nearly spat my tea out when he said they'd put up 'one of them *gazeebras*' earlier, so no one could see.

5.25 p.m. Dreadful news – it's a death, possibly a murder. The victim is male, according to Hal. I mustn't spread rumours; the police aren't saying much yet but they're already questioning people. Oh my God. My mind's racing. Who could it be? Hal is alive and texting, which is a relief. Perhaps it's Billy. He's not been in good health recently. I can't bear to think about it. There are so many older people there – it's a tragedy. Must be someone living alone, otherwise this would all have happened during the night when they didn't come home from their allotment – or maybe it did? Moonshine Man! He could have been murdered by the scary white van man, or vice versa? Wouldn't put anything past that dodgeball.

Let's hope it's someone who passed away quickly and painlessly at first light this morning, doing what they loved best in their favourite place on Earth. Relatives informed and already agreeing it's exactly how they wanted to go. Could be the case – older people get up before the birds. Now there's a murderer on the loose, as well as a bloody stalker. They'll need to form an orderly queue. Making light of it but in truth, I'm terrified. We'll find out the facts in time. Need to make tea and calm down.

11.00 p.m. An evening of texts and speculative calls from: Sam, Hilary (who'll let Chrystal know I'm okay) Sara, and Simon, all secretly worried I was the victim. They'd seen it on the local news. Feel like I'm party to inside info as they didn't say it was a 'male' – to use police lingo.

Monday 15 September

Awake at 3.22 a.m. thinking of Moonshine Man and the big white van. Can't believe I'm laughing at the rhyme when this is so traumatic. Were they dumping a body?

Text from Hal: *Victim isn't anyone with an allotment. Discovered in the corner, not far from our friend's shed, by Tommy.*

How appalling for Tommy. I was nervous going out for milk and checked the rooms for murderers when I got back, poking each door open with a broom handle before venturing in.

The plot thickens. I can't stop making inappropriate comments. Please excuse me readers – I am not making light of death. Back to my 3.22 a.m. theory – maybe the body *was* dumped? Forensics (real life *Silent Witness*) will tell us. They'll work that one out in the first episode – they're an immensely clever bunch.

11.30 p.m. Update – GIBS is the victim. I can't believe it's him. Poor Chrystal must be in total shock. They're still not giving anything away, but the police told her tonight and have asked when she last saw him – it's suspicious. What the hell was he doing there? Looking for Chrystal, no doubt. Maybe Gibs was my stalker?

Confession: my next feeling is relief that it isn't someone I liked – Billy, Scott, or the kind, gentle man who cuts the communal grass for the benefit of us all. Granted, the victim was a mother's son and a brother, but to me he was akin to a mythical beast; a monster glimpsed from a distance, usually at night, always on the prowl. He was capable of dreadful acts and yes, the man needed help. BUT would help have come too late, after he had created his next victim? Another statistic to add to a long line of women murdered by their ex-partner. And finally, perhaps my most uncharitable thought of them all, dear friends – where *was* Chrystal last night? May the good Lord strike me down and, in an act of irony, carry me off to what I had always thought of as *non-existent* hell with the other unbelievers, mocking us all the way. I'm so sorry for such evil thoughts. Chrystal wouldn't be capable of such a thing … would she?

Email from the committee: *The police would like to hear from anyone who was at the site after 5.00 p.m. last night. If anyone interviewed today has reported seeing you, the police will contact you to assist with their investigation into the serious incident that took place at the site.*

OH MY GOD – that's me! I was there. There was no sign of Gibs, just Moonshiner – was it him? Deep breaths are required. What has Gibs seen, or uncovered? My detective head and heart are racing (I'm not a *real* detective, you see). This is awful. What if they saw me? They'll know I'll 'grass them up'. Simon's genuinely concerned for my safety – he knows more than the others. Now it's changed overnight from *Miss Marple* to *Line of Duty*. Sadly, this is not TV – it's reality. I've had nervous stomach all day and now I'm going to be sick.

Woah there, hold your horses everyone – where was trained killer Hal last night? Now I'm getting carried away. It's becoming too surreal for words.

Tuesday 16 September

7.25 a.m. Trying my damnedest to banish shameful thoughts about my friends becoming murderers overnight, which is the effect nighttime can have on your otherwise rational brain. Hal has already texted to tell me not to mention I'm suspicious about MM.

Hmm – I was rather hoping for a trip 'down the station' and a free ride in a panda car, but I gave my statement without a lawyer present or a dubious-looking tape recorder, in the comfort of my own home. Of course I did – I'm not a suspect. Don't big up your part, Moffitt – but you could be classed as a key witness if turns out MM is the murderer. Officers Becky and Ian left after an arduous time dealing with a nervous, forgetful, menopausal, sweating woman. In my defence, I just wanted to get it right. They were very patient, even when my shaky hands slopped tea on Ian's boots. After that, I was convinced they'd think I was the killer, which made me shake more.

They wanted to know my relationship to the victim – and to Chrystal. They dropped the hideous bombshell that the time of death was 7.30 p.m. - 9.00 p.m. I arrived around 8.45 p.m. UGHHH! Did a murder pass me by without my realising, or was there a dead body in the corner of the site before then? The very same corner I've been snooping in and am rarely out of, these days. I could have been the victim – perhaps Gibs was just unlucky, and a serial killer is at large. I was reeling from the shock and having a vindaloo-style hot flush, though it wasn't as bad as it used to be pre-HRT.

Suddenly, it gushed forth, pouring out in a jumbled, random gabble: the suspicious moonshine shed; the to-ing and fro-ing; potatoes; never seeing him gardening; cauliflower vandalism;

stalking; carnation decapitation; the white van. I even threw Moonshine Man's 'dirty looks whenever he passes me', into the mix for good measure but when I admitted I had absolutely no idea of his name, I sounded like a time-wasting fantasist. When I finally paused for breath, they both stared at me, wondering whether I should be sectioned there and then under the Mental Health Act and said, 'Okay, can we start again with that?' AAAARGH!

Methodically, Becky teased it out of me with her fine-tooth comb, dissecting it word for word until I was losing the will to live.

Becky: So, a friend told you they thought he was up to no good in the shed?

Me (singing): She said, there's something in the woodshed.

Becky (nonplussed): Who's she?

Me: No one. It's from a Divine Comedy song. Except this one's just a shed. And *she* is a *he*, I think.

Becky: I'll just write *they*.

Me (thinking, *Hal will literally kill me*): No, I meant the song says *she* but he's a *he*. I'm not sure because I've got no recollection of who told me about the woodshed er, I mean the shed.

Then more verbal diarrhoea about sneaking around the shed and the smell that comes from it when no one else is around.

Me (thinking, *Simon will literally kill me*): It wasn't just me. I was with my friend, Simon. I'm sure he's making alcohol in there. Out of potatoes. He grows a lot of them and not much more. There are recipes on the internet.

Becky: For potatoes?

Me (trying not to laugh): Alcohol – hooch, vodka or whatever, apparently. Not that I've looked.

Ian asked if Gibs could have known Moonshine Man. I said I doubted it otherwise Chrystal would have known. Told them about the stalking she'd endured, that we'd seen him parked outside the allotments when Chrystal was visiting and walking her dogs. Expertly I was steered away from the irrelevant anecdote of the unruly dogs' visit; I was rambling again. They thanked me for the information and said they'd be investigating the shed. When I quipped 'see if you can *shed* any light on the murder', tumbleweed rolled across the lounge floor and followed them out of the room. I'd overstepped the mark, too much levity for such a serious matter. However, I loved that they called it the 'woodshed', which meant they were taking notice of my singing, and it wasn't wasted. They were almost certainly spent with exhaustion, as I am. Feel drained, wrung out like a wet pair of old and very unflattering knickers relegated to a cloth.

I'm cringing now at how toe-curlingly embarrassing it was! I'm furious I hadn't taken the van registration number, but we can't all walk around making mental notes of every vehicle reg on the off-chance it might come in handy one day. You'd have no room in your head for anything else. Anyway, do NOT ask someone my age to remember seven characters in order without recording them; I had to think twice about the colour!

Opened wine. Wondering if I shouldn't have said anything, as instructed by Hal. No! He's not pushing me around; it has nothing to do with him. Nothing at all. Mind your own bloody business *James*, or I'll be the one asking awkward questions, mate. On reflection, I'm not sure if the worms will go back into the opened can as willingly as they slithered out of it. I locked all the windows and chained the door again.

Wednesday 17 September

9.00 a.m. Can't stop worrying about poor Chrystal. No, you lot, I haven't changed my tune and don't for a minute think she has any responsibility for this death. Conflicted, is my guess – to answer my own question. That decent, beleaguered woman whose life was made a misery by the thug Gibs, will be feeling something much less than hate. I know she may have a sense of relief, but it will be closely followed by guilt for feeling that way. She'll be running the whole gamut of emotions – poor soul.

8.00 p.m. Had a long chat with Hilary: Chrystal is shocked but not distraught and is certainly not blaming herself in any way. Phew! What a relief. When it came to Gibs, she developed a protective shell over the years and is now describing her feelings as 'ground zero' – which is an elevation from negativity and hatred. She has no reason to hate him now he can longer harm her. I love her logic. Sensible, measured, pragmatic. The police told Chrystal that Gibs had been struck with a blunt instrument which hasn't been found yet, and he was discovered face down in the cauliflower bed on plot sixty-two. 'He couldn't stand cauliflower,' she told Hilary with a hint of a smile. She said to tell me she's sorry for bringing all this trouble to my door, or garden. Bless her heart – she's got nothing to apologise for. When I asked Hilary if she thought Gibs was looking for Chrystal, she said, 'No. I think he was after Scott.'

More wine.

Friday 19 September

Hal's texted, claiming he's worried about me; perhaps it's an excuse to get in touch. Met him at the allotment and had a camping stove coffee. The pungent smell of paraffin is very nostalgic and reminds me of camper van holidays as a child. I tried to avert my eyes from the scrap books on the shelf – the scene of *my* crime. Hal was very calm but, considering his background, death is not as shocking as it is to the rest of us. Asked me what my thoughts were, saying I usually had a theory about 'our friend', pointing to moonshine corner. I began to flush again. Am I now a very easy person to read thanks to the menopause? I expect there was a thought bubble floating above my head containing the words, 'Well, you're on the list for a start.' He'd already told me he'd been interviewed. On Saturday, he was at the allotment, saw no one, then went home alone. Therefore, he has no alibi. Told him I thought it could be a random person and that I wasn't going up there unless there were other people around, which of course was a huge mistake because he said he'd come with me if I let him know when I'm going! So now I can't go to the allotment without him, or he'll be huffed. WHY must I always open my big mouth just to unleash more trouble on my life? He said that any genuine friend would do the same. *Genuine*? How genuine is that man? Anyhow, he thinks it's more likely to be Moonshine Man. Given that he was seen leaving the site that night, he could have been there all along. Hal says he didn't see anyone but hadn't walked over to the corner, and MM could have been inside the shed doing whatever he does in there.

Told Hal I'd mentioned MM, the van, and the shed, but added that I was so vague and rambling that they probably won't take me seriously. He didn't pass any comment, and I managed to keep schtum about the police searching the moonshine shed – so it wasn't *all* bad.

Everyone at the allotments is gossiping about the murder. Why wouldn't they? It's big news. Now it's Agatha Christie meets Alan Titchmarsh. As per usual, I steered well clear of Miriam; today she's number one on the list of people to avoid. She passed Hal's shed, excited about the murder.

'Couldn't wait to get down here. It's like something out of a film with all these police around!'

Ghoulish. Something has happened to occupy her mind; something other than alcohol and how to hide it from her husband. Maybe she and Gibs had a brawl? A vision of a brawling Miriam and Gibs flashed through my mind, with her whacking him with a full bottle of vodka purchased from a man in the corner shed – now there's a thought! There's an idea for my new career: private investigator and private security duo Moffitt and Halford. It has a certain ring to it.

Sunday 21 September

Went down to Hilary's flat, or 'apartment' as she calls it, with its amazing views of the bridges. Unbelievably, Miserable Jeff has a new woman. I'm fascinated to know which deluded sucker swiped right on his sour mugshot. Perhaps he was holding up his payslip. Eventually they'll discover that Jeff's only true passion is his bank balance and the two are seldom parted. All things considered, he has absolutely nothing whatsoever to offer. Scroll on.

Chrystal was there. I was taken aback by how tired she looked, wearing no makeup and casual clothes. Poor love. Naturally, she's stressed after the past week. Yesterday the police questioned her again about her movements on Saturday night, whether she kept a snow shovel or a spade in her car ('blunt instruments'?), *and* they searched it. They must seriously consider her a suspect. She was walking the dogs at the time of the murder, alone. The rest of the night she spent at home, also alone. She can't remember seeing anyone as it was very quiet on the Town Moor. She's taken to driving a very long way round, in and out of housing estates to check Gibs isn't tailing her then parking up and walking to the moor from Fenham or Gosforth, so he won't know where she is. It's no surprise that she can't remember her exact route that night.

'Aam not sleeping. Not even a wink a night,' she said, tearily.

This poor woman has been through enough. If ever there was anyone less likely to possess a snow shovel or spade, let alone plan a murder and whack a six foot hulk of a beast with it, it's her (yes, I'm well aware of what I said earlier). She relaxed after a glass of wine and even managed a few laughs about Jeff's new status as an internet stud. At the exact moment we waved her off in a taxi, a car pulled out of a space and followed it from a discreet distance. Hilary says I'm paranoid, but I texted Chrystal later to check she was home safe. I'm very concerned about her mental health.

Monday 22 September

Email from the committee confirming that the Allotment Show will go ahead as planned on Sunday – that's excellent. It would be a great shame to cancel the highlight of the allotment year. Spoke to Simon about the police visit. He's sworn not to tell Sam anything about MM and I told him about the white van. He's still acting very grown-up about this, which isn't an unreasonable expectation to have of a man in his forties.

Sam called – she's fretting about me, so I distracted her by asking if they've decided to find out the sex of the baby. Good news: it's a surprise! They'll be great at avoiding the pink v blue scenario anyway and will choose neutral clothes for the little person, whoever they are! My grandchild – I'm so grateful for the positive distraction. It's giving me something lovely to think about rather than death, crime, and what I shouldn't have blabbed to the police. I really don't know what I was thinking of last year, contemplating leaving Sam and my friends in favour of a man! Yes, I was following my heart, but my little gang occupy most of the space in that fickle generator of love, anyway. I must have been crazy.

Didn't sleep well and am still having flushes despite the HRT – could just be stress. Giving the police statement really highlighted how irritating they can be. In the dead of night, I'm reliving every moment of the murder night in very slow motion and wondering if I'm sweating or merely doing my great big beetroot impression. That reminds me, most of the tomatoes have turned red in time for the show! Must stop eating them or there'll not even be five left to enter – they are so moreish. They've taken forever and getting them through their final stage was an uphill struggle: the children who need to be pushed into doing homework or revising. It feels like they're never going to make it (after all that work you've put into them!) but they surprise you in the end and pass everything with flying colours or find a job they enjoy. They've ripened – they have triumphed. Success is not about money or academic achievement – it's about happiness and fulfilment. It comes in many forms.

Wednesday 24 September

3.00 a.m. Still awake, wondering if Moonshine Man's been interviewed yet. He's going to know it was me who snitched if he saw me that night, though I kept well hidden. But if he's a hardened criminal he'll have been all eyes and ears. Have they searched the shed yet? What's the usual timescale for such things? Not long on *Vera*, though sometimes the 'intel' arrives late, delivered by a very serious Kenny. Then Vera flies into a rage (or a *radge*) blaming someone for the oversight and sending them scattering to various corners of Northumberland. This is reality – though I still can't quite believe it. Got up for a wee brandy. I'm drinking more. It's the stress. Need to sleep, not lie awake listening for every terrifying creak of the windows or floorboards. I'm safe enough – I think.

11.00 p.m. Slept well in the end thanks to brandy and have felt better all day. Went straight up to allotment. Hal was there hovering around my plot. Asked why I hadn't texted so told him I knew people would be there at this time. Mornings tend to be busy. I refuse to encourage such dependency and though it goes against my instinct, I'm keeping my distance here, relatively speaking – after jumping into bed with someone. Ugh – cold shudder races around body. He had arrived early and saw the police opening up the shed. They'd blocked off the path, so he wasn't close enough to see inside. Poor Hal, everyone's trying to keep him at a distance. Oh no! I wrote 'poor Hal' – I mustn't lower my guard.

Billy was there looking very distressed. Then the ice cream van pulled up and he insisted on buying some for me and Hal. When he came back, he was licking the ice creams, shouting 'Eeh mind, you'll have to be sharp. They're disappearing!' I was laughing so much that I accidentally on purpose dropped mine as soon as he passed it to me and was lucky he didn't have any more change to replace it. He's lovely, but there are limits! I watched Hal dump his in the blackcurrant bush and turn expertly to Billy saying, 'Thanks mate, that was just the job.' It provided a few minutes of light relief.

On a positive note, I'm feeling less nervous now that the miscreant's been busted and, with a bit of luck, is on his way to jail. But what if he doesn't get a sentence and finds out I'm the 'grass'? I'm running away with myself again – too much TV drama and soap-watching. He'll not know, and all will be well. I'm also erring towards Gibs as the most likely stalker. His very last visit to the allotment was probably not his first, and with his penchant for following women, he'll have known where I live. Me, the evil one who went on holiday with Chrystal, introduced her to the allotment and to Scott, who's *obviously* a new boyfriend because he's male. That would be his excuse to continue to stalk and destroy her. Only, it backfired this time – well and truly. Speaking of which, I've just leapt out of bed to investigate the unholy racket outside – fireworks? The opening round of the annual Northern Region Sheet Metal Hammering Competition? No. It's a Tesco van delivering beer to the students.

Thursday 25 September

I know you're all intensely irritated by this now, but I'm missing Lucas. Go on, tell me again – I'm never satisfied, change the cockadoody record, blah blah blah. I can't help it! Anyway, I'm allowed. Remember, this is my diary and no one else's.

12.00 OH MY GOD – a courtesy call from the police *thanking* me for the information on Moonshine Man and telling me there was nothing in the shed bar a load of gardening tools.

Full to the brim, apparently! NO WAY! He's moved it. In fact, on the night of the murder he was dropping off a lawnmower with his mate's van. When I asked if they'd searched the house, I detected a hint of sarcasm creeping in when he answered, 'Yes, we thought of that too.' Cringe! I stuttered, 'But, but, but …' only to be politely but firmly cut short. 'Thanks again, bye now.' I mean, why on earth would they listen to the middle-aged rantings of a busybody? The absolute bloody snake! Nothing there, my arse. He's given them the slip. The van! Of course – it all fits now. He was probably loading up the produce (we're not talking leafy greens, here) and came back another time after the murder to clear the shed. That's hardly likely as there would have been police officers there daily. What's more plausible is that he murdered Gibs and cleared out the gear pronto. How else was it not uncovered? Surely, they must see that. He's *got* to be a suspect. Dropping off a lawnmower? Of course he was – to fill the shed with legitimate gear in place of the missing moonshine factory.

Texted Simon with the new revelation – knew he'd be shocked, but he turned super-serious and he's offering to stay over if I feel unsafe. That in itself is worrying. Not sure if I ought to tell Hal the new info. Would be wrong on two levels:

a) it will encourage him
b) if he's involved in the murder, he shouldn't be given any information

However, if b) is correct, then a murderer is not someone I want to upset or offend in any way – any more than I already have done, that is. I'm sleeping on it – if I can.

Friday 26 September

Texted Hal. Suitably encouraged by the attention, he called me immediately. It's my own fault. I'm a disaster magnet. He's either a BAFTA award winner (another secret past?) or is genuinely shocked. Called our moonshine friend a 'dangerous pro who's making muppets out of the lot of us – and the rozzers'. Hal, no one calls the police 'rozzers' nowadays (I didn't say those words out loud). That aside, he's as baffled as I am. Then again, it doesn't take much to confuse me.

The whole sorry business is more and more disturbing. Where's MM's distillery vanished to? Not his house. What about white van man – an extra-fine needle in a giant haystack. Remember him? Come on, rozzers, can't you lean on him (not Giant Haystacks)? Trouble is, he's too 'respectable'. He's cunning and arrogant. I risked my safety telling the police, but Hal knows about him too; he knows he's dodgy. I can't sit here like a plum doing nothing – I must get to the bottom of this. He may not be the murderer, but I know what I saw in that shed.

No Country Casual-wearing asshole is going to muppify Lizzie Moffitt. Let's get on it – as they say.

Sunday 28 September

The allotment show was FANTASTIC! A welcome break from the traumatic events, a day of normality, apart from the small matter of a police presence – true to TV dramas, where they attend funerals to observe the suspects' behaviour. The spectres at the feast. People I've never spoken to before stopped to talk about the murder, an extreme way to make friends. Our beloved place won't be the same until it's resolved, and I hope they don't think

I've brought trouble to the site by attracting Gibs. Despite our poor climate for grapes, the grapevine is extensive, and everyone will know the connection by now. It's not exactly my fault that my friend's ex was a vile, controlling bully. You may be shocked to know I'm relieved, no, *happy* that she no longer must live in fear of that man, in fear of her life. I'm not exaggerating – do the research if you don't believe me.

I loved chatting to everyone about what they were entering; selecting and picking the entries; pulling up several leeks before choosing two potential winners; deliberating over which four tomatoes are not only the most beautiful, but the same size; arranging them carefully; leaving the judging tent with your fingers crossed; returning after what feels like eternity with the greatest anticipation.

Nevertheless, nothing could detract from the childlike delight of discovering your first attempt at growing tomatoes has been honoured with first prize – and a certificate to prove it! And third best red cabbage – it's still a prize. When your child is recognised in some way at school – star of the week, a certificate of achievement perhaps – it's on a par with that. Pure elation, but don't tell Sam! Horticultural showing is not about the biggest, but the best, well displayed produce. If you plonk six raspberries of varying sizes on the paper plate, you won't stand a cat in hell's chance of taking home a piece of paper. You'll be overheard saying, 'I'm not disappointed,' in a disappointed voice. But any level of competitive spirit on show today pales into insignificance compared to the notorious leek shows of old. All manner of skullduggery and sabotage took place at those events – it was all about the prestige. The nearest social club would auction off the giant beasts that weighed in at well over one stone! That's some puddin'. And to think, each and every one of them started life as thin as a blade of grass. It's a miracle. Fascinating stuff. Don't argue.

OCTOBER

Thursday 2 October

Felt wary about what I might find at the allotment, but I refuse to be put off going there on such a beautiful day. The sweetcorn excitement has been building for weeks as I've watched the cobs growing fatter and hopefully ripening. You check they're ready by peeling back the protective leaves, where the corn is swaddled inside like a baby, to unveil the jewels within. Their pattern is so intricate – a mini crocodile skin but completely uniform, in lines, like squashed pearls. They must be a buttery yellow; any paler, stop peeling and step away from the sweetcorn.

I ate my first one tonight, steamed and smothered with butter (we'll lower the cholesterol another time). It's a delicacy in every sense of the word and I relished every niblet, each one exploding with flavour. All is well with the world.

Saturday 4 October

Awake most of the night hatching a plan: a stakeout. Debated the pros and cons of asking Simon but he's far too serious now. It's likely he'll try and talk me out of it then blab to Sam who will emotionally blackmail me into abandoning the idea, saying it's highly dangerous. Then she'll get heavy, asking if I really want my grandchild to grow up with photos only, never having met me. If I stop to think about it and commit it to paper, I get the collywobbles with the odd hot flush thrown in for good measure.

Calmer now and think I've sussed it. Called Hilary to sound her out and ask her along. I've had to tell her everything of course – it was a long conversation. She and I are seasoned PIs – that's Private Investigators to you lay folk, after we successfully caught Malcolm bang to rights in Gosforth Park. She doesn't know about the second one with Simon when we caught MM cooking up his wares, which makes me a fully qualified PI, I guess? Okay, our first target was merely embarrassed, rather than likely to kill us, but it still counts.

Chrystal can come and we'll look less like undercover police if there are three of us. I know she has an assortment of wigs (naturally!) – she's mentioned her Cher wig before, so I'll wear that, and Hilary can be the getaway driver; he'll never recognise her from the allotment. Might stick Chrystal in the back as she stands out in a crowd, even more than someone in a Cher wig.

So, where's our friend stashing his gear then? I'm getting into the role now, sounding like someone from *The Sweeney*. Hal once let slip that MM lives in one of the streets next to Jesmond Dene, beside a friend of his. We could park up, wait until he leaves the house then follow him. We'll pose as three mates having a coffee in the car before a walk in the Dene. Sorted!

Sunday 5 October

Chrystal's up for the stakeout – somehow, I knew she would be! She's an incredibly courageous woman and I have nothing but respect for her. Her response was, 'Of course, man! Love a good steak, out; fillet's me fave. Is it that new place down Dean Street?' Classic Chrystal. Joked about wearing dark glasses and bringing a copy of *Hello* magazine with eyeholes in it.

'Might have the one with our Kelly in it so I can stick holes in his photo. Hate him.'

'Who's your Kelly?'

'That dodgy rapper bloke.'

'Ah, you mean *R.* Kelly!'

'Yeah him,' and looked at me as if I was clueless.

Now I'm beginning to doubt the wisdom of inviting her. The Three Musketeers? Three Stooges, more like. Calmed my nerves by texting them the code name: Operation Fillet. Now can't stop giggling to myself!

Wednesday 8 October

Allotment for a therapeutic session of blackberry picking to take my mind off the stakeout. Wow, those thorny devils do a sterling job of protecting their babies from thieving fingers and hungry beaks, with overenthusiasm and unnecessary violence; I've got the scars to prove it!

Billy came to chat, and I declined his offer of a cream cake – had enough trauma lately! It was a welcome act of kindness amidst the manure-infused quagmire we've found ourselves in. 'Terrible business, this isn't it? Aye terrible,' he kept repeating.

As predicted, I'm resorting to past habits: drinking to help me sleep. Never a good solution, when you end up feeling more anxious than you were before the alcohol. A very vicious circle indeed – grrrr.

Made blackberry and apple crumble and watched an old episode of *Line of Duty*. That bunch are a load of snoopers (usually on each other) and snitchers (usually on each other). I wondered if the car that followed Chrystal belonged to undercover police putting a tail on murder suspects? Or is it my fertile imagination compensating for the other bits that aren't? It's too scary to think my lovely friend has been labelled as one of them. It would be extra ironic if we were tailed on the stakeout and funnier still if one of them was also being followed – real life AC12!

We're gonna need a bigger street…

Saturday 11 October

Operation Fillet minus one! Unlike when we tailed (my new favourite word) Malcolm, Hilary is understandably jumpy about this one. She's the designated driver – in case he recognises my car. We've exchanged several texts to discuss the minutiae of the plan. I accept we're not dealing with meek and mild (except when in the front seat of a Skoda Fabia) Malcolm, but is there really any need for:

When we're having a coffee in the car, are we both going to turn round and face Chrystal and if so, what if he leaves the house at that precise moment?

At the time, I wanted to scream like I do every time Jacob Rees-Mogg opens his mouth, but she's wholly justified in her apprehension. Now I sound like JRM – AAAAGHHH! We're trying a morning shift at first. Told them to bring snacks and this was the sensible add-on from Hilary:

Odourless. I don't want food stinking out the car.

You always see them on TV with a dashboard full of junk food. I'm with her on this one. Manure – fine. Burgers – not fine. And no crunchy stuff. I'm not listening to Chrystal chomping her way through a giant bag of nachos for three hours. Yes Hilary, that's how long a morning lasts and no Chrystal, you can't bring the dogs, or they'll trash the car, fart, and need to be taken for walks which will instantly give the game away as he'll have seen you at the allotment or with Scott. By the way, no one can know about this. No, not even Simon and *obviously* not Hal. Bloody hell, I'm beginning to think I ought to go it alone.

Sunday 12 October

7.00 a.m. The day of Operation Fillet has arrived at last. Needless to say, I didn't sleep well so I'm whacked. Not used to getting up so early. What a great start. Chrystal is renowned for keeping the conversation going i.e. incessantly chattering, and although she's generally subdued these days, the adrenaline will perk her up. Hilary can be a tad serious, and I don't want to nod off if it's a long shift! Feeling really nervous. Here we go.

11.00 p.m. GOTCHA – as the tabloids would say – my new career starts here! 'Straight Outta Spooks' tee shirts are on their way – still buzzing from the experience. Aside from one near mishap, it was mission accomplished. Moonshine Man's work ethic ain't what it used to be. We arrived at nine, but he didn't leave the damn house till half past eleven! Chrystal kept us entertained to the point of near exhaustion, and produced a surprise item which almost blew our cover – a SHEWEE! Yes, you Shady Pines readers will be perplexed about what that could possibly be as they were invented after your days of festivals, outdoor events, and long car journeys. Determined to ramp up the drama, she kept her surprise well under wraps until at least ten thirty when we were beginning to flag. Her timing was perfect. She started moaning about needing the toilet, prompting an earbashing from Hilary about not drinking so much coffee. In reply, Chrystal produced a weird, bright pink funnel-like object and a plastic sealable bag, declaring triumphantly, 'No probs, man, I've brought me own!' Well! We all needed the Shewee after that. Didn't stop to think about the risk of attracting attention with the racket we were making, screaming and laughing. Not only that, but the movement of the car as Chrystal wrestled with her jeans, knickers, *and* Shewee in a half-squat position, was enough to make any passer-by look twice.

I was horrified at the bag, thinking my car would become a tiny portaloo, complete with wee on the floor and judging by the swearing and, 'Eeeh man, ah NOOOOOO' coming from the back, it was a distinct possibility. It was hilarious and revolting in equal quantities. Unlike ourselves, at the end of the escapade the wee bag proved fit for purpose and was safely sealed in Chrystal's backpack for disposal at home.

Our chief entertainer wasn't finished yet. Bladder empty, she showed us a pack of photos from happier days: family occasions and holidays with the girls, each with an accompanying funny anecdote, as you can imagine. I insisted on silent breaks of ten minutes, which weren't silent because both of them ignored the strict rules regarding crunchy food and brought crisps. Don't know why I bother!

We parked in a perfect vantage point a few doors down from his house. I was slightly jumpy about the neighbourhood watch types, but we struck lucky, and most were out sticking their noses in elsewhere. At eleven thirty, suspect leaves house, gets into car and drives to an industrial estate on the Coast Road where there are self-storage units. Hilary's priceless comment: 'He might just be moving house'! All very tricky and as it was a tiny car park, we had to drive really close to him with a squealing Chrystal biting her finger to stop the noise. An hour later, suspect emerges with a large black bag in each hand. OF COURSE! IT was a lucky strike. He must have put a few bottles in each one, or maybe they were full of equipment? Whatever it was, it needed to be kept away from his house and the allotment. I was sure he'd be off to Sainsbury's or somewhere irrelevant but no – the jackpot! That's why there was nothing in the shed – and he wasn't going to take the gear home with the police sniffing around.

'Could still be packing?' Hilary broke the silence. We both looked at her in disbelief.

I'd had enough by then. I was boiling in the wig, and it was itching like mad. We screeched out of the car park just before he came too close, causing Chrystal to yell, 'Hey Lewis Hamilton, calm down pet!' Cue more hysterics from Team Stakeout. Another hairy moment followed when the suspect overtook us on the Coast Road, looking straight ahead so we got away with it. To celebrate, I tore off the wig and wound down the window to air my sweaty head. Somehow, I let go and a sudden gust of wind sent Cher flying gracefully through the air, only to splat onto the windscreen of the car behind! Naturally, they put the wipers on and either panicked or decided on the deluxe wash option, because water sprayed everywhere as the wig swooshed back and forth across the screen like a bedraggled Peruvian guinea pig. You've probably guessed that the Three Musketeers in front laughed until we couldn't breathe; even cool-headed Hilary nearly crashed! Miraculously, the now filthy wig was flung from the wipers just in time to avoid a multi-vehicle pile-up and landed on the central reservation – dead. Poor little silky guinea wig Cher, you gave us so much joy in your short life that even your tragic demise was indeed, worth it.

Thursday 16 October

Spent a few quiet days in recovery after the big adventure, plus post-excitement drinking while dissecting it with Hilary and Chrystal. Rang the police to report our findings. I'm not one hundred percent sure they took me seriously, even though I stopped short of blurting out the wig story. In fact, they gave me a telling off about the dangers of vigilante behaviour, stalking and harassment laws which is a damn cheek when two of us are *real* victims of those crimes! What's more, if the police are still tailing Chrystal, they'll have seen him too and won't need to check our story. If he's running illegal alcohol, maybe he's the murderer. I mean, that level of organised crime involves mega bucks and dangerous individuals. You don't have to be a real officer of the law to know that. Every time I think Moonshine Man may have spotted us, my stomach turns somersaults. If Sam knew, she'd be livid.

Saturday 18 October

Went up to allotment to find Hal had watered the winter veg in the greenhouse. I was disappointed and irritated because I love watering and he's also too attentive, to the point of overbearing. I'm constantly suspicious of his actions after the discovery and can't help thinking he has something else to hide. He stopped by before I left, asking what I'd been up to. Oh my God! Immediate thought was: what if he followed us? Now this is getting ridiculous, the convoy of snoopers could have stretched back for two miles by the time they all kept their distance from the target in front! No, Hal wasn't following us. He was here last Sunday – but are there any witnesses to that? He's not seen Scott or Sandy since the murder either. Told him Chrystal texted Scott who said he's okay. They haven't spoken to the police because they weren't there when it happened, only earlier that afternoon.

I wandered over to their plot. It looked well-tended. Perhaps Sandy's not well or is spooked by the murder. The place is less populated during the day than it used to be. I'm not surprised.

The police have left and there is a murderer on the loose, who may well be walking among us. Shuddering as I write. Yet again, I envy your knowledge, readers and Shady Pines residents who remember what happens next in this diary. You may have been there, and if not, you could flick through and sneak a look at the later months. Then, I would hopefully know not to be afraid, or who not to trust. Strange times. Life has gone from one extreme to the other. I guess that's the essence of life, and there's not a thing we can do to change it.

Monday 20 October

Some plants are coveted by birds. Others are ignored. It's the luck of the horticultural draw as to which group you're in. Wood pigeons are crafty and destructive. They are also tenacious and will sit on a perfectly sturdy brassica cage, plastic hoop, or bamboo cane, until it breaks, and they end up bang on top of their target plant below. Then they gorge themselves until they have barely enough strength to lift their greedy hulks off the ground to take off. They call, 'Take two pies Ratty' repeatedly, which is infuriating and encourages rats. Typical shabby pigeon behaviour. Having said all that, they are so ungainly they're comical, and I love the way they waddle about the plot.

While I was removing slugs from the winter brassicas today, a thought struck me – I am officially a 'grass'. And I've successfully tailed a criminal. I could add these accomplishments to a CV, should I ever need to apply for a job as a professional Private Investigator. I'd call myself Brassica Cage, my alter ego; a formidable character who takes no prisoners, except if they've committed a crime. Not that I have any time to apply for a job these days, with my busy *amateur* crime-busting schedule. Must confess, I'm thoroughly enjoying it.

Tuesday 21 October

Hal texted: *Our friend was seen getting into a police car today by my mate from his street. Must want to question him again – not at home this time.*

Aaaaagh! Dilemma. Act natural.

Me: *Interesting! I wouldn't be surprised. Maybe they've found something in the shed.*

Hal: *Lizzie, making your own beer or vodka isn't illegal, only in the eyes of the committee.*

Followed by a winking smiley face.

Me: *We'll see.*

Hmmm. Called the team about the latest development and our friend being taken in for questioning. I'm all jittery. Much whooping and hollering all round. Premature, methinks. He's a sly old fox that one, too clever by far. Maybe the murder weapon had been in the shed and was taken along to the lockup with the other stash. I bet that's it! They'll have found that along with bottles of hooch, labels, jars and all that jazz. What if there was a safe in his house full of dirty cash – or a secret panel in the library. Two things:

1. Hope they've found and charged Gibs' murderer.
2. If it's MM and they haven't, hope to God he didn't see us yesterday.

Windows are locked and table is rammed up against the back door. What have I done? My nerves are shredded. Blood pressure will be through the roof, and they'll never give me any more HRT. Drank wine and listened to salsa music before bed. Missing Lucas like mad. It's the music – happy memories of dancing in the lounge, dizzy with love. Now I've made myself cry.

Wednesday 22 October

Woke up feeling very low. Decided not to update Sam on her mother's antics, she'll only worry and it's not good for the baby. I'm so obsessed with the goings on at the allotment that I'm missing out on the excitement of my only child's pregnancy. I am officially stupid. Right, Moffitt – get up and get sorted. Meeting Sam in an hour and don't want to bring the mood down. She's so bloody perceptive and will see straight through any attempt at faux positivity. What do the Americans say? Oh yes – 'turn that frown upside down'. Ugh.

10.30 p.m. Feeling lots better now I've spent the day with my inspirational daughter, even though she sometimes acts like the first woman ever to have a baby. She just wants to get it right, but I wish she wouldn't read *all* the textbooks and compare them like she's preparing to write an essay!

We had a bit of a cuffuffle in the Biscuit Factory. It's fine, I can laugh about it now, but I shouldn't be allowed in such places. Sadly, the Biscuit Factory today has nothing whatsoever to do with those delicious sugar-packed treats and has been gentrified into an art gallery. Not a jammy dodger in sight. We ate upstairs in the bright, airy café overlooking the rooftops of the industrial Ouseburn, over to Byker and the River Tyne. It's a feel-good place, or at least it was until we began wandering around the ceramics downstairs. It was all going swimmingly until drip, drip, drip – I looked down to see three huge crimson spots: two on the floor and one on a beautiful white bowl. AAAAAAGH! Had simultaneous hot flush and panic attack and when I looked up Sam said, 'Mum, your nose is bleeding!' In my scramble for a tissue, two more drops splattered onto the once-pristine collection of ceramics by Kiki. At the speed of lightning, we wiped off every last trace of the red bodily fluid before any of the staff noticed. The boot was on the other foot – I'm the criminal today. As a punishment, the God of Law had a sneaky surprise up their all-seeing sleeve. A tiny Snowy Owl stared up at us menacingly from the display table, its face spattered with blood. I grabbed it and to my utter dismay realised that the glaze was matte with a chalky texture to it, not a shiny wipeable surface like the others. As I rubbed, the blood smeared across the beak and dried into Snowy's face, turning it into an ideal centrepiece for Damien Hirst's kitchen, or a butcher's shop. 'He's been hunting, that's all,' said Sam, with a smirk, which didn't help. Worse still was the look of disgust on the face of the young man who worked there as he approached, realising he was going to have to don protective gloves and deal with this horror show. He smiled sympathetically but was clearly repulsed.

'Oh dear, never mind. That's forty pounds please. The till's this way.' At this point, Sam disappeared, rushing upstairs to hide her raucous laughter from me. Bloody owl – bastard owl, more like. It now looks like it made a pathetic attempt at war paint and got bored halfway through. At the time, I wanted to smash Mr Extortionate B Owl to smithereens because that smug little git just made off with the rest of this week's pension. GRRR!

Sam had the genius idea of going for a drink. She knows her mother well. Though I'm not concerned about my alcohol intake this year, I am going through a very stressful time and can't share it with Sam. That's my way of justifying the late afternoon glass of wine which worked a treat. She was on a calm-offensive – distracting me with baby talk, such as describing the paraphernalia and teeny tiny clothing she had bought in preparation for their arrival. The strategy worked, and now I'm thinking of the positive things in my life to soothe my frazzled mind.

Unbelievably, I'm feeling more charitable towards Snowy B Owl! In fact, before I came to bed, he was gently removed from my bag and displayed in a prominent place as a salutary reminder that I should be kept well away from expensive items.

Friday 24 October

NEWSFLASH: Hal has a contact in the police – hardly surprising considering his past line of work – they're detaining Moonshine Man! He'll tell Hal later if it's for more questioning or something else. There's no point in *not* speculating – he *must* be on a murder charge. Allotment this afternoon. Had an out-of-character conversation with Miriam – she was unusually friendly and sober as a judge. We discussed the murder like two sane adults which was nothing short of a miracle. Told me how frightening it all is, and I was sorely tempted to tell her not to worry because it looks like the killer has been arrested and we can now sleep soundly in our beds. I'm happy to hear that she wasn't interviewed by the police – for both parties. If they thought I was hard work, Miriam would have finished them off. Hal came by for a coffee and we had a good chat. Had to be ultra-careful not to mention Operation Fillet.

Saturday 25 October

You know that you've not only arrived in the land of middle-age but are a good few hundred miles into its nether regions, when the prospect of Apple Day fills you with excitement. Unable to persuade any of the others to indulge in such a rare treat, I went alone and loved it.

It was gorgeous! A sticker on the wellbeing chart and yet another benefit of having an allotment. It was a perfect autumn day: bright with only a trace of crisp. Crisp equals cold and I don't do cold. We brought leftover apples or windfalls, preferably free from unwanted residents in the form of slugs and worms. I expect many of the little varmints would slip through the net, however, rendering the apple juice unsuitable for vegetarians. When I arrived, there was a well-dressed older chap sporting a Barbour jacket and a flat cap (definitely not *Peaky Blinders*-inspired) standing outside looking lost.

'Are you looking for the Apple Day?' I asked in a friendly, community spirit-like way.

'What? No,' he snapped, in an unfeasibly posh voice.

'Would you like to come along to it anyway? It's in here,' I persevered.

Then, in a tone that would be appropriate had I asked if he wanted to eat his own vomit, he said, 'Why on God's earth would I want to do *THAT*?' and stomped off to buy the Daily Mail. The cheek of it! Hey mate, it's not every day you get a proposition from a younger woman to live dangerously and do something you just might enjoy. Clearly any social filter he ever possessed was now well and truly broken beyond repair. Nonplussed, I strolled past the beautiful fairground organ blasting out the happiest of tunes, while advertising funeral services on the side. That's right, *funeral services*. Now, that's what I call juxtaposition. I pondered on the connection and drew a complete blank. It will remain one of life's mysteries.

It was literally a hive of activity inside, with a beekeeper selling Air Bee and Bee Hotels! All manner of apple themed cakes, jams, and chutneys were on offer. A genteel lady on the stall told me that this was a Mary Berry cake but didn't laugh when I said I hadn't realised Mary was coming; Apple Day is no joking matter. Miriam appeared and plonked a bowl of sliced apples and oranges floating in clear liquid onto the table.

'My special fruit salad with a lemonade marinade. Have some!' she slurred. Worried it might be *gin* and lemonade, and with all the kids lining up for a taste, I tried some in the name of health and safety. It was even more revolting than expected – don't try this at home, folks.

Shrieks of delight rang out whenever the lever of the apple press was turned, forcing the precious brown nectar out of the fruit and into the tub below. Kids hurled apples at a wooden monster's mouth, getting carried away with excitement and told not to be silly, or they'd be taken away in the fairground organ van. I lied about that bit – this is Jesmond after all, and 'I heart Jesmond' parents never tell lies to their children in the name of discipline. Unlike I did, apparently. Sam often reminds me that when she was tiny and had a habit of running out of the garden gate, I once told her that the River Tyne Monster was at large and on the lookout for little girls to eat. Of course, I denied using such appalling shock tactics, but remember saying it! At least I didn't tell her that when you hear the sound of an ice cream van, it means they've run out of ice cream.

Sunday 26 October

I've been vindicated after speaking ill of the dead: a call from the police to reassure me Gibs was responsible for ripping up the cauliflowers and leaving the carnations on the step. He kept photos on his phone – trophies from his crimes, to feed his sadism and cheer himself up when feeling low; a happy reminder of how clever he is to terrorise women. Therefore, Moonshine Man giving me evils was my only punishment for sticking my nose in his dodgy business (said DI Brassica Cage). I've made two enemies at the allotment accidentally – I suppose MM was my own doing if I'm entirely honest. Other people would manage to make new friends here. I suppose Hal falls into that bracket, though I spend most of the time avoiding him, having made a complete monkey of myself. My God, why can't I manage to be normal and find a happy medium? Speaking of God, they have another job to do – I need striking down for wondering if Hal was the stalker! I'm off to take the hair shirt back out of the wardrobe.

I'm beginning to think Mr Moonshine may have been above stalking – perhaps murder is more apt for his level of crime after all. I'm so relieved he's in custody. I know I'll sleep better in my bed tonight. It seems you must add 'in my bed' when there is a murderer on the loose. It's very strange because a bed is always my first choice of sleeping location. I only hope we're not lulled into a false sense of security. It's still very unnerving.

If you have ever had a child, or been a child, then you'll know what I mean by a 'punking'. The site is full of them at this time of year, as they gear up to Halloween. Some are the size of beach balls! I didn't grow any myself but might have a go next year. I don't think it's a novice's vegetable.

Monday 27 October

Since the murder, Hal has really stepped up to the mark. He also zoomed up the esteem charts from thirty-two to number five when I discovered he wasn't my stalker. I must admit, some of it has been exciting (think Operation Fillet), but for the most part it was extremely upsetting. I'm now craving stability and Hal is providing that – though I must bear in mind he has a dubious past and could be unstable in the future. Oh yes, and he lied about his whole identity. There's always the other awful possibility that if he *is* a Steady Edward despite that, he'll always be on the boring side of reliable. Rock and a hard place.

Might see what he's up to tomorrow. Maybe the moon's full again?

Tuesday 28 October

There's news – not good this time. Hal's contact reported MM has been charged, but *not* with the murder or anything at all to do with Gibs. 'Unconnected' was in there somewhere. That's terrifying and means there is still a murderer out there. Back to feeling nervous in our beds. I ought to celebrate the fact that it'll be about the moonshine and all down to Brassica Cage and the No. 2 Ladies Detective Agency. But I'd rather the killer was detained and be proved wrong on the alcohol front, instead of the other way around. My treacherous thoughts are turning to Hal, whose alibi, in my humble opinion as a seasoned detective, is not watertight. In fact, it's leaking buckets: he lives alone with no one to verify he was at home all evening *after* he went to the allotment. No! It makes no sense that he's the murderer, other than he is a real live trained killer. STOP! Enough for one night or I'll never sleep at all – in my bed.

10.00 a.m. Met Hal at a café – sounded jittery, anxious. No I'm NOT imagining it, Shady Pines folk, I'm sure he was! Trying to be rational here and suggest that he's bound to feel like that as he was also certain MM was the murderer. Did Hal just hope they would pin it on him because he's a dodgy character with the moonshine stuff? Or, and here's the million-dollar question again, has Hal something to hide? He offered to see me home – no thanks, my guard has been reinforced with steel and is firmly back in place.

Wednesday 29 October

A day of revelation. There are many life messages, like the Buddha quotes, e.g. 'Don't be an idiot all your life', and, 'I could have told you that', only worded differently. But one of my mantras is, 'Expect the unexpected' with the optional add-on 'at a time when you least expect it'. Hal has fessed up. I'm serious – no he's not the killer – well he could be but hasn't admitted to it yet. Technically, it was entrapment, because I was feeling in a niggly mood and asked which were his best and worst sales rep jobs. Reeled him right in first by ranking my best and worst schools when I was teaching. Then I hit him with my favourite anecdote of all: the little boy who had a sore 'winkle' and couldn't go swimming, and how his loyal friend came with him to snitch on the nasty kids who'd laughed when they found out, and it wasn't funny, you know 'because it happened to his Grandad and his went rusty, then it fell off and he had to put makeup on it.' Followed by faces of sheer horror. I held it together until those last few words then I could contain myself no more! I laughed and they laughed along with me, but only to patronise me. They were adorable. I'd love to tell them that story now, because of its cuteness, though they'd be mortified!

Anyway, less nervous than the day before, poor Hal was lured into coming clean. Buddha would not be pleased with me. It was a full confessional; a 'Lizzie, I haven't been completely honest with you,' moment. Assuming I was going to hear a murder confession, my throat tightened, and I choked on my fruit scone, causing him to stop in his tracks and slap my back so hard that it made it worse. But at least he didn't do the Heimlich manoeuvre on me.

He told me about his army days, mentioned 'dreadful experiences' in Afghanistan and how he still suffers from PTSD. He moved into private security after leaving the army, which was fine until it started to get heated – a shootout in Brazil, for example. That's when he realised he couldn't handle it and came home for counselling. He found it a waste of time and the only useful thing the counsellor told him was that the pound shop sold raspberry canes for one pound fifty, which is wrong on so many levels.

It was true that he'd had jobs in sales before joining the army, the worst was as a Hush Puppies rep. Said it was 'soul destroying', without a scrap of irony, so I couldn't laugh. Not that I wanted to after what he'd told me; I'm still taking it all in. It explains his short temper and occasional outbursts.

Hal walked into my trap, then I pushed him through the safety net onto spikes and forced him to relive a traumatic past he was trying his best to forget. What kind of person does that? I'm ashamed. A spiteful, conniving, judgemental wretch. How did I let it enter my head that he could be the stalker, or the murderer – ugh! I felt sick afterwards. Don't say he should have been honest with me, but thanks anyway.

He's changed in my eyes. PTSD is an insidious, debilitating condition. The poor man's only crime was to wear a blazer, shirt and tie. Perhaps I should make it up to him. I'm not fessing up about the snooping or Operation Fillet, though; some things are best left as guilty secrets. Been thinking of him all evening. Now I'm confused but I'm certain of one thing: you must never fall into a relationship out of pity or guilt; that trap is very hard to scramble out of – the sides are greased with the slipperiest of oils.

In truth, I'm trying not to think about Lucas, who loves Halloween, which is on Friday. Last year we spent it like a couple of teenagers, laughing till we cried. Such is life. Goodnight.

Thursday 30 October

Most of the day I've been righting wrongs regarding Hal: a procession of confession with Simon, Sam, Hilary, and Chrystal. Might have missed out the bit about the scrapbook to Sam – pointless dragging up past misdemeanours now. Simon the cynic reckons this doesn't rule him out as a murder suspect and are we sure about that alibi? That's above my paygrade, Simon. I'm refusing to believe Hal is responsible. It's got to be a matter of time before they find more evidence to charge MM. Hilary's reaction was one of relief and said she always thought I was too hard on 'that lovely man' when all he wanted to do was please me (she doesn't object to a blazer and tie when, actually, she should). I had to politely remind her of the jealous outbursts, a red light warning me not to collect two hundred pounds, pass Go, and drive on into a fully-fledged relationship, ending up in need of a Get out of Jail Free card. On the other hand, maybe he just needs more professional help and time to heal. Chrystal distrusts all men and also reminds us Hal could still have done it. Nevertheless, he's redeemed himself considerably and I'm the one harbouring a guilty secret: snooping into his private belongings in the shed.

In protective and cynical mode, Sam warned me not to be too forgiving on account of poor Hal being 'extremely dull'. She's grouchy and not sleeping well because of the pregnancy. I stopped short of saying, 'You're tired *now*?' because I'm sure her friends won't have held back on that one. I'm certainly not going to be the voice of doom and gloom.

Friday 31 October

Developments at the allotment: Scott turned up looking gaunt and ill. Chrystal mentioned she hadn't had a response to her last text, so perhaps that's why. Then the police arrived and took him away in a car – yes it was obviously a police car. No, he wasn't in handcuffs, so it must be for further questioning, though no one knows if he's already been questioned so it may be just 'for questioning'. Poor Scott. I sincerely hope the murder has nothing to do with him. Maybe his alibi hasn't checked out because he was out for a walk on his own then home alone – oh stop guessing! I'll drive myself mad.

11.45 p.m. LUCAS!!!! More tomorrow – urgent business to attend to!

NOVEMBER

Saturday 1 November

Okay friends. Been caught up in a supersonic whirlwind and I'm still spinning! Shady Pines folks, you might have had the decency to warn me about this. Don't ask me how, but you could have hinted, when I was listening to salsa music before bed, drowning in nostalgia about last year, Lucas was walking up the garden path and about to knock on the door! Expecting trick-or-treaters, I just stared, speechless, then threw my arms around him and squeezed as tight as I could. He replied with an even tighter squeeze, and we stood for a while as tears streamed down my stupid cheeks. I apologised, and when I heard him say, 'It's okay Leezie,' in his irresistibly soothing voice, I felt an overwhelming sense of calm. The moment I opened the door, I realised just how much I was in love with him. I've missed him more than I've ever allowed myself to think, scared it'd be worse if I wrote about it and if I didn't, the feeling would go away.

Pulled him inside and opened wine to calm the nerves, then the interrogation began. Said he had a feeling from my lack of communication that things were either very good (new job or relationship) or very bad and was worried about my depression returning. He'd contacted Sam who gave him the green light to come; I'm glad she did. Lucky for her, I'm not in the throes of a clandestine relationship, like mine and Lucas's once was, or the late-night caller would have been ignored!

I'm so excited (and I just can't hide it). After a night with him, the butterflies have emerged from hibernation. *Of course* I slept with him – and why not? It's a free country. Though there is one butterfly stuck in the ointment in the shape of Hal, I refuse to let it spoil my day. It's none of his damn business and he doesn't need to know. Wonder how he'll take it? Stop! I'm not having a jealous man interfere with my life, that's for sure. Anyhow, there's too much going on. Told Lucas all about the murder, Moonshine Man, and the detective work. His response was, 'Bloody hell!' in a London accent, which I wasn't expecting. I laughed because it was cute, a moment of light relief among all the angst. He said he didn't know having an allotment was so dangerous.

He's had enough of London and the expensive lifestyle. A glut of Salsa instructors from every corner of South America means he must teach Spanish classes at night, which isn't nearly as exciting as the dancing – I can vouch for that! Although he's enjoyed being part of the Colombian community, his quality of life is poor, spending every weekday evening at home and rarely going out at weekends. That would kill me. His next move is to find a job as a Spanish language teaching assistant in a school up here and give Salsa lessons at night to boost his income. There's so much to take in – my brain's doing overtime and there's stomach gymnastics to boot!

We're so relaxed with each other; it's like he's never been away. He's dying to see the allotment but I'm lying low because I can't face Hal. Think I'll text him, so he has time to get used to the situation in case he's still harbouring thoughts of a romantic nature. Now I wonder if I'm being too presumptuous. I'll do it tomorrow and put a very positive spin on it – because it *is* very positive, like it or lump it. In fact, I might sign off with that when I message – or maybe not…

Sunday 2 November

Woke up and slid my foot towards Lucas to check it wasn't a dream. Another delicious night, though I can no longer starfish in bed. Oh well, every silver lining. I was beginning to wonder if the shop downstairs had closed for good, but it reopened for business with a fanfare (no puns please). I'm sure the HRT has worked its magic; it was even lovelier than before he went to London. I'm a confirmed HRT-vangelist – my new religion.

Now to the *other* business – the text.

Me: *Hi Hal. Had a surprise visit from Lucas last night. He's spending a few weeks here. Hope to introduce you to him soon.*

Followed by a smiling emoji as if it's no big deal.

Okay, so what if I didn't mention he's moving back – one step at a time. Now I've sent it I'm nervous as hell. Aaaagh! These men and their precious egos. I refuse to frantically check my phone for a reply, so I put it in the drawer out of reach. Doing that attracted Lucas's attention, so I ended up lying, saying I was trying to reduce my screen hours, like a saintly, clean-living type. Now I feel crap about the lies – as if I'm having an affair! I made sure I told him about Hal helping me with the greenhouse and raised beds, but started babbling when explaining they were nothing to do with actual beds, which set off an enormous flush and a flashback I don't wish to document.

6.00 p.m. Just back from a stress-relieving walk on the Town Moor and a drink at the pub to warm up. Lucas said he'd missed Newcastle and the simple pleasures of life, in spaces that are never overcrowded. Sadly, there isn't enough greenery to go round in London, so everyone must share nicely. I'm always surprised how calm and philosophical he is. He fled his country after death threats for his trade union activity as a teacher, leaving his family and friends behind. It's still not safe to contact them. It's unthinkable, yet here he is, supporting me – he's awe-inspiring. Can't believe I resisted looking at the phone until we came back.

The reply: *Okay*

Clever. He's giving nothing away.

Monday 3 November

I bit the bullet and took Lucas to the allotment. Thought it best to warn Hal we were going. He was wearing one of his smarter outfits and looked quite spruced up. Trying to be casual, I asked where he was off to. He was embarrassed and said, 'Nowhere.' I felt for him. Throughout the excruciating twenty minutes, I was a human pendulum, swinging one way then the other in a desperate attempt to maintain the equilibrium. Tried to make Hal feel good about himself by showing Lucas the famous greenhouse and raised beds, praising his extensive gardening knowledge and practical skills to the hilt. Then, suddenly aware of making Lucas jealous, and not wanting Hal to feel *too* good about himself (though he was quick to add anything I'd forgotten to mention on the list of skills!) I'd switch to rambling about Lucas's dancing prowess. It was draining, but I survived – just. Hal was perfectly polite, but I wouldn't describe him as 'welcoming'. Didn't think Lucas noticed, but he said later, 'I think that guy likes you.' OH NO! Luckily, I wasn't facing him so he couldn't see the colour of my face, blushing in response. His logic was, 'His face is softer when you speak to him.' I brushed it off with a laugh and, 'Have you forgotten – I have that effect on all the men!' followed by, 'Phew, it's boiling in here.'

The upside of the visit: Lucas loved the allotment, despite the time of year. Like the rest of us, it doesn't look its best in winter.

'It's beautiful and a happy place, though not for the Gibs man.' Looking pensive, he then asked, 'What type of work did your friend Hal do before the gardening stuff?' After my heart stopped thumping, I said, 'Oh I don't remember.'

Don't ask why I lied. It's all very worrying – but *much* easier at the time.

Tuesday 4 November

Simon came round for a drink this evening armed, in his trademark style, with a story.

'Viv got an ASBO in Corbridge,' he announced with glee.

He'd spent the day there with his friend Theatrical Ian who dresses eccentrically to match his dog's name Vivienne (as in Westwood). Now, if ever there was less of a doggy double for Vivienne Westwood, then this scruffy little brown, (not ginger) *very* cross breed terrier, is your pooch. With Ian's purple Mohican hairstyle, large hoop earrings and red and yellow striped blazer, they would have raised a few rural eyebrows the minute they drew up in their thirteen-year-old pink Toyota Yaris. By contrast, the picturesque market town of Corbridge is so refined that it is most definitely *nestled*, rather than situated, in the heart of the Tyne Valley. Close to the river, it has a drive-through (definitely *not* a drive-thru) square brimming with exquisite independent shops, each painted a shade of environmentally friendly sage green. It's the type of place that hosts a 'Knit the Nativity' event at Christmas. Every single one of the delicately interspersed sought-after houses is a 'character property', every square metre an estate agent's dream. On entering the village square your first thoughts are:

1.   Am I posh enough to step out of the car?

2. Will Neighbourhood Watch report me for parking without a private registration?
3. Is there a ducking stool?

Back to Vivienne. Like many small dogs, Viv behaves appallingly towards other canine would-be friends so, when an elderly Corbridge resident dressed in a combination of tweed and Barbour approached with her springer spaniel, all hell was let loose. Theatrical Ian boomed at the snarling little terrier, 'VIVIENNE, STOP IT! CALM DOWN!' The lady's stress levels rocketed from traumatised to completely freaked out. 'No, YOU stop it, before I call the police! How the devil do you know my name?' Theatrical Ian was laughing so hard that Simon had to step in and apologise, not just for savage Vivienne's antisocial behaviour, but for the unbelievable coincidence of having the same name as her victim's owner. I can imagine the chaotic scene, more easily illustrated in the form of a classic chemical equation:

horrendous dog-fighting noises + loud shouting from strange townie + screaming from genteel local lady = hideous noise pollution of sleepy Corbridge ambience + inevitable attraction of a crowd

The two Vivs were finally placated and parted on good terms. Human Viv tottered away to repair her shattered nerves with a pot of Earl Grey in one of the many tearooms, basking in the dulcet tones of Classic FM. Simon blossoms with an audience, and Lucas giggled away all evening. It was so relaxing. Except when Simon started whispering about MM, 'the drugs guy'. Told him not to exaggerate and never to mention his ridiculous theory in front of Lucas or he'll worry about me even more and I don't want him pecking my head.

Wednesday 5 November

Hal texted with dreadful news – Scott has been questioned further and released on bail. It's awful. He's a suspect, then. Not charged with anything but he must be in the house by ten at night. It's shocking. Being friendly with Chrystal, Scott will be seen to have a motive and the police may think they're secretly in a relationship (they don't know her like we do). What if Gibs came to the allotment and there was a fight – I really can't imagine Scott physically fighting anyone at all, let alone Gibs. He's so gentle and I'm certain he'd come off worse. Hal made no mention of Lucas, then why would he? He's a man, after all.

3.00 p.m. Hilary rang. Not good. Chrystal says Scott's alibi hasn't checked out as there were no witnesses. Even Sandy was at her only friend's house that evening. Apparently, he'd laughed about the bail conditions because he's always at home anyway. I'm surprised the police haven't stopped him from seeing Chrystal, as another bail restriction. Maybe they want to watch how close they really are. We know he was at the allotment earlier in the day too. Chrystal is frantic. Of course, she doesn't want her friend to be the killer, but must accept there's a remote chance he may be. I've seen cases in the news of people wrongly imprisoned because they had no alibi, while the real killer has outwitted the police. Mustn't catastrophise. Poor Sandy – she must be out of her mind with worry.

They need to do some serious digging as I bet bloody Moonshine Man has a watertight alibi, courtesy of his partners in crime. It's INCREDIBLY frustrating.

Friday 7 November

Chrystal's been supporting Scott – she's distraught and blames herself. I'm concerned in case they also suspect her. It's sending my blood pressure sky high yet again. They'll come round and confiscate the HRT if I'm not careful. At least I'm not facing a potential jail sentence. Need to keep calm.

Lucas is a great help. He's been cooking with my homegrown winter veg: kale, purple sprouting broccoli, two colours of cabbage – red and green, if you're struggling with that one! He's using herbs and spices that haven't seen daylight since he left a year ago! I've never had the gumption to cook creatively. Basically, I CBA. It's been a real treat to see the produce used to its full potential, rather than boiled to death or stir fried beyond recognition.

I've loved waking up next to him again (someone I actually intended to sleep with) and am enjoying every second of it. During this stressful time, he's the perfect antidote. There was no need to broach the subject of living arrangements for when he moves back here – he's already said he'll find his own place to rent as he respects my need for space, and my own life. That's a relief! I wasn't sure of his expectations at first. I'll see how it all pans out and we may end up living together later, if Hal approves – that was honestly a joke! I'm struggling to occupy my mind with matters other than the predicament of Scott – and Chrystal.

Saturday 8 November

BREAKING BAD NEWS: Hal's contact says MM was charged with *production of a Class A drug!* IT *WAS* A METH LAB – crystal methamphetamine, dissolved in water to disguise it. It can be drunk or injected apparently. Simon was right all along. It's absolutely TERRIFYING. The worst part is having to admit to Simon that I was wrong. Called Hilary and Chrystal who were astounded. In fact, Chrystal was momentarily stunned into silence, which was a first. In her unique way, she joked about naming a drug after her, saying at least Class A was better than Class B. She is indeed a class act – and I love her!

Haven't recovered from the stark realisation that not only was this taking place on our site, but we also snooped around then followed him to his lock-up as if it were a silly game. A man who will undoubtedly be part of a chain, a dangerous network of organised criminals – drug dealers. I shook when I read the text and felt compelled to tell Lucas the whole truth. He looked at me as though I was utterly bonkers and said, 'You could have been killed.' He's right. I can't believe we were so stupid.

Meth Man (we at least had the right initials) must have slipped up. I'd like to think we set the ball rolling by discovering the lock-up, but I suspect there may have been more sophisticated surveillance taking place for such a serious crime, which makes me wonder – has Scott been framed for the murder? Drugs gangs will have the means and the motive to do it, cleverly choosing a quiet man like Scott – maybe one of them tipped off the police? Gibs must have been wandering around looking for Scott, or me, and came across something he shouldn't have. I bet he knew what crystal meth smelled like. Ugh – it's making me shiver.

Lucas is turning protective on me, but I'm glad not to be alone in the house given everything that's happened – and is still evolving. Although Meth Man is locked up, I'm scared of the associates who are at large. And he knows where I live. Might have told them about my snooping around the shed – how stupid! Should have heeded Simon's advice and kept out of it. As with manufacturing Class A drugs, hindsight is an exact Science.

Lucas was right – I could have been the one lying face down in the cauliflowers.

Sunday 9 November

I was awake in the night, seeking medicinal brandy. Couldn't get back to sleep and didn't want to wake Lucas. Feel rough as a badger. I'm anxious but trying to play it down. Went for a walk around Leazes Park. The swans calmed me down with their serenity. Like them, I'm paddling away manically below the surface, in an attempt to keep it together. My paddling is often visible, if truth be told. One positive – I'm loving Lucas's company. Luckily, Hal's been keeping a respectable distance and has been excellent at updating us via his secret source. He's inscrutable these days, sending matter-of-fact texts to deliver the message and nothing more – which is better than him sulking in my face.

Monday 10 November

Ventured to the allotment to pick more veggies which cheered us both up. There are some perfect leeks for Lucas to transform into edible heaven, rather like himself – the heaven bit, he's not a leek. There's not a lot to do at this time of year, apart from digging up and composting stems and leaves after the growing season.

Billy was there, a rare sight these days. 'Aaful about Scott. It's never him, he's a canny lad. Wouldn't hurt a fly. There's rumours abroad that it's the girlfriend that dunnit. Aye, apparently they didn't get on.'

'Where are these rumours?' Lucas asked. I explained that he wasn't referring to another country.

That's right, blame the abused woman. It was red rag territory, and there was nearly another murder as I tongue-lashed Billy within an inch of his life to scotch such nonsense – no they weren't from Scotland either. These are locally grown rumours from Jesmond, presumably organic.

'Aa just thought you should know,' Billy said meekly. In a strange way he had good intentions, but I don't regret acting the way I did; sometimes the messenger must be shot.

Tuesday 11 November

Positive news, at last. Lucas has seen a job as a Spanish language teaching assistant at a school in Heaton and is going to apply for it! I can hardly contain my excitement. It's exactly what we need now, and for the future, which is looking decidedly promising. As a refugee, he already has his Indefinite Leave to Remain and will apply for Settled Status too. I'm thrilled about that; it's an indication of how happy he is here. Mustn't build my hopes up, but it's impossible not to.

Wednesday 12 November

Needed a change of scene, so we drove up the coast to Seahouses for the most wonderful boat trip to the Farne Islands; it was magical! This trip wins first prize every time for 'highlight of the holiday' on the visitors' itinerary, and I love the family-run boat company who have taken many thousands of tourists for an unforgettable experience. They started when I was born and are still going strong. Now that the fishing industry has shrunk, it's a means for the family to earn a living and stay in the local area, unlike many who have had to migrate to the city for work.

Inner Farne was inhabited by St Aidan and St Cuthbert (separately) who, coincidentally, wore habits, and were hermits, but had nothing to do with crabs. We donned our layers and were rewarded with a bright sunny day and an unseasonably calm sea. Simon kindly gave Lucas a warm coat as his London jacket was far too thin against the North Sea wind.

Like many families, the resident puffins take their holidays in July or August, heading out to sea and returning in April for the breeding season. It's a strange choice of winter destination, but the seafood will be good, if not the weather or the hotel. It's a long time to be away; I suspect it's an offshore tax dodge of some sort. So, no puffin-spotting for us *but* we caught the very end of the seals' breeding season. There's always something to delight the tourists with and today was no exception. We were treated to a spectacular dolphin show, far superior to any on offer at Sea World, because these splendid creatures are in the wild, where they belong. A pod of six of the bottlenose variety raced alongside the boat then leapt out of water, twisting in mid-air. Lucas had never seen dolphins as his home city of Bogota is ten hours from the coast – unlike mine, which is ten minutes. Loved the commentary, delivered in a gentle, melodic, Northumbrian accent.

Not to be outdone by their extrovert, cousins, the grey seals made a crowd-pleasing gesture of their own, lolling around on the rocks and bobbing in the sea. They're dog-like, with appealing puppy eyes and a tendency for playfulness; their whiskery snouts giving a cartoon-like appearance. The pups are adorable in their cream coats of fluffier fur – shockingly the target of hunters in colder climes. We were privileged to sail very close without them batting an eyelid; they didn't mind us admiring their beauty.

During the birds' breeding season, you'll see puffins scuttling in and out of their burrows, like penguins who've popped on a technicolour beak as a clever disguise. But you don't fool us, you funny little clown-birds. I promised Lucas we'd come back in May to see them. The seals, dolphins, guillemots, and gulls offered us more than enough entertainment. It's totally life-affirming. David Attenborough loves it too. According to another friend, the Chronicle Live, it's his favourite place in the UK to watch nature. Accolades don't come higher than that, pet, and Sir David should know, as he's the King of Wildlife.

Selfishly, I didn't want to take Lucas to beautiful little Craster as it would evoke memories of Hal and the fateful evening that followed soon after. Instead, we had delicious fish and chips in Seahouses then drove home, chatting all the way about the visit. Feels like we've been on another planet, yet it's on our doorstep. I realised I'd not thought about Chrystal, Scott, or MM until we passed Morpeth. Then I came back down to earth, with a jolt.

Friday 14 November

Visited Sam and tried to play everything down as usual, except for how happy I am to see Lucas. After all, she is responsible for him being here. She's excited and nervous about the birth. As expected, I'm on standby in case Ben can't be contacted when she goes into labour. It's unlikely, but Sam likes to have all bases covered.

Went to a little Malaysian restaurant in town near the football ground. It's a wonderful snapshot of Newcastle's diversity – packed with students from the many regions of Asia – the sign of an authentic restaurant. I love the laid-back, café style atmosphere and you know everything on the extensive menu will be tasty and fresh; many dishes come to the table sizzling.

Saturday 15 November

Hilary says Sandy is frantic with worry and driving Scott crazy with talk of being 'fitted up' for the murder by criminals. She could be right. He's tried reassuring her by saying they're bound to find evidence from somewhere to prove that it was Meth Man or one of his mates and it will all be fine. He's very calm, on the surface anyway. We shall see.

Monday 17 November

Bombshell. Chrystal called – the police and a forensic team came to search Scott and Sandy's house. Why? They claim it's routine, but it suggests there's no more evidence to pin it on the drugs gang and are back to clutching at straws. Scott wasn't too clear about the exact reason. They've searched his bedroom already and spent hours in the utility room and garden shed. Poor Sandy was screaming at them and was warned about obstruction. Scott said it was awful. They've taken samples away in bags. Samples of what, he wasn't told. He's still very calm about it but we're all panicking. I'm not sure Scott appreciates the implications of this. He doesn't agree with the theory that he may have been framed, which is just as well at this stage. Or perhaps there's a police officer on the gang's payroll. Now I've *definitely* been watching too much *Line of Duty*.

I pushed the tables up against the doors again. Lucas thinks it's extreme, but I need to do it to feel safe.

Tuesday 18 November

Update – Scott's been taken in for questioning again. This is serious, considering it follows a forensic search – it's horrific.

3.00 p.m. Called Hal for news from the contact – nothing, other than he's still being questioned. Chrystal hasn't heard either and says Sandy has no idea what could have prompted this move. We just have wait. It's physically painful. Poor Scott. Or should we prepare ourselves for the worst – the possibility that Scott killed Gibs, in self-defence, or otherwise?

Inundated with support from my lovely friends. Hilary says Chrystal isn't bearing up well. She's worried about Scott's wellbeing and is in no doubt of his innocence, but can she be certain? Can anyone? I'm like a politician, flip-flopping all over the place. Trying not to involve Sam who's in the uncomfortable stage of her pregnancy and not sleeping well. I don't want her fretting about me. A long chain of angst has been created here. Though it's arisen out of care for each other, I feel I'm at the beginning of that chain and responsible for it by having the allotment in the first place.

Lucas has been an absolute rock. He has the knack of doing the right thing – suggesting a walk, a coffee, a drive to the sea, ice cream, anything to divert attention from the horrors unfolding in front of our eyes, and any unwelcome secrets that may be revealed in the coming hours or days. I also respect Hal for accepting the relationship and leaving us alone – or is he keeping a low profile for another reason?

This is all driving me mad. Need to think positive – ooh yes, the baby's due in a month's time!

Wednesday 19 November

8.00 a.m. Hal texted: *Scott's been charged with murder.*

No! They *must* be wrong. It's clearly a mistake. I feel really sick. Poor Scott, and Chrystal – unless she knew? Can't write any more.

10.00 p.m. Another awful day. Called Hal to see what else he knows but said it was to do with the forensics – they have evidence. Tried to calm me down by saying it could have been self-defence and he'll get a lighter sentence. *Sentence*? He shouldn't have *any* sentence – he can't be capable of killing anyone. My head's spinning as it is. I just can't bear the thought of Scott in prison. He's so gentle and mild-mannered and he'll be a target for bullying – like he was at school. It could tip him over the edge. Hal hasn't a clue how to say the right thing. I wish he'd said nothing.

Chrystal's in shock. She's seeing Sandy tomorrow. She's a braver woman than me. I hope Sandy's not ranting and raving about it, because Chrystal feels responsible for the whole tragic escapade as it is – she and I both. I'll never sleep. Lucas made me a lovely meal and we shared a bottle of wine, then opened another one.

Thursday 20 November

Slept dreadfully. Too much alcohol. Woke up in the night with a terrible thirst and had to drink loads of water. I feel vile. Lucas is up and I can smell coffee and toast – usually very nice, but today it's making me want to be sick - again. I'm so ungrateful.

11.00 p.m. News about Scott and the evidence. Sandy was in floods of tears when Chrystal saw her. I can't imagine that. Didn't think she was even capable of crying. Told Chrystal the evidence was blood spots in the utility room but that it was rat's blood so they must be wrong. Or it might be something else they've found. It was garbled and difficult to follow, which isn't surprising, coming from Sandy. Chrystal assumes they've had rats in the house sometime in the past. Poor woman. I can't imagine how she's feeling. She insists she's fine alone. Chrystal kindly offered to stay longer but she was adamant. Sandy had started ranting again by the time she left, back to her old self, so Chrystal took that as a good sign and will keep in touch by text.

I'm surprised she doesn't hold Chrystal responsible for befriending Scott and leading Gibs to him. There are a few rats at the allotment from time to time, but they don't tend to follow you home. Shouldn't be joking. Does Scott have blood on his hands after all? I flatly refuse to believe that.

Hilary called, worrying about Chrystal, and has insisted she stays with her for the next few days in her Quayside flat. Not sure how that one will pan out as it's like taking a bear to a beehive, staying so close to the bars and clubs in town. Shouldn't be so mean. That girl needs a break.

Spent a sober evening watching films and eating pizza to satisfy the post-hangover carb cravings.

Friday 21 November

Texted Hilary. Chrystal's fine. They'd been out but she was very tired, and they went home after two drinks – definitely for the best. Sandy had texted to say not to worry about her as she was having an early night. Chystal was relieved she didn't have to speak to her and she seemed better, judging by the text. I'm not sure you can assume that, but I didn't query it. I keep thinking of poor Scott being grilled by detectives, unable to prove where he was when the murder took place. Or sitting in a cell frightened, wondering what's going to happen next.

Picked parsnips from the allotment. The frost has made them sweeter. We made a great veggie curry with heaps of rice – comfort food. Bizarre that we produce pure, wholesome food on the same site as others who make drugs. Drugs that wreck lives and kill. It's an ironic juxtaposition, that's for sure.

11.00 p.m. Chrystal called this evening. She can't get in touch with Sandy and is worried she might be struggling. Wants us to go with her and Hilary tomorrow to check on her. She's very spooked about the possible involvement of the drugs gang and is convinced they could be threatening Sandy, or perhaps have already got to Scott. Maybe he's given a false confession. But if he's being threatened, why didn't he do that sooner, and what's the significance of the forensic evidence?

In the absence of truth, nonsense creeps in to fill the vacuum.

Saturday 22 November

Arrived at Sandy's house to find two police cars and an officer at the door. A wave of panic swept through us all as we drew up. Chrystal jumped out and ran to the door shouting, 'What's happened – is Sandy okay?' It was awful waiting for the response. She calmly replied that Sandy was talking to detectives inside. Yes, she was fine. No, Chrystal couldn't come in. Then she 'strongly advised' us to go home. So, we came back and waited.

Lucas made strong coffees and Chrystal requested 'something even stronger'. We talked her down by offering cake, but I didn't blame her for asking. We stayed up talking ourselves round in circles. Lucas sat aghast while Chrystal told him the details of the stakeout and the fate of the Cher wig. I hadn't told him about the lighter moments, and it was so refreshing to enjoy a laugh amid our chronic state of limbo. Bundled them into a taxi at midnight and fell into bed, shattered.

Sunday 23 November

Total shock – woke up late to missed calls from Chrystal, Hilary, and a text from Hal with the news.

Hal: *Scott released. All charges dropped. Sandy's confessed and been charged with murder.*

Me: *WHAT? Are you sure about this?*

Hal*: Positive.*

I called Chrystal. Scott rang her a few minutes ago. It's true. Of course, he's devastated. Says he wishes he could swap places with her – it's horribly sad. A few days after the murder he noticed a spade from the allotment in their shed at home. Sandy told him she'd brought it back to wash after she'd used it to kill a rat – I suppose that was partly true and one word to describe Gibs. Again, I shouldn't joke. Hence the blood spots in the utility room, barely noticeable to the untrained eye, but glaringly obvious to the real-life *Silent Witness* crew. The police told Scott that Gibs had gone to look for him at the allotment after he'd left to go for a walk. Sandy was still there, digging. In fiercely protective lioness mode, she wouldn't give anything away that could possibly endanger her son's life. Apparently, he 'became violent', and we can only imagine the rest. I'm wondering where MM was; perhaps he saw it all from his shed, or arrived later, saw the body then summoned his crony to bring the van and dismantle the drugs lab, knowing that the police would arrive in the next twenty-four hours.

Scott asked the detective why he'd been arrested in the first place, and how they'd known to search the house. They told him he and Sandy had been seen at the allotment earlier – I bet it was MM giving them a tip-off in exchange for a lighter sentence on the drugs charge. We'll never know. It was therefore suspicious that they hadn't come forward at the start, after the appeal went out for anyone who'd been there. Sandy assured Scott there was no need, as they weren't there at the time of the murder and didn't see anyone when they were on their plot earlier. When his alibi from the walk couldn't be corroborated, on top of a possible motive as Chrystal's close friend, they decided to question him. Considering all that, it's not surprising Scott was in the spotlight as a suspect. Little did they know that Sandy was infinitely more capable of despatching an aggressive man, given her strength and temper of a wild cat. After questioning Scott, they also checked out Sandy's alibi with her friend, who'd confirmed she was there, which turned out to be *after* the murder, of course. She'd had time to rush home, wash the spade and hide it in the shed, then leave the house before Scott came back from his walk.

It explains why she was in such an awful state. She'd told the police she was waiting for Scott to be charged, hoping the forensic evidence wouldn't stack up and he'd be released. Highly optimistic of her – maybe she's done it before and got away with it …do NOT go there! After Scott was charged, she called the police to confess. When we called round, they were about to take her away. It's all so upsetting, and I feel for them both. I'm sure she'll be able to plead self-defence when she's spoken to a lawyer, given Gibs' vindictive, abusive nature and tendency for stalking. But we don't know exactly how these things work. She'll go to court in a few weeks and there will eventually be a trial. Hopefully her confession will have helped her case and she'll get the support she needs for her mental health issues in prison too.

A mother will go to the ends of the Earth to protect her child. Gibs picked on the wrong one there – especially the mother with a spade in her hand.

Another mean thought just popped into my head: Hal dodged a bullet earlier. Sandy was clearly interested in him a few months ago, and if things hadn't gone her way, who knows what might have happened?

Monday 24 November

Can't stop thinking about Sandy. Of course, Chrystal still feels dreadfully guilty. Hilary had to sit her down and 'give her a stiff talking to'. I thought she was going to say 'a stiff *drink*', but that would have only been a short term solution.

She'd explained that while it's heartbreaking for Scott, Chrystal is in no way to blame as she didn't kill anyone. It feels weird to think I know someone who will be referred to as a *murderer* – it somehow doesn't feel appropriate, knowing the circumstances.

Hilary also explained that it was far better than the other possible scenario, which was that the drugs gang were responsible. That could have impacted massively on us all. I'm now hoping and praying (yes *praying*) that no one in the police is on their payroll (again, too many TV crime dramas) or they'll know about the stakeout and the lock-up information. Still, we need to keep a close eye on Chrystal during all this.

Keeping everything crossed for a boring, normal existence in the next few months, with Lucas, obviously. I'm dropping the idea of a detective agency and going to calm myself down and grow old gracefully. Like a good granny. FAT CHANCE!

Tuesday 25 November

Lucas has an interview for the teaching assistant job next week! He's already started preparing. We're both thrilled but trying not to build our hopes up.

Felt I owed Hal a face-to-face catch up so met him at the café as the greenhouse is rather too cosy (this greenhouse ain't big enough for the both of us) and that's obviously his fault. It was good to see him, although he appeared a little awkward at first. Wondered if it was because of Lucas, then he told me he'd been referred for counselling again for his PTSD – excellent news. He also announced he's going to take the plunge into internet dating, and that he might need help setting up his profile. I'm delighted he's moving on in leaps and bounds and also means I'm off the hook. See how selfish I am?

Wednesday 26 November

Scott's gone to stay with his dad. He deserves some TLC, and it takes the pressure off Chrystal. He's in a complete daze, a poor lost sheep, according to her. It's not surprising – he's spent much of his life caring for his mum, though she didn't portray it that way. He's hopeful Sandy may be able to claim diminished responsibility, depending on assessments in the next few weeks. She will be able to handle herself in prison – she's tough, on the outside at least, and might even learn a skill, provided they don't let her loose on the gardening tools.

She'll not attend court until after Christmas and the trial will be a long way off, same as MM's. I'm not sure how well he will fare in prison with his well-to-do background and arrogance. If he's grassed on any of his business friends, he could be in for a rough time. Who knows? We can always hope.

Went out with everyone to The Cluny in the Ouseburn for a drink. It's a wonderful pub and music venue, and it was so good to go out together after the recent stress. Lucas persuaded me to host a birthday meal for them – he'll cook, of course.

Thursday 27 November

I've invited Hal to the meal. I feel sorry for him, and he's been so helpful updating us via his contact, invaluable in fact. He has no family and never mentions friends, only 'contacts'. I texted him and included the celebrity guest list so he can decide what to do:

Lucas, Sam and Ben, Hilary, Chrystal, Sara, and Simon, who's single again. Hilary's been asking me about Hal – she's denying it, but I'm convinced she has designs on him. I've watched her turn into Mrs Smiley when he's around. They'd actually be good for each other, both calm, serious types. Hmm…

No reply from Hal. He's probably thinking about it, or maybe needs an excuse not to come. Overthinking again – I shouldn't be so impatient.

Friday 28 November

Everyone's confirmed they're coming to the meal, apart from Hal, who still hasn't replied. To chivvy him along, I rang and left a message. It's short notice, but we need to buy the food and I don't want to waste any if he's not coming. Maybe he's still sulking about Lucas. Okay, so it's not all about me; I hear you. He could be going through a bad patch mentally.

Saturday 29 November

My Birthday. Still nothing from Hal. He's not going to turn up unannounced. It's a pity, and Hilary will be disappointed! Spending the day cooking and tidying for tonight.

Sunday 30 November

What a night! Just what I needed. I was showered with gifts and love – I adore my friends. Sara and Chrystal drank too much but were funny, not annoying. Sara reckons she's in a steady relationship with Adam who came to the allotment, which is why we haven't seen her for ages; watch this space! Sam and Ben came along for a short while. Lucas did a spectacular job with the Mexican themed food: spicy, colourful, and delicious. Scott and his dad looked after the dogs so Chrystal could stay longer. It was a lovely gesture. Sandy's doing better than expected and has seen a prison doctor who persuaded her to try some new medication. She certainly needs it.

Everyone thinks I'm over-reacting about Hal's lack of communication but I'm seriously worried now. Spoke to a few people at the allotment but no one has seen him for several days. Called at his house. No answer. Curtains were closed, car in drive. Very strange. Maybe I should report it to the police. I might have regained my credibility after I was right about MM. Hal's either a missing person or just one that CBA.

11.00 p.m. Text from Hal: *Hi Lizzie. I'm away for a few days. Don't worry about me. See you soon.*

How does he know I'm worried? No mention of the invite or *happy birthday*. Where's he gone? He's never been anywhere all year. At least he's alive and hasn't been in a car crash. He could be lying low in the house, feeling unsociable.

DECEMBER

Monday 1 December

When will this end? I'm drained and in a state of shock after a horrendous day. Hal texted from the Assessment Suite at the hospital. Apologised for not coming to the meal, which made me feel terrible when I found out what happened. Wouldn't tell me why until I arrived. His face was gaunt, and his lip was swollen. Responding to my open-mouthed stare, he said, 'I'm fine, just a few cracked ribs, that's all,' in a forced cheerful voice. But that definitely *wasn't* all.

Whispering, he revealed he'd been *kidnapped* by two men connected to the drugs gang, higher up the chain than Meth Man. I thought my head was going to explode trying to process it all. He claimed it wasn't torture, merely 'questioning', but two huge thugs came to his house, forced him into a van, broke his ribs, then locked him in a room somewhere for three long days where I expect he was threatened with more violence. I'd say that counts as torture, and I'm solely responsible for it because they thought Hal tipped off the police about MM, when it was me in my witness statement. He must have feared for his life. They took his phone and made him text anyone who'd been in contact, hence my message.

Thanks to his training, he stayed calm and didn't tell them about me. They left him to sweat for the first night, which was really tough. He persuaded them that MM was useless at his job, a liability, and had drawn attention to himself with the chemical smells and by acting suspiciously. Told them he would have blended in had he not been rude to people and blatantly wheeled the goods back and forth. Hal said he 'couldn't cook an egg' let alone crystal meth. In a very shrewd move, he name-dropped an ex-army acquaintance and another from his private security days, who had become involved in organised crime. He assured me these people weren't his *friends* but told a different story to his kidnappers; it saved his life. He thinks they must have checked out his connections because on day three they blindfolded him and dropped him at the hospital, presumably fearing the gangsters Hal had mentioned.

I'm in absolute awe of his bravery and quick-wittedness. His background will have helped, but you need to be able to carry it off and sound convincing, which is admirable. And to think, this unbelievably dangerous, *real-life* drama was taking place when all I could think about was my birthday invite. Pathetic!

Hopefully he'll be out tomorrow.

Tuesday 2 December

Slept badly thinking about poor Hal's ordeal. It's inconceivable that something so awful happened to someone I know, a friend, because of me. Lucas was horrified and needed convincing that Hal isn't involved with the gang, so I explained the whole story about his past – not about snooping in his shed, though! It's not surprising Lucas has trust issues after his experience in Colombia, where someone he worked with reported him to the authorities for planning another teachers' strike. That's why the death threats arrived. Until then, he thought he could trust his union colleagues with his life; instead, he feared for it.

Was too shattered last night to mention the brief moment of craic from the Assessment Suite – an unlikely setting for it, I agree! Just before I left, a team of medics marched in and gathered around a young guy in the next bed to Hal. Pulling the soundproof curtains around for 'privacy', they sent his partner to the corridor and loudly asked him how many sexual partners he'd had in the past two weeks! We all held our breath until he mumbled, 'Just my fiancée,' and when they assured him of confidentiality (ha ha) he confessed he'd strayed on his stag night in Amsterdam! So, a disease and a dilemma. The curtains were whipped back to reveal a red, anxious face, while the rest of us looked away as fast as we could, trying to hide our smirks. The high-heeled partner clip-clopped back in saying, 'Aww babe – you okay? What did they wanna know?' At that point I made a sharp exit, leaving Hal to report back later. I'm only allowed to tell Lucas about the kidnapping. Hal's so thoughtful, he doesn't want to heap any more guilt onto Chrystal. Crucially, the fewer people who know, the safer it is for all of us. We're dealing with the most ruthless criminals who have their own way of punishing those who stand in their way.

Text from Hal: *Fireworks! He told her what they'd asked but bottled out of the rest. She asked about the stag do and he denied it – just blethered away sounding guilty as hell. She stomped out, told him to stuff the wedding and is off into town to flog the rings.*

Me: *Good on her!*

Wednesday 3 December

Collected Hal from hospital and took him home. Luckily nothing more serious than cracked ribs and bruising. Told them he'd fallen down a hill onto some rocks while walking in the Cheviots – the cover story we're telling everyone, and that he was staying at an old friend's house in Wooler when it happened. We'll add that there was no phone signal, so he hadn't seen the invitation or subsequent messages. I hate lying to anyone, especially friends, but we can't afford to take risks with those dangerous thugs.

He was very grateful to Lucas for coming to help and was more relaxed in his company. When we walked through his lounge door with some food shopping, he said, 'Excuse the mess,' referring to an upturned coffee table from the scuffle. It was a shocking reminder of the trauma – yet another in his life. I wish I could go to the police and nail those animals who are still peddling their poison to vulnerable adults by exploiting equally vulnerable county lines kids trapped in their network. Don't worry, I won't be telling *anyone*.

It dawned on me just how different the outcome might have been if it wasn't for Hal's army background, and he'd stayed as a Hush Puppies sales rep. That's made me smile. I'm perverse.

Thursday 4 December

8.30 a.m. Lucas's interview today! He's so nervous, and so am I. Simon lent him a suit. He looks so gorgeous in it – I'd give him the job.

10.30 p.m. HE GOT IT! We're elated – and shattered of course! Waiting all afternoon for the phone call was nerve-racking, and of course we had to tell everyone afterwards – *and* celebrate.

Friday 5 December

A much-needed allotment day. The place was deserted – it was bliss. We cleared away all trace of a growing season from the greenhouse to make space for two chairs – a winter conservatory again! Tomato grow-bags, pots of all sizes, trays and shelving for the seedlings, tools, canes, and netting are all stored safely away. It's a reassuring feeling, having done a great job and tying up the loose ends, ready for the spring.

Also, we have another treat in store for tomorrow – football! The loyalty of Newcastle United fans is legendary. One example is Simon's cousin, who drives from Cirencester for *every* game – that's dedication, or is it madness? Either way, Simon's not a fan and is giving us the tickets for the game against Chelsea. I asked if his cousin had broken a leg as it was so rare for him not to come. Simon told me he would have two broken legs if he came to the game because he had a family birthday party with a three-line whip for attendance. We're both mega-excited.

Saturday 6 December

Match day. Lucas was like a child at Christmas. The Toon are doing really well so far this season and the atmosphere was unbelievable – like nothing I've experienced before: the noise of the fans; joining in the chants; the camaraderie and feeling we're all in this together – unlike when a politician tells you that, because it's a lie. To some, football is a religion, followed to the letter by fans who travel far and wide to all games and attend the hallowed turf of St James' Park.

We had a great view of the pitch, in contrast to the away fans who are squashed into the highest corner of the stadium, requiring oxygen and Sherpa assistance. There's an acceptable amount of spite and zero tolerance involved in Geordie football. Here are the rules. Note – the list may not be exhaustive:

- anyone who's ever played for Sunderland must be booed

- anyone who's caused injury to or fouled one of our players must be booed
- if an attempt on goal by the opposition is wide of the mark it must be cheered
- if Toon are winning comfortably and the game is nearly finished, every pass must be cheered
- any singing from the away supporters must be drowned out

Drinking Bovril at half time is not a rule, but is encouraged, unless you're vegetarian or vegan.

We won 2-1. Lucas jumped up and down as if he was born on the banks of the Tyne. The game was so absorbing. The moment you step into the stadium, you take on the new identity of a football fan and leave the stresses and banalities of life behind. The wind carries the roar of the crowd over the Town Moor and all the way up to the allotments. I love to hear it there, and it was even more exhilarating to be part of it. I'm convinced there's copious amounts of dopamine released during the ninety minutes, as long as we're winning. On the walk to and from the match, city centre traffic gives way to pedestrians. Cars are outnumbered and normal rules of the road don't apply. I wouldn't fancy the chances of any motorist who knocked over a fan – not with fifty-two thousand others prepared to rush to their assistance if there was any road radge. No need to worry, we walked on air all the way home, carried along by euphoria and a wave of black and white.

Sunday 7 December

Lucas made a meal to take round to Hal and wrote a label that looked like 'bear casserole' instead of 'bean', which made us all laugh (and poor Hal's ribs hurt). He said it was worth it as it cheered him up, and wanted to know if Bear Grylls was in it. That's the second joke he's cracked recently and I'm now resisting any obvious puns about ribs – it's too cruel. He was very grateful and had slept a lot following the three-day nightmare, plus another thirty-six hours of mental torture in hospital with 'all the shenanigans' as he put it: people coming and going; sleepwalking; shouting at the wonderful staff; arguing with their own visitors; breaking off engagements – no wonder he's worn out!

Monday 8 December

Allotment again, to collect more delicious purple sprouting broccoli spears – the veggie version of Britney, though there's not much meat on her, either. Miriam thundered through the gate and down the track, muttering. No clinking bag today. Asked if she was okay (foolish) and she ranted about how bad it was that her plot neighbour's been locked up for 'brewing a drop of beer'. I explained that it was all over the national news that it was drugs, not home brew. Said she doesn't watch any news, it's 'too bloody depressing' and he was a 'very decent fellow'. DECENT! Heard it all now. Evidently, she thinks that no one with a posh accent could possibly be involved with drugs. How naïve! She wasn't having a word said against him, even when confronted with the facts. Aaaaagh! 'Too many jobsworth meddlers round here,' she snarled, and rambled on about how disgusting it was that everyone assumed he'd killed, 'your mate's boyfriend'. At that point I snapped, '*Ex*-boyfriend, Miriam, *ex*!' and went into the greenhouse before there was another murder. How can she defend such pondlife from the bottom of a drugs chain? She's a funny fish, that one.

Wednesday 10 December

Town is filled with Christmas cheer, superficially, at least. The lights and shop windows are bright and atmospheric, but the faces of the daytime shoppers tell a different story as they tear around from queue to queue, tempers fraying. At night it's a far happier affair, when several work parties and good friends come together with large measures of Christmas spirit. My mind drifted back to my first staff Christmas night out as a teacher, so I found the diary entry entitled 'DISASTER AREA!!!'.

It was during the heady era of *trebles* i.e., three shots of vodka or gin for an irresistibly cheap price, signposting the road to disaster. According to my long-suffering colleagues, I couldn't understand why I was totally non compos mentis within an hour because I'd, 'only had three drinks' – which turned into a stuck record for the rest of my short evening. Of course, I'd downed nine shots of vodka and cranberry juice without weighing up the consequences. Shocking! It's no wonder I couldn't follow the rules of the drinking game and kept demanding they be repeated. I was a complete pain. Two lovely colleagues escorted me home, but not before causing them more embarrassment by putting up a child's plastic dome frog umbrella, borrowed from my goddaughter en route to meet them. What's wrong with that? I hear you ask – it's hardly the worst sight Toon has seen on a Friday night. Well, friends, I insisted on keeping it up inside the metro station, hanging onto it for dear life in case anyone had any heroic ideas about confiscating it. They finally talked me into putting it down before the train came, while I wailed, 'But I *like* it,' on repeat. How cringe-making! However, it served its purpose as an effective anecdote when Sam started to experiment with alcohol; no young person wants to be *that* embarrassing.

The baby's due in a week's time – I can't wait! Not too close to Christmas, though first babies are notoriously late.

Friday 12 December

Sara's organised tickets for an Abba tribute band at the brewery in Exhibition Park tomorrow night. It'll be brilliant! I declined the offer of a wig, after the last itchy experience, but Hilary wants to go as Frida, if Chrystal will be Agnetha. I'm slowly getting used to the new version of Hilary, who's willing to let her hair down, excuse the pun! Oh yes, about all that, I've decided not to embarrass them about the holiday incident – some things are best left. Also, you never know when I might need to refer to it in the future!

Sunday 14 December

Woke up with a fuzzy head, even without a wig on. Prising open my mascara-clogged eyes, I laughed out loud thinking of last night's exploits at the brewery gig. We'd donned our best seventies gear, and Chrystal's outfit was fabulous: white satin flares and matching top with frills galore, and the pièce de resistance of course: a luxuriant Agnetha wig. We expected nothing less. It was just what we needed, and we all danced wildly. Once again, it was Chrystal who provided the after-show entertainment – luckily a one-woman event this time.

We'd just left the brewery on an Abba-tunes high, singing at the top of our voices, when a bottle of beer was triumphantly produced from inside her coat. Holding it like a microphone, she belted out a rendition of 'Waterloo' with accompanying dance moves. Naturally, the exiting revellers joined in and soon

Chrystal was leading a conga through the park, dangerously close to the side of the lake. The door staff tried in vain to calm everyone down, but an all-singing all-dancing cast of *Mamma Mia* were taking a telling from no one.

Suddenly a familiar shriek rang out from the front, followed by a loud SPLASH! I dashed to the edge of the lake and spotted (surprise surprise) Chrystal, flailing around in the murky depths with the bottle of beer held high above her head – a glass Excalibur. She tried frantically to right herself with the other arm, the Lady of the Lake clinging on to her prize possession for dear life. Streaked from head to toe with muddy green slime dripping miserably from the top of her blonde wig to the bottom of her flares, she cackled like a Scandinavian Medusa in a cross-cultural horror film, 'EEEEEEEE HEE-HEE-HEE EEEEE MAN!'

She could hardly stand for laughing, nor could her merry band of conga-ing disciples, who instinctively reached for their phones, rather than help her. She must have her own YouTube channel by now. Next, we'll have Chrystal on demand. It was sheer luck she hadn't dragged the entire line in with her. The furious door staff were shouting at her to get out, as if she'd deliberately wandered into three feet of putrid mud and freezing cold water for an evening dip.

Still giggling uncontrollably, and with emerald locks of pondweed flowing, she finally emerged to a round of applause, due largely to her success in protecting the bottle of precious beer. It was a freezing cold night; luckily a stern-faced doorman appeared with a foil blanket to wrap around the clumsy turkey (seasonal). Surrounded by mayhem, he was slick and professional, and I suspect it wasn't the first nor the last time it's happened. Unimpressed, he snatched the holy grail from her frozen hand, ordering her to hold the foil blanket instead, which flapped in the breeze like a superhero's cape, adding to the mythical element of the whole spectacle. Show over, the conga-joiners dispersed, leaving their sodden heroine in our capable hands so we frogmarched her across the park to my house for a late-night shower and a change of clothes. Continuing the fairytale theme, we walked in the door as the clock was striking midnight, before hypothermia set in, and the hilarious anecdote turned into a hideous ordeal.

Now do you understand why I woke up laughing?

Monday 15 December

IT'S OFFICIAL – I have grandmother status! Sam went into labour during the wee small hours and at 11.10 a.m., Rosie Elizabeth arrived a little earlier than expected, with the sole purpose of brightening up our lives. I was ecstatic to read her middle name – it's a very special privilege. They're both fine – exhausted but no complications. Ben has already sent a photo. You've guessed, she *is* adorable. I think Granny Lizzie has a certain ring to it. I'll see them when they come home tomorrow. Sam's not great without her sleep – she'll need to get used to that. Messaged everyone and now enjoying their congratulatory texts. I'm overcome with emotion – I love my friends, and my expanding family!

Tuesday 16 December

Spent a wonderful couple of hours with my new granddaughter! Selfishly, it's lucky Ben's parents live in Yorkshire, so there's not a queue of visitors. Lucas insisted I go alone for the first time as he didn't want to intrude or overwhelm them. He's a star. I'm sure

Rosie knows me already. I'd forgotten how tiny their little fingers are, with perfectly formed nails. And her toes – so weeny! She's the most exquisite little treasure that's ever been created and I can't stop thinking about her.

Wednesday 17 December

Took Lucas over the river to Gateshead for a walk around Saltwell Park and the wonderful winter art trail – a stunning collection of light installations and performances. It was family-oriented, but unaccompanied adults were also allowed. An immersive experience that left me feeling loved-up and gushy, which might have been annoying.

Told him my story about a class trip there in my last year of teaching. The park's infamous parrot, Percival, told a six-year-old child to eff off when they attempted to strike up a conversation with him. Yes, he honestly and truly did exactly that. There was lovely Dahlia, innocently greeting him with, 'Good morning, mister parrot', when the rebellious teenager snapped, 'Fuck off', in a scarily deep voice. A bird possessed by an evil avian spirit, perhaps? Dahlia's response was almost as priceless, 'Er, that's not a very nice thing to say,' in a teacher's voice that rivalled my own. Naturally, the whole class erupted into fits of giggles. We tried to silence them while they imitated Percival's cheery reply for the rest of the trip. I snitched on the feathery devil to the park keepers who explained he was rescued from a house where he spent all day locked in a tiny filthy cramped cage and arrived with two words of gratitude. There was nothing they could do except try and convince the public he was saying, '*Knock* off', but were rarely believed. Apparently, it's a sign that he's happy. I dread to think what he says when he's in a bad mood!

It amazes me how very young children learn to self-censor their language when they're in school. Even those from a super-sweary household can step out of the environment and never repeat it to another adult. They are so clever and could teach parrots a thing or two. At least the children on that trip had something to write about and it was timely practice for their 'k' sound in phonics – every cloud.

With visions of a barrage of complaints from parents, I gave a 'swearing isn't big or clever' lecture on the bus home, telling them that unless they wanted to see Percival banged up in Parrot Prison, to remember this very important message: what goes on in Saltwell Park, stays in Saltwell Park.

'Where is Parrot Prison?' asked Dahlia.

'Next to Budgie Borstal. No more questions. Now, let's sing 'The Wheels on the Bus''.

Thursday 18 December

To compensate for the disappointment of the growing season coming to an end, we are allowed to have small bonfires at the allotment during the winter. Lucas was beside himself with excitement and couldn't wait to use the new incinerator from B&Q. I think *incinerator* is bigging up its part, as it's a metal bin with holes, not something recycled from Consett steelworks.

We bought far too much barbeque food, along with chestnuts and homegrown potatoes to cook in the *incinerator*. I made some mulled wine, and we wrapped up warm and spent a wonderful afternoon outdoors, appreciating the peaceful environment, enjoying the smell of woodsmoke and the crackling fire.

Saturday 20 December

Just when you're least expecting it, another secret or two comes out of the woodchip! Hal called with some very interesting gossip from his contact. Apparently, Meth Man is 'singing like a canary' (luckily not a parrot) from his cell and has named one of the gang leaders in an effort to reduce his sentence. Unlike me, he mustn't have watched enough TV dramas because everyone knows that's not always the best idea. That man is so arrogant he probably thinks there'll be no repercussions for him. I expect he'll learn the hard way. On a lighter note, he said he paid Miriam in bottles of wine to keep quiet about his dodgy business in the shed, not that she knew the full extent of it. How funny – Miriam, the gangster's moll! Hal said he was recovering nicely until I started laughing about it, which set him off too.

I've invited him for Christmas Day. Hilary's kids are having the pleasure of Miserable Jeff's company, so I've invited her too. Might be time for a spot of matchmaking if I'm not mistaken. Chrystal's going to her sister's, but we'll get together on Boxing Day. Rosie is bringing her parents along if they're not too exhausted.

Sunday 21 December

Lucas and I wandered down to the Baltic for the most moving photography exhibition I've ever seen. Chris Killip lived in a caravan on Lynemouth beach during the eighties, alongside the sea-coaling community. It was fascinating – what a tough life those amazing, resilient people led.

Stepped out into another world on the Quayside, resplendent in winter sunshine, bustling with people enjoying the Christmas themed market and fresh air. The food stalls are a snapshot of how the city has evolved in its diversity. When I was young, the choice was fish and chips, burgers, or hot dogs. Now there's something for everyone, from everywhere in the world, to suit all manner of diets. There's even a vegan stall in a horsebox – horses are vegan too! Lucas swerved the Latin American food and opted for fish and chips – let's not stereotype, that's diversity in action.

Monday 22 December

I've already bought Rosie a cot, so we braved the crowds to go baby clothes shopping for a small gift from Lucas. Cuteness overload! Steered clear of anything perceived as girlie e.g. unicorns and fairies, but something I found strange was the abundance of pandas, crocodiles, and lions as a motif of choice. Don't get me wrong, pandas are ostensibly adorable, but as bears, they have a vicious streak. Crocodiles have very few redeeming features, bar the ability to say 'snap', and let's not forget how deadly they are at a watering hole – though not quite as bad as hippos, who also feature on many a sleep suit. Last but not least are the cuddly lions – don't get me started; they'll rip your throat out as soon as your back is turned. How about a gnu, an aardvark, or a similarly benign creature. Why not a sloth theme? They're very gentle and I expect they fly off the shelves in Colombia.

We settled for something with monkeys on it – although on a zoo trip when I was six, one yanked my hair, so they're not all they're cracked up to be either.

Wednesday 24 December

Please God, don't punish me with any more nasty surprises; this year has brought more than its fair share and I promise you faithfully, my meddling days are over. I've had the very best experiences too: a granddaughter; the allotment; Lucas's return; his job; new friends for life (HRT included). I'm confident we can all rub along together well – not literally; I still have flashbacks from the date night. Back to positivity – the new year is looking distinctly rosy from here on in!

Thank you, my lovely Shady Pines friends. You've stood by me for another year of ups and downs. I have a special message for you: remember to tell your family and carers that you were once as young, vivacious, and independent as they are. You deserve the very best in your autumn years.

Walked to the allotment in a reflective mood. I'm proud of the work I put in to transform the plot and can safely say that every minute was worth it. I'll learn from my mistakes and successes in preparation for next season, as I did with every new class I taught, as we all do in our work or relationships – if we are lucky enough to get a chance to change, or to change them.

Enough of this heavy stuff, I came here to pick sprouts, red cabbage, broccoli, leeks, and parsnips! Together with the potatoes and carrots stored in the garage, they'll be my first homegrown Christmas vegetables. Simple pleasures…

ABOUT THE AUTHOR

Maya George is the author of *Look at me Now,*
to which *Lizzie Digs Deep* is the sequel.

She was born in Newcastle upon Tyne where she now lives with her husband. Maya has travelled extensively, living and working in London, Mallorca, and Colombia. Throughout her life, she has continually campaigned for social justice and equality for all. She loves retired life, people, animals, and her home city.

mayageorge18@yahoo.com

Printed in Great Britain
by Amazon